THE SINNER AND + THE GUNSLINGER

THE SINNER AND THE GUNSLINGER

A Sinner Sisterhood Novel

LANA PECHERCZYK

Prologue

Amidst the clamor of the bustling city, a starving woman jangles her coin cup. She shouts to be heard above the din with a sense of urgency.

"Repent, sinners! War is here. The path to redemption is almost lost in darkness!"

Clouds block out the sun, shrouding the street in shadow. The woman stops and looks up. Rushing denizens crash into her back. Her coins spill onto the street, rolling until they disappear down the storm drain.

She grabs the offender by the collar and snarls, *"Do you believe in second chances?"*

ONE
THE PAST

Leopards didn't crawl through third-story bedroom windows. They lived in the forest or jungle. The boy was only six, but he knew that. So when he woke in the middle of the blackest night of the year and saw the dark shadow of a large cat slink into his room and sniff around, he thought he was dreaming.

He rubbed his eyes. Blinked. But it was still there . . . hunting, leaving embers in its wake. A scream would wake his baby sister. She'd cried all day, and he was so tired of hearing her wails. She'd cried like this since they lost their mamma and papa. Sometimes he would put his thumb in her mouth to stop the sound. Today he did it twelve times and accidentally made her choke. The matron smacked him with a wooden spoon on his bare bottom until he couldn't sit.

Sniffing.
Sniffing.
Sizzling.

He gasped and hid under his covers. Maybe it wouldn't notice him. If he tried not to breathe, it might walk by, and he would wake up. Maybe if he said his prayers . . . but he couldn't remember the words. All he had was the little red knotted bracelet his mother had bought his sister. She said it was for warding off evil spirits, but he'd been jealous of the gift and stole it for himself.

The fiery-eyed creature slinked around the room, its nose leaving a line of soot as it poked and prodded. It stank like rotten, burned things and horrible dreams. The sniffing stopped. *Oh no.* The boy clenched the charm.

He peeked over his covers and whimpered. The leopard had risen on its hind legs to look over his sister's bed. It straightened until it looked like a man—if a man had a tail, whiskers, taloned fingers, and blazing eyes.

The boy should scream. He should say something . . . but . . . she would cry, and he hated when she cried.

"Snuggle time," the leopard-man hissed as he picked up the sleeping baby.

"No!"

The leopard-man's head twisted toward the boy so fast that embers spilled from his eyes and caught fire on the bed. Flames licked up its legs, burning and smoking. Leopards didn't crawl through third-story windows, but demons did.

Two

The Past

"Go on. Go join the others."

At the sound of the impatient voice, the boy paused the flipping of a coin over his knuckles. He lifted his head and saw the matron shoving a dark-haired girl into the group home's courtyard.

The girl was a scrappy thing. Dark, tangled hair hung down her thin shoulders. Her dress was too big for her willowy frame. She hugged a stuffed bear to her chest. When she darted a wide-eyed look about, the boy skulked backward and hid further behind the potted plant in the foyer. She didn't see him watching her. The boy thought she might break down and cry like all the other newcomers, but just when he thought she'd run the other way, she lifted her chin and stepped into the slate courtyard where the other children played.

Brave girl.

The boy went back to his coin—practicing rolling it over his knuckles like he'd seen the cowboys do in the Wild West movies, but then he stopped again at the sound of a voice he hated.

"Oh, what do we have here?"

"Fresh meat," said another.

The sounds that followed were unmistakable. A little girl crying out. Shoves and grunts. Then curious hissing and snarling. More grunts and shuffling. Anger flamed the boy's cheeks. He captured the coin and squeezed so hard it hurt.

Getting to his feet, he strode into the courtyard. The other children had her toy and were tossing it over her head.

"Hey!" he bellowed.

Everyone looked at him, but he only had eyes for the redheaded ringleader, who just couldn't keep his trap shut. The boy stalked forward and shoved the bully hard enough that he fell on his ass, then said, "You wanna pick on someone, Puck? I'm your huckleberry."

Every brat in there jumped on the boy. But he was no shrinking violet. Since his sister burned, he'd been in and out of foster homes and learned to protect himself. They all thought he'd killed his baby sister. They thought he'd had enough of her crying and got rid of her himself. No one believed his story of a fiery-eyed leopard demon who did the deed. They called him a baby killer, and they beat him up. Repeatedly.

Sometimes he was pinned down by three or more kids. Sometimes, the boy learned to improvise, just like now. When he was overpowered, he found sticks and used them like nunchucks. When the sticks broke, he used his coin and shoved it against their soft bits. Anything could be a weapon if used properly. Eventually, he forced Puck and his bullies to scatter.

Standing as the victor in the courtyard's center, bleeding

from his chin, he limped to where the stuffed bear had been dropped. He knew the toy was different when his trembling fingers touched the fluffy surface. It had a smokey scent. His instincts wanted him to be creeped out by the strange, beady eyes that seemed to follow him. Their red glint reminded him of the demon that burned his sister. One of the eyes was falling out of its socket. When he poked it back in, the toy seemed happier.

He used his shoulder to wipe the blood from his chin, then reverently wiped the dirt and dead leaves from the bear. Much better. He limped to the new girl.

Up close, she was even prettier. One day, she would grow to be a beautiful damsel worthy of any Wild West movie—no, not a damsel. She had a wild look about her . . . A free spirit shone from her eyes and refused to be cowed.

He handed her the stuffed animal. She bared her teeth and hissed at him.

The boy laughed. "You're a real wildcat, huh?"

She swallowed. Nodded. Then walked away.

"See you around," he mumbled, watching her go. It wasn't until she'd turned a corner, leaving the courtyard, that he returned to his spot and flipped the coin around his knuckles.

The smell of smoke remained.

THE GIRL STOOD at the front of the line for the school bus and hugged her backpack to stop herself from turning and punching the bully in the face. He tugged her pigtails. She clenched her jaw. She'd already been in two fights at this new school. She mustn't make it a third, or another mark would be drawn on her naughty card at the group home. Who would adopt her then?

Her thoughts immediately traveled to the boy with dark, messy hair and intense eyes who always seemed to be around when she needed him most. They'd only known each other for a few weeks, but it would be sad to leave him. Maybe he would be adopted at the same time as her and they could be family.

Another tug on her pigtails yanked her head so hard that her neck cracked. A snarl ripped from her lips, and she spun to face the same freckle-faced bully from her group home. He laughed down at her with unhinged glee. He was five years older than her and taller by two heads, but she didn't care. She torpedoed his midsection.

It took two teachers to pull her from the bully's body.

"Detention. Now," barked Mr. Diplo, pointing to the school gates, glaring at her from over his glasses.

"But . . . " She glanced at the bright-yellow bus as it pulled up to the curb. If she missed it, she'd have to walk home alone, and—she shivered—creepy things followed her in the shadows. Without Snuggles to comfort her, she felt the bad things get closer. But bringing Snuggles to school at her age would get her teased. He had to remain home on her bed, waiting for her safe return.

Sniffing, she forced back tears and scowled at her bully. He climbed onto the bus and sat by the window, where he gave her a cocky finger wave. *Not fair.* She didn't start the fight. This wasn't fair!

"Now," Mr. Diplo repeated.

With a frustrated whimper, she picked up her backpack and stomped toward the school gates. Someone grabbed her shoulder—her fist clenched and swung, but the boy from the group home stopped it inches from his face.

"Easy there, wildcat. It's just me."

She relaxed and tried to smile, but her chin trembled. With everyone else, she was brave. With him, it was hard to pretend.

"You okay?" His brows drew together.

"I have detention," she blurted. "It wasn't my fault and now I have to walk home late." She hugged her backpack. "Bad things follow me in the shadows."

He watched her intently for a moment, then glanced over his shoulder and checked what Mr. Diplo was doing—he was too busy wrangling the kids in the bus line to notice he'd waylaid the girl. He got down on his knee and pulled something from his pocket.

"Here," he murmured, holding it out. "I've been meaning to give you this."

"For me?" Her voice was full of awe as she took the red knotted bracelet. A tiny white bead was in the center. Upon seeing it, she scrunched up her nose. "Is that an eyeball?"

He nodded, puffing out his chest. "It's called the evil eye. In Turkey, where my parents are from, they use this to ward off evil spirits."

She allowed him to slide it onto her wrist and tighten the red straps. It was creepy. But it helped her nerves a little bit.

"You," Mr. Diplo shouted from amidst the hubbub, pointing at her. "Stop dawdling and get to detention."

The boy stuck up his middle finger at the teacher's back, and the girl chuckled.

"I'll be here when you get out," the boy said, his hazel eyes turning warm as he straightened her pigtails.

"Promise?"

"Cross my heart, hope to die." He sliced a finger across his chest twice, then pointed to her and said, "Now you say 'stick a bullet in your eye' and pretend to shoot me." He took her hand, folded it into a finger gun, and made her point it at his head and shoot. He feigned a dying action before continuing with the last bit. "Then we both say, eat a horse manure pie and make gagging, puking sounds."

"That's a weird game." She frowned.

"But it's fun. Do it."

"What does it mean?"

"It means if I break my promise, you get to do all those things to me."

"Oh." She bit her lip. "That's . . . serious. I don't want you to die."

"Neither do I. That's why I'll never break the promise." He rubbed the back of his neck and nodded. "I'm not going anywhere."

Three

From the front steps of the abbey, I watch the male interlopers leave the limousine. *Team Saint.* The name churns in my stomach, and I spit to remove the bad taste. Five men invite themselves into *our* sanctuary, intending to tell us how to do *our* jobs. To say their arrogance grates against my bones is an understatement. I know what this is, and it's not an offer of help. It's the sharpening of a blade before it cuts.

Typical.

The world is in chaos, demons wreak hell on earth, and these patriarchal asswipes think it's the best time to assert their authority over a secret society of female assassins.

As they unload their luggage, my brows lift. I expected doddering geriatrics who are set in their ways, but at least four are in their twenties or thirties. The Monsignor is the only old-timer among them.

My gaze skates over them, and I catalog interesting details that might aid in me unraveling their purpose here. The priest has a hard look about him—his eyes are unforgiving as he darts a glance at us all standing on the steps, scrutinizing him right back. Then his cheeks brighten in a very obvious, and, I sense, uncharacteristic blush.

One of my Sinner sisters says something I don't quite catch because my attention has shifted to the fit black man in an Italian designer suit. His muscles virtually burst the seams on his jacket. But unlike the priest, his eyes are warm, and—dare I think it—even nervous as he takes us in. The third man looks like a blond version of Clark Kent. But less buff and in a crinkled, three-piece suit.

Another of the girls snarks something, and another shoots back a retort.

"Ladies," the Reverend Mother warns.

I glance at my sisters. All of us are decently clothed except Mercy—our redheaded, voluptuous team leader. Her silk robe has fallen open, allowing her pale bosom and rosy-pink nipple to be out for all to see. No wonder the priest blushed. I roll my eyes.

"Put your tits away," I mumble.

The girls keep bickering, drawing me into their drama. Usually, we're not this fractious, but the tension in the air has us by the balls. Our organization has operated in the shadows of the male-dominated church for centuries. Now that the Vatican has discovered us, they're here to control us. We all fear the possibilities. So when I tease Tawny about being lazy and she launches at me, I face her with a set jaw and a hard look. If she wants to fight me, so be it. She's a hot-headed Sinner pretending to be a peaches and cream sweetie pie. *Bring it.*

Thea steps between us and gestures with a severed hand she brought back from a recent mission, complaining about us not warning her about this visit. Seeing the sweaty corpse limb flail about is enough to shock me back to the reality of our situation. I stuff my unsettled nerves down.

I had no idea Team Saint was coming either. None of us did.

The world falls away as I retrain my gaze upon the interlopers and finally take in the fourth younger man as he drags a heavy trunk toward us at the abbey steps. Voices warble. The sun dips behind a cloud. I shiver. There's something familiar about him. Something in the way he moves. His gait is familiar, yet so foreign. When he stops at the base of the steps, straightens, and rubs the back of his neck with his hand, my heart stops.

It can't be.

Zeke?

He blew into my childhood and cared for me in the group home when no one else did. Even though I was six and he was eleven, we were instant friends. He became my world—my protector. My hero.

Now, decades later, I stare at him from the steps of the abbey. So much has changed between us. I am no longer a frightened little girl but a world-class assassin. He is no longer an unwanted orphan but a gunslinging demon hunter.

He's so grown up, strong, and . . . handsome. His hair still sits messily around his ears, but somehow his devil-may-care attitude gives the uneven texture a cool vibe. The gun belt slung low on his hips is missing the pistol holsters, but I recognize the shape. Pride swells in my chest. He'd always dreamed of being an expert marksman; here he is, dream verified. God has miraculously returned him to me . . . despite my sinning ways.

Then the introductions start. The Rev begins by pointing us out. With each name called out, my traitorous heart leaps a little further into joy. Surely when he hears my name and focuses on my face, he'll put two and two together and remember me. I might not have the pigtails falling out, but I'm not that different. Surely he'll run up the steps, tugging me into his arms and—

"And Leila is our weapons expert."

His eyes skate vacantly over me like I'm a stranger. Like the years we spent together in group homes were made up. Like he'd never played at rescuing me from bad Cowboys or had eaten my burned cookies.

Not him.

Not Zeke.

How could it be? He's dead. He died in a fire . . . a fire everyone blamed me for setting. A fire he courageously ran into, hoping to rescue the stupid stuffed toy I should have been too old to care about, except it was the only thing my birth parents gave me before leaving me on the doorstep of a church as a baby.

So it can't be him. This man just looks like him. He has the same crooked smile, hazel eyes, and look on his face as he rubs the back of his neck. But it's not him.

My stomach drops. I blink rapidly, hating how my eyes are burning. It's so stupid of me to think he would be alive.

The Monsignor's voice breaks through my thoughts. "Zeke is our gunman, yes?"

It *is* him. So why . . .? I glance down at my body—at the curves, at my hips, and the swell of my breasts in the tight black workout attire. I hadn't even had my first period when he died . . . left . . . whatever this is. He either doesn't recognize me or doesn't care. Maybe he never cared. I mean, why would he pretend to be dead? Why would he make it look like it was my fault?

Zeke and I had once sat on the group home couch, watching a movie on the tiny television in the darkness. I was maybe thirteen by then. Or twelve. Something close. He was ready to age out of the system. We knew our tiny family was about to be disrupted, so we decided to do a movie marathon of all the old movies we first watched together. The first movie I had ever wanted to watch was Dracula . . . which was a mistake because of my overactive imagination. For years after I'd watched it, I had nightmares and an obsession with all things vampire. Zeke had steered me toward his favorite Westerns.

But this one night, at a scary part of the movie, I crawled toward Zeke and cowered in his arms. For a moment, he hugged me close, as he always did. But then, suddenly, he shoved me off and told me not to be stupid. It was so abrupt and gruff that I watched the rest of the movie with tears stinging my eyes. After that night, he wasn't quite the same with me.

Maybe he'd truly had enough of me. Maybe his death was faked because he knew I would have followed him anywhere.

Unable to stop the fury and indignation bubbling in my blood, I can't focus. Can't breathe. Can't see beyond the red veil of rejection burning before me. And when the Rev dismisses us, I walk inside and don't look back.

Four

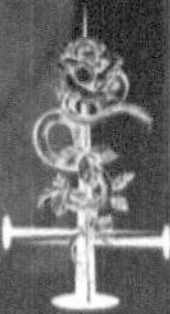

Wesley is back from the UK and has the healing staff. Or rather, Thea has it. I stare at the message on my phone again, hardly believing it.

> Hey mate, we got it. Thea says it will work more than once. It healed me from a mortal wound. See you soon.

I give my reflection a last look in my small bedroom mirror behind the closed door. I'm shocked to see the whites of my eyes are yellow. My energy is waning. Up until now, I still had the strength to work out a little. But this morning, I struggled to eat. This disease is eating me from the inside.

I shouldn't care. I should be happy to die, but something keeps pulling me back. Shoving my hand deep into my pocket, I pull out the charred remains of the red bracelet I'd given Lei Ling all those years ago. The red string symbolizes fate. Some cultures believe there is an invisible red thread that joins two souls together no matter where they are. The evil eye bead is still bright, despite the charcoal residue. I have no idea if it actually worked to ward off the evil spirits Lei Ling feared, but it helped her sleep at night . . . until it didn't.

I'd only been gone from the group home for a few months, but the pull to return to Lei Ling had been strong. I'd barely begun to scratch the surface of demonology. There was so much to learn, so much bullshit to wade through. And gathering contacts in the city's underworld was proving harder than expected. I hated being away from her, but I needed guns, ammunition, and supplies, yet I had little to no money. I couldn't go back with empty hands.

I always kept one eye on Lei Ling. Always checked in. But this one time, I was late. I lost track of which home she'd been shipped off to, and then when I found it, the news report came in.

ORPHAN GIRL DIES IN HOUSE FIRE

I dropped everything and returned to her. I was so fast that the charred remnants of the house fire still smoldered when I arrived . . . and half buried under rubble was a bright-red string with a white bead barely hanging onto the thread—the evil eye. My wildcat . . . dead. I should have been there. I should never have left.

My fist swallows the red thread and clenches. I give myself a hard look in the jaundiced eyes and say, "She's in a better place. And you'll never get there. All you can do is keep hunting the evil things that made your life miserable."

I don't know why I keep thinking about Lei Ling here, in this abbey filled with Sinners and whores. It's probably because one of them has a name so close to hers . . . but apart from them both being Asian, there are no other similarities. From the moment I saw Leila on the abbey steps, I knew she was a different person. She was the furthest thing from innocent. My lip curls in disgust. These women are nasty and dangerous. Don't get me wrong, they're fucking sexy as all hell. And if I'm being honest with myself, I'd probably bang them all. It's just sex. Empty, soulless sex. Why not do it with someone who feels the same way?

I shove the bracelet into my pocket and storm out of the tiny room, then crash headlong into my neighbor—Leila. Her perfume zings into my abused lungs, and I wheeze as we become a tangle of limbs and confusion.

"You fucking kidding me?" She shoves me away.

I stumble back and grin. Irritating these women is like a drug I can't avoid—especially this one. The feisty brunette with a name like the one I lost. Every time I flirt with her, it's like I'm torturing myself with ghosts.

Leila slams her shoulder into me as she walks by. Pain bursts in my bruised flesh.

"Psycho," I grumble and hold my arm. Shamefully, I can't take hits like I used to.

She pivots to face me, eyes wild. "As if you can't take it."

She inches closer, and I feel the heat of her body. Her pupils blow to giant black saucers. My pulse quickens, and I drop my gaze to the blush of her plump lips. She really is stunning. I think I'm getting hard. Yep . . . a semi is poking into the fly of my jeans. I don't know how she does this to me, but I react with arousal every damn time I smell her. I guess seduction is what these women know.

I can take it . . .

"But I can give a lot more," I drawl and let my gaze rake down her mouthwatering body.

Her spitfire attitude brings life to my sluggish heart. If Thea's relic works, if I truly get healed, maybe I'll knock on her door in the middle of the night, slip in, and see if she's up for—

"You're revolting," she snaps.

My grin widens. "You love it."

"I want to puke."

I stifle a groan at this tension. My cock is rock hard now. All she needs to do is look down and see . . . but I can't help messing with her further. "You want to fuck me."

"I want to *murder* you." Her shriek thunders in the hallway, and I step back, eyes wide.

Okay . . . maybe she's not playing with me. But in all my time here, she's always been happy to trade insults. I honestly thought it was a game. My bad.

"What's your problem?" I ask.

"My problem? Are you serious?"

"Yeah, your problem." I shove her shoulder with two fingers.

Leila goes so still that I fear I've turned her to stone. Fear licks down my spine as I realize she's switched into Sinner mode . . . and my fingers are still pressed into her shoulder. This is why Team Saint is here. This dead look in her eyes. I should step back, but I'm worried one move and she'll snap.

With a measured, deliberate motion, she lowers her eyes to where I touch her. Then she slowly returns her icy gaze to my face. There's something in there beyond the cold death—it's personal, pained, and too real. And I feel like it's all my fault. I quickly avert my gaze, shove my hands back in my torn jeans' pockets, and jog down the stairs as fast as I can . . . away from the psycho.

"If you're spoiling for a fight, Zeke," she shouts after me, her voice husky. "I'm your huckleberry."

The world screams.

Not the world.

My heart.

I pause halfway down the steps. My knuckles whiten on the rail. Can't breathe.

The big dumb redheaded bully from the group home is picking on the wrong kid. I hate his fucking guts, and he's just given me the best excuse to start a brawl . . . Time to rescue the damsel. I charge into the courtyard to a game of piggy-in-the-middle. Four or five other foster kids tease the tiny new girl. But she's snarling and hissing at them like a wildcat.

My lips curve as I take in her moxie. Brave little thing. But they should pick on someone their own size.

"Hey!" I shout. They all look my way.

I stalk forward, my death stare zeroed in on the fuckhead who thinks he can just take what he wants. I shove him so hard that he falls on his ass. I snarl, "You wanna pick on someone, Puck? I'm your huckleberry."

My fingers slide into my pocket and touch the charred bracelet again. It can't be. Has Lei Ling been in front of my face the whole time? Who died in that fire? Why was her bracelet there? Why couldn't I find her in any of the hospitals? She's dead.

Lei Ling is dead.

Or . . .

Have I been so caught up in my pity party that I didn't recognize the miracle before me? I face her so slowly that my heart thuds in my ears. And words . . . what are words? My throat is dry. My lungs feel like an elephant sits on them. But I force myself to look upon the stunning beauty's face with fresh eyes, hoping against all hope that I didn't imagine her last words.

"Wh-what did you say?" I murmur.

"You heard me." Her scowl deepens, and she jogs down the stairs, passing me without a second glance. But as she goes, I see her scratching her inner wrist—the same wrist that used to wear the bracelet. Her hair is shorter now, but from this angle, I can imagine she and Lei Ling are the same person.

"Wildcat?" I stumble down a step, but she doesn't stop.

She keeps walking, and I wheeze out a pained breath. I'm unsure which hurt more—the day I thought she was dead, or today, when she looked at me with nothing but hate.

Five

The Past

Screams woke the boy from his sleep. He smelled smoke. Fire. His first thought was that it was back— the fiery-eyed demon. It had burned his baby sister before his eyes, and now it had returned to burn him too. But it wasn't the bed beside him on fire. This room was the same as before he went to sleep.

Through the window, moonlight shone bright enough that he could make out the rows of beds and orphan boys still sleeping in them. Smoke curled from beneath the door.

The screams and fire were out there . . . where the girls slept.

Wildcat.

His heart leaped into his throat as he tossed his blanket and stumbled out of bed. When he wrapped his hand around the doorknob, it sizzled against his skin. *Hot.* He hissed and shook it. Eyes darting about, he searched for another exit—the window.

"Get up!" he bellowed. "FIRE."

The boy was almost a man now. His voice had deepened, and his body had changed. Too old for adoption, but too young to live on his own. So he stayed here in the group home with the other rejects. It had never bothered him because here, he had her. His wildcat. Like two peas in a pod, they'd gravitated toward each other upon meeting. And, although she was half a decade younger than him, they'd found so much common ground.

She was a fighter. She was his only friend. For the better part of a decade, she was his life.

They tried to adopt her out, but she always returned because the fire followed her too. And now it was here, for both of them. He would age out of the system in a year, then he would take her, and they'd leave together. He'd find a way to take care of her.

He broke the glass with a chair and then tossed his blanket over the shards. They were two stories up, but he'd climbed down the drainpipe many times before.

"You did this," snarled one of the boys behind him. "You and your evil pet."

He didn't bother defending himself. They never believed. So he climbed out of the window and didn't look back. The moment his bare feet hit the ground, he ran.

"Wildcat!" he shouted, his throat already hoarse as he jogged around the large house.

The front door burst open with a plume of smoke. People spilled out. One. Two. He tried to catch their identities as they screamed and ran past him. So hard. Too many shadows. Too many screams.

"Wildcat!"

"I'm here," a feminine voice piped up. He turned and located her in the chaos. They locked eyes, and she ran into his arms.

"Huckleberry." Her nickname for him sent shivers down his spine. Her thin body trembled in his arms. "It found me. It found me."

He put her down and smoothed her dark, sweaty hair. Bright eyes full of fear glimmered at him.

"We're safe," he said, tugging on her red bracelet. "It can't get you out here."

"But Snug . . ." Her bottom lip trembled. She swallowed her words and sucked in a breath, trying to be brave. The other kids teased her for keeping Snuggles at her age, but it was the only link to her past.

"Where?"

She looked at the house. The alarm blared. Black smoke billowed from every window, and more people streamed out. Now that he knew she was safe, and the demon hadn't taken her, he was no longer afraid. This was probably a simple house fire. It was all in his imagination.

Probably.

"Wait here," he said to her. "I'll find him."

"No," she cried and tugged his sweatshirt. "It will get you."

He stared into her teary eyes. "You will be safe out here until I get back. The demon doesn't want me, remember? It had a chance, and it walked on by. I will return with Snuggles."

"Promise?"

"Cross my heart and hope to die." He dragged his pointer finger over his heart twice. "Now you say the next part."

She pouted, fashioned her fingers into a gun, and pointed at his face. "Stick a bullet in your eye."

"Eat a horse manure pie," they said together and then made puking gestures.

She giggled. It was all he needed to hear. The world was empty without that sound.

He pushed her away and then jogged into the burning building.

Six

Leila - Today

Sometimes you meet a stranger and know they'll be in your life forever. There is no quantification of this knowledge. It's just a feeling. A sixth sense. It's like you've already spent time with them. You've laughed and cried with them . . . yet . . . you've only just met. Sometimes this feeling comes from future friends, lovers, or mentors. But sometimes, it's from an infuriating boy like Ezekiel Cohen. He blew into my childhood and cared for me when no one else did. Even though I was six and he was eleven, we became instant friends when he saved me from bullies and called me wildcat. He became my world—my protector. My hero.

Then he made me believe he was dead . . . and that I killed him.

I confronted him, but the coward hasn't spoken to me since. I keep waiting for him to man up and explain why he left, but he can barely look at me.

Good. I don't care, either.

I turn my attention to the front of the abbey classroom, where Thea and Wesley recount what they've translated from the lost gospel's prophecy. A week has passed since the demon prince Asmodeus played us for fools and broke out of his prison. Thea found an angelic relic only she can use to heal all manner of ailments . . . but we still lost our sister Prue. We still found the Monsignor crucified to the wall in our dining hall, and the nuns still tried to kill each other.

It's been a week since the start of the apocalypse . . . we think.

So far, we've not heard a peep of proof that Asmodeus is truly the Horseman of War and causing havoc amongst the streets. But he knows how to infect innocent people with the urge to fight. He knows how to teleport. He could be anywhere by now.

I glance at my Sinner sisters on my side of the long conference table. Mercy, Raven, and Tawny look as tired and concerned as I feel. The Reverend Mother appears older than I've ever seen her. None of us slept well. Not with the knowledge that any of us could be next. And Tawny—I give her a sideways glance—that demon prince *kissed* her. She's paler than usual and fidgets continuously. Probably wondering if the demon did something to her . . . left something evil inside.

Across the table, the surviving members of Team Saint listen warily. Zeke appears bored, but I know he's listening. He used that bored face whenever I wanted to watch baking shows at the group home, but then knew exactly what ingredients to buy me when I asked for help.

Father Angelotti sits next to Saint Dominic. I try to place their expressions . . . They look lost, hopeless, and upset. The discovery of Mary Magdalene's gospel has rocked the foundations of their faith.

She wasn't a prostitute. She was Jesus's favored Apostle and wife. A woman. A prophet.

Thea's angelic relic and Asmodeus's prison break prove Mary's apocalyptic prophecy to be real, so it stands to say we should all take the rest of her manuscript as, well, gospel.

If this gets out, then it changes everything for the Catholic Church. Priests will be allowed to marry. Women will be allowed into the seminary. The question is, what does Team Saint plan on doing with this information? It's no secret they were sent here to dismantle us—a secret society of female assassins. But that was before one of theirs fell in love with one of ours. That was before we found out the Mother of Demons, Lilith, is spearheading the antichrist's arrival. Thea and Wesley insist our factions must work together to stop this apocalypse, but I'm unsure.

Zeke is a liar. The Saint is too quiet. Probably has a Rolex hidden beneath the cuff of his expensive Italian suit. Father Angelotti doesn't seem so pious with those prison tattoos hiding beneath his white collar. Old scars batter his olive skin. I don't trust any of them. For all we know, they've already tattled to the Vatican, who had already spent centuries hiding Mary's gospel so the patriarchy can retain power in the church.

They might sneak in during the night and burn us all down. It would save them drama . . . and keep their power in balance. I should double my fire hazard checks tonight. Just in case.

Now is the time we should be watchful. Wary.

A loud bang whips my head to the front of the classroom. Thea has just slammed the gospel down and now glares at us.

"Did anyone listen to a word I said?" Her brown eyes blaze with aggravation.

Wesley stands to her side, arms folded, suit crumpled.

"Bloody hell, enough of this wallowing," he tells his team. "We don't have time for egos and self-pity. Yes, we've suffered losses—from both teams. Yes, things aren't what you thought." His tone softens as he focuses on the Saint. "I know it's a hard pill to swallow, Dom, but your God is still here. He's still the one you put your faith in. It's the institution here on earth that's messed up."

Interesting that he didn't address the priest first. Dominic gesticulates and shoots rapid-fire Italian I can't quite understand.

Wesley purses his lips, then opens the gospel to a page and writes a passage on the chalkboard. When he's done, he adjusts his spectacles and points at the board with his chalk.

Five relics of the divine borne by
Five sinners of saints to mend
Five heralding horses

He says, "One thing Thea and I learned on our journey was that nuances in the prophecy can be misinterpreted, but some words will not change." He circles the words: five, relics, divine, sinners, saints, and heralding horses. Then adjusts his glasses before addressing us. "It's undoubtedly clear five relics will be the key to stopping the horsemen. We've seen what Thea's staff can do and that it will only allow *her* to harness its powers. And it's clear the Sinners and Saints must work together to locate the remaining four relics."

"Do we know which relics?" The Rev asks as she adjusts her habit around her wrinkled face.

"That's one of the unclear parts," Wesley confirms.

"But," Thea adds, her eyes hopeful, "more words have appeared on blank pages. We're working hard to translate. In the meantime, I suggest we all get involved with researching known holy relics and—"

"Wait just a goddamned minute," I growl. "Is no one going to talk about the fact these men wanted to dismantle us a week ago? Are we just going to sweep that under the rug, hold hands, and sing 'Kumbaya' because the book tells us to?"

"Will you *Sinners* keep killing men because they're in your way?" the priest asks.

"If the shoe fits . . ." Mercy mutters. But he doesn't cower. His eyes rake up and down Mercy. My hand twitches for a weapon, but he loses the anger in his eyes as he answers.

"*Non uccidere.* Thou shalt not kill," is all he says. Silence expands in the room.

A mix of fury, guilt, shame, and defiance churns in my gut. How dare he? There isn't a single drop of blood spilled in the name of the Sisterhood that isn't rotten. The men we kill are rapists, murderers, and disgusting, corrupt souls. Mercy slams her palms on the table, stands slowly, and leans toward him. Her copper hair falls like a waterfall around her face, but her expression is fierce as she growls through clenched teeth, "God can suck my white, freckled—"

Thwack!

The Reverend Mother's cane slams on the table. Mercy

flashes a guilty look and then sits without a word. But she holds the hate as she glares at the priest.

Father Angelotti turns a deep crimson around his neck and ears. I can't tell if it's anger or a blush. Mercy's not wearing her usual revealing clothes today. Hasn't since Prue died. She's just in modest black workout attire. So maybe the priest's reaction is anger . . . but when I give him a second glance, his eyes are unfocused, and his fingertips tap the table irritably.

He's probably thinking of a creative penance for her. Our resident priest ran away a week ago, so if Father Angelotti doesn't fill the gap, we'll have to find another priest willing to take a vow of silence and come to the Sisterhood.

The Rev softens her gaze toward Father and removes her cane before sitting her old body back down with a wince. She straightens her habit with gnarled fingers, clutches her rosary beads, then sighs loudly so no one mistakes her exasperation.

"No, Father Angelotti," she says. "The Hildegard Sisterhood has suspended all Sinner missions until the Lilith threat is over—not just here, but around the world at our other chapters."

"And then?" he asks.

"We might all be dead by then." She harrumphs. "There's no point arguing hypotheticals, but I can promise you that my girls will work openly with your boys. And *we* will not keep secrets. We expect the same respect from your team."

"*Sì.*" The priest gives a curt nod, but from the clench in his square jaw and the hardness in his eyes, it's clear he has reservations. "We will put aside our differences for the soul of the world."

"What about the Monsignor?" Dominic's accented baritone rumbles from the base of his throat. "We will send him home for a burial, yes?"

My brows lift. That's the most I've heard him speak.

"Considering the changing nature of Mary's gospel," Wesley says, his expression grim. "It's better that we bury him here alongside Prudence and keep this information to ourselves. At least until we understand more about the holy relics we're hunting."

Dominic abruptly stands, buttons his Versace jacket, and walks out. Father Angelotti gives Wesley an unreadable look and leaves.

Wesley pulls off his spectacles and rubs his eyes. "This is my fault. I should have been honest with them from the start."

Thea touches his back. "It's not your fault."

"The Monsignor is dead because I brought us here. We lied to them. I lied to myself."

"Sometimes shit happens, Wes," Zeke says, standing up. "Can't go beating yourself up about it."

My scoff is audible. The lie had something to do with him and Wesley manipulating their team to come here. He almost hijacked the relic from Thea, and we all saw her use it on Zeke after they returned to the abbey. But still, none of them are talking. I have no idea what happened.

"Decisions have consequences," I state, then shift my glare to Wes. "We're not privy to your reasons for lying to your team, but I hope it was good. Because you've clearly lost their trust and have done nothing to gain mine."

"Leila," Thea admonishes.

"It's true," I reply. "Anyone can see. And I, for one, would like for people to stop lying."

"I agree," Mercy says.

"Me too," Tawny adds.

Raven stays quiet, probably because her psychic gift has given her enough information. She has a habit of keeping valuable thoughts to herself. I used to hate her for it, but she once explained that it's because half the time, she never knows if her visions will come to pass or remain a dream. I get that. I suppose, what's the point of adding to the confusion?

But these men . . . there's no excuse. They can't preach about us working together while simultaneously lying to us.

"Sometimes the truth is more painful than the lie," Zeke mutters. I don't get a chance to tell him that's irrelevant bullshit because he lifts his chin to Wesley and says, "It's about time I speak to them."

"I'll come." Wes gives Thea a loving goodbye kiss on the forehead, then collects his books. "This is my mess too."

SEVEN

ZEKE

I leave the classroom with my hands in my pockets, one hand running over the rosary beads Cisco gave me after he baptized me and the other toying with the red charred bracelet.

It feels like two opposite ends of the spectrum. One represents my absolution from all my sins. Another represents the reason.

I thought I could stay here in the abbey and help piece back together the lives of these innocent nuns. After all, this chaos was partly my fault. But I can barely sit in the same room as Leila without falling apart. The guilt is eating me alive.

She's alive.

Alive.

Not dead. All these years, I'd done a good job of forgetting her. So good that I'd failed to recognize her when I arrived at the Sisterhood. I spent the week mentally berating myself and trying to figure out why. How could I forget someone who made such an important impression on my soul? The only answer I came up with was that I thought she was dead. Ghosts don't grow up. They remain the same in your mind as the day they died.

My little sister is still that gurgling, baby-powder-smelling child. Lei Ling is still that sweet, innocent girl who sometimes got hives and itched when she worried about making a good impression.

I'd built her into something pure and saintly in my mind— someone so kind and good that there was no equal. But here she was, all grown up, a Sinner—a killer. No trace of the innocent girl exists in her hateful eyes. It's funny how emotion can change one's appearance. Anger and hate can turn you hard, even ugly. A smile can make anyone beautiful.

Leila had stewed for a week, thinking that I couldn't care less about her when the opposite was true . . . and far more painful to admit. Because I'd failed again. I'd let her down and now there was nowhere to hide.

"Zeke, wait up."

Wesley's footsteps quicken behind me, but I walk faster towards the stairs leading down from the archives.

"Zeke." Wesley grabs my arm a few steps down, and I spin to face him.

It hurts to look into his concerned eyes where my failings live with glaring clarity. All I've done my whole life is mess things up. Couldn't save my sister from the fire demon. Leila is a goddamn assassin now with blood on her hands. Wes lied to Cisco and Dom because of me, and now they don't trust us. My illness was why Wesley arranged for that gospel to come here and why Thea used her angelic relic on me, but I'm not sure it was worth the cost.

How far can you fall before your feet land on brimstone?

"You all right, mate?" Wesley's British accent is thick today. It happens when he's tired.

"Better than ever," I drawl. Since Thea healed me, I feel like a new man . . . health-wise. I'm eating like a horse. Packing muscle on like I'm a teenager. All my old fighting injuries no longer ache when I work out. If only that relic could heal what's inside my head.

Wesley looks at me as though he's not convinced. I consider confessing about Leila, about how we used to be so close I considered her family. How in the end, when she started blossoming into maturity, I started developing confusing and deep feelings for her. Then, how I failed to recognize her as an adult but still acted like a dick and tried to fuck her.

He's the only person I've come near to revealing everything, but I chicken out every time. I haven't even told Cisco during confession, and he's the only team member who can relate to what I'm going through. He knows about my old criminal lifestyle . . . but nothing about Lei Ling.

She was a precious secret I held in my heart.

If it weren't for Wes, I'd have died in the gutter, in a prison cell, or by the bullet of an old enemy. Either way, I would have been alone and miserable.

I suppose, at least, I'm not alone now.

"Right, well," Wes says, "I think it's time we sat down with the lads and have a little heart-to-heart."

I groan. "I know. Let's get this done with."

He nods and runs his hand through his short blond hair. "And there's something else."

"More bad news?"

"That's a matter of perspective." He sighs. "But you should all know. No more secrets, yeah?"

A sick feeling churns in my stomach. Consequences suck. I never thought I'd be around to deal with them. Being diagnosed with a terminal illness was poetic justice—my penance for all the shitty things I've done, including those people I've killed. I never truly believed Wes would come through for me with this holy relic business, but he did. That morning I got his text message, my view of the world started to claw its way back to hopeful. But it wasn't just Wes. Thea's a Sinner—a supposed evil-doer and bad person—but she came through for me too.

Maybe there's hope for Leila. Maybe there's hope for me.

Now . . . now I have to start facing the consequences of my actions. I look down at my hands and swallow a lump in my throat.

"Lead the way," I say.

Wesley claps me on the back, and we head down the stairs, exit the abbey, and take the long path to the small church at the back of the estate. Dom and Cisco seem to be spending a lot of time hiding out there lately, and I don't blame them. Their world has been turned upside down with Mary's gospel. We should have had this conversation a week ago, but we've all been preoccupied with damage control after Asmodeus. Nuns keep slipping back into chaos. We monitor them around the clock to ensure they don't kill each other.

The time never seemed right to say, "Oh hey, you didn't know about those holy relics, but we did. We just never told you in case the relic only worked once, and we had to betray these women to get first dibs."

The walk down the winding path beside the large lake is beautiful. I must admit the estate scenery is second to none. If I lived here, I would have a hard time leaving. Sweet-smelling nature is on both sides. A babbling brook flows down a hill, under the path we cross, and into the lake on the other side. Further up the hill behind the abbey is an enormous walled garden where they grow much of the vegetables and fruit used in the cooking. It's also where the chickens are kept.

Forests and trees are everywhere else.

It's a nice simple life. Peaceful. Free. The kind of life people crossed oceans and wild country to claim. The kind where death was around every corner, but they fought tooth and nail to live in freedom.

It's paradise until I see the twisted clues sprinkled around. A rope hangs from a tree where the Sinners take turns hanging from a noose to strengthen their necks. Then there's the bark on trees worn down from shins repetitively meeting it—training to toughen their skin. Let's not forget the garden of beautiful, deadly plants waiting to strike, just like their mistresses. This paradise has fangs.

We're silent as we walk, but I sense Wesley has something to say. Normally, I'd love the challenge of teasing words out of him. But this past week, the air has been as thick as water, and I have no illness as an excuse.

At the sound of scampering behind us, I reach for the Colt Lightning holstered at my hip. Since Asmodeus, I've worn two pistols everywhere. Cisco blessed the cartridges, and I've engraved them with the Enochian sigils from an occult spell. While I can't kill demons, I can sure as shit slow them down.

My pistol is aimed and cocked before I register the small dark, iridescent ex-demon galloping toward me on all fours. I put the gun away. Jinx arrived at the abbey with Thea and Wes from London but has spent more time with me in the past week than her saviors.

I open my hands, and the scaled animal half scampers up my legs, half jumps, until she crawls around my neck, burrows under my hair, and settles like a stole. Thea said Jinx's demon form appeared like a grotesque fish with fangs and legs, but after Thea healed her, she morphed into what looks like a tiny mythological serpent.

Definitely not evil.

Something about her appeals to me. I think it's the redemption . . . the second chance she's been given. I like to believe she's drawn to me because we've both been on the receiving end of angelic healing, and we're both equally stumped as to what made us worthy of this miracle, but maybe she's just after me because I keep treats in my pocket.

I interpret the tiny dolphin sounds in her throat as a scolding for leaving the main building without her.

"Sorry," I mumble and pat her warm body. "No treats today."

Wesley's brows raise above his spectacles.

"Don't say it," I warn as we continue toward the church. I used to hate pets . . . Anything I had to look after was too much responsibility.

He shuts his mouth, but I can feel him smiling at me. As we arrive, the large double doors open, and out walk two resident nuns dressed in habits. The Sinners affectionately call them Magpies. Wes and I stand aside, giving them plenty of room to pass while offering friendly smiles.

The Hildegard Nuns keep a vow of silence and only speak during mass. Then they let loose. Sometimes they're so loud I hear them singing from the abbey. Before I was healed, I tried to get them to break their vow and spill Sisterhood secrets. I figured, at least one of them must think the work these Sinners do is evil. But the most I've ever received was a warm smile and a dishcloth slapped in my hand so I would help in the kitchen.

Before heading inside the church, I watch the nuns meander back toward the monolith limestone abbey with ivy creeping over the facade. This place isn't what I expected. When Wes told me about an organization of assassin nuns, I had insane Hollywood notions involving corruption and evil. But the nuns who live here are the kindest, smartest, and most generous women I've met. And the Sinners, they're not nuns. I know they've made some kind of vows to the Sisterhood and to God, and they often assume the identities of nuns out and about, but they're not nuns. They're . . . interesting.

Wesley no longer believes they're evil, but I'm sure Cisco and Dom still have reservations. Me? I've done worse things than these Sinners. I rest my palm on my pistol and think about my own wild country—the urban jungle I tamed after I thought Leila was dead, and how, for a time, I was its god. My apostles were drug runners and arms dealers. My gospel was the word out of my mouth.

If evil and disgust are afforded to these women who kill for honorable reasons, then what am I owed? That was a part of my life when I lost all reason.

Movement in the distance catches my eye, and I squint to see better. Two Sinners jog around the estate. I've not seen the girls take a day off. If they're not working out and training, they're in the archives researching and preparing. I squint harder and recognize a familiar lithe frame and dark bob framing a pale face. Leila. She attacks the path with single-minded ferocity. It's like she wants to carve grooves in the ground with her feet. The curvy redhead behind her is almost the same, but when I look closer, it seems like something is chasing her. Like maybe this is a distraction for her too.

I smile—Leila runs headfirst into a challenge while others are chased by it.

Jinx flexes her claws on my shoulder, urging me to keep walking. A placating pat on her head calms her down.

"Come on," Wesley says.

Inside the church, incense wafts from the modest wooden altar at the front. Arched stained windows are bright and cast a turquoise light. A single column of pews with red velvet kneeling pads takes up the nave. A gothic fan-vaulted ceiling makes me feel small and inconsequential . . . as I'm sure was the purpose.

Cisco's black shirt sleeves are rolled up, and he fusses about the inside of the wooden tabernacle in the sanctuary. Something must have spilled.

Dom's hulking figure kneels behind the front pew. His bald and cross-branded head is bowed in silent prayer. He prays more than the priest.

Wesley stops to dip his hand in holy water by the door and then makes the sign of the cross. I always forget this part but mimic his movements. Maybe I should have left the ex-demon outside.

Jinx wakes briefly, as if she heard my thoughts, and grumbles.

"Behave," I warn as I walk the left aisle and then slide onto the front pew Dom kneels behind. Wesley genuflects at the crucifix behind the altar and then quietly sits beside me. Guilt flushes my cheeks. I forgot that part too. I'm not a very good Catholic.

This probably isn't the best place to break the news of our subterfuge, but I have to admit the atmosphere is calming.

No one else is in the church except us four.

While we wait for Cisco and Dom to finish, I gaze around the gothic architecture in awe. Arcades of marble columns lead to a triforium on either side of the nave. One has a pipe organ, and the other holds a confessional. To the right of the sanctuary, a half-open door leads to a shadowed room. I glimpse more twisted clues that this paradise has teeth—a rack of weapons on the wall, a vintage wooden confessional, and perhaps the kneeling pad from a pew . . . only there's no padding like that out here. It's hard and worn. The words, *The Sin Bin* are carved into the door.

On the opposite side of the sanctuary, another door is open. The room beyond is filled with priestly robes and supplies. Cisco has accepted the Reverend Mother's offer to be the abbey's priest until another is sourced from the local diocese. The priest who'd been here upon our arrival—Father McBride—didn't last long.

My brow furrows as I wonder what kept these priests from confessing Sisterhood secrets to the Vatican all these years.

They were probably threatened. Or maybe they really did hold to their vows of silence.

Just as well Father McBride didn't last long. He could have ended up like the poor Monsignor, crucified. Asmodeus painted a bloody message on the wall beside the body: *Ezekiel 18:4.*

The actual Bible verse is:

> Behold, all souls are mine; as the soul of the
> father, so also the soul of the son is mine:
> the soul that sinneth, it shall die.

Wes thinks it's Asmodeus's promise of a little payback to the ancestors of the woman who locked him in a stone prison, but I fear it's much simpler than that.

My name is Ezekiel. Eighteen is the number of people I've killed, and four is the number of years I spent doing it.

EIGHT

ZEKE

"C*iao*," Cisco greets softly as he walks down the sanctuary steps, wiping his oily hands on a cloth.

The Italian priest's body language says he's full of goodwill, but an unmistakable flash of wariness exists in the depths of his eyes. Fransisco Angelotti's muscular body is carved not from hours in the gym, but from years of brutal physical activity. I know because I walked the same roads.

I recognize the scars on his knuckles, the muscular frame, and the hardness ingrained into his facial expression. While I don't know his full story, I know his supernatural talent for sensing evil is what saved him from life in prison and brought him to the priesthood, much to the Italian mafia's dismay. He was their best enforcer. Ever. And they paid him well. Like me, he was a god in his world. I'm sure they intended to spring him out of prison, but the church came calling first.

I confided in him about my history with gun runners here

in the States. He shared secrets of his time with the mafia—enough that I know he's ashamed of what he's done. He said he was absolved of his sins and that when he baptized me, he absolved me too.

It can't be as easy as that, can it?

I slide my hand into my pocket. My fingers graze the smooth rosary beads. Temptation comes in all shapes and sizes. Anger. Violence. Sex. Addiction. Each is a gateway to another, and after I thought Leila was dead, my life was a miserable never-ending cycle of God's punishment—until this team showed me another way to focus my energy.

Love had no place in my damned life. I existed purely to serve as a tool in this holy war against the dark forces that claimed my sister and taunted Leila. But now that I see her all grown up and the sole reason my heart exists, I know I'll either come out of this in Heaven or Hell. There is no in-between.

The wooden seat creaks under Dominic's weight as he sits behind me. His warm brown eyes hold more forgiveness than the priest's as he takes me in. Sometimes I wonder if any crime is bad enough to wipe that look from his face. Sometimes I want to try and test it.

Wes adjusts his spectacles and says, "We have a confession."

"*Si*. I must get my purple stole," Cisco replies. "You are both overdue."

Wesley gestures for the priest to return. "I think, perhaps, Dom needs to hear this too."

The determination in Wesley's eyes makes me nervous. He's going to try and accept the blame—I can feel it. I can't let him, so I take over the confession . . . sort of.

"I asked Wes to use his connections at the Vatican to bring

us here. I'd heard a rumor about a prophecy and a healing relic that only Sinners could . . ."

My voice trails off under our priest's disapproving glare. He continues to wipe spilled sacramental oil from his hands with a cloth. It's hard not to imagine him as an enforcer cleaning himself after a bloody crime. I suspect that hard look is all repenting parishioners need to reveal their darkest secrets.

He knows I'm lying.

"Mate," Wesley says to me. "I appreciate your effort, but you didn't *make* me do anything. And I came to you with the idea." To the others, he adds, "A while back, I found a passage in an old, discredited prophecy about holy relics and Sinners and Saints—you know that now as Mary Magdalene's lost gospel. When word came of a secret society of Sinners, I felt the prophecy might be real. The fact I learned this about the time Zeke revealed he was sick felt like fate. We're here today because I manipulated events so that we'd be the team sent to dismantle the Sisterhood . . . and, in doing so, be in a prime position to use that relic on Zeke before Thea could use it on Prue. As you know, events worked out better than anyone anticipated. I trusted Thea, and she's the right person to hold the power."

"You lied to us," Dom states, his brow furrowing.

Wes nods. I glance at the crucifix on the wall behind the wooden altar, then nod too.

Cisco exhales and sits on the sanctuary steps. He closes his eyes and asks, "Why?"

"We didn't think you'd approve," Wes replies. "And that you'd stop us."

That they'd tattle to the Holy See's agents about our plans. I never believed the Entity—their secret service—

existed until Wes revealed a few insider stories. On the surface, the Vatican's espionage team includes priests, cardinals, and bishops . . . not that they'd admit it. But if the papacy faces danger, it is swiftly and mysteriously eradicated. Whoever they are, they're well-funded, shrouded in secrecy, and have untold power.

"Did you know before you joined our team?" Dom asks me.

"No. I joined because I was running from the life I had. I needed an outlet for my urges, and you not only gave it to me, but I felt like I finally had a purpose for it—hunting demons. I mean, I started to hunt demons, and then . . ." I frown, still unwilling to share details about Leila with the rest of the team. "I guess I went off the rails."

"He wasn't sick until after he joined," Wes pointed out.

"*Sì*." Dom nodded, remembering.

"I'm sorry we kept it from you." Wesley's eyes are full of sincerity. "And I'm sorry I didn't give you the heads up about what was inside the gospel, should it be proven authentic. I know this alternate version of history will take time to wrap your heads around, but you can't deny that miracles have come from it."

Jinx unfurls herself from my shoulders and drops behind me to climb onto Dominic's lap. His eyes widen at the ex-demon. Then his big hand lands on Jinx's head, engulfing the skull. He strokes until the creature is calm.

"No, we can't deny miracles have happened," Cisco agrees, then gestures to my shirt. "You were healed too, yes?"

I nod.

"Show me."

"My wounds were mainly on the inside." The fighting scars I have are gone, but they were old.

"I mean your tattoos," the priest replies. "They are now broken like Wesley's?"

Wes looks at me. "Bloody hell, mate. I didn't even think to check."

I grab my sweater from behind my neck and slide it over my head. The Rolling Stones t-shirt comes off too. I glance down at my torso. Rich black lines and arcane symbols are littered over the bronze flesh. "Looks fine to me."

"No," Dom says from behind me. "*Sono guarite.* Back tattoo is *guasto.*"

"He's right, Z," Wes says, inspecting my back. "Healed scars have disrupted the tattoos."

I crane my neck and see near my lower back where a decade ago, a thirty-eight-caliber slug hit, just missing my kidney. The healed skin has purged the tattoo ink. None of these arcane spells will work if the lines aren't joined.

"The sooner you get those fixed, the better," Cisco points out.

"These little miracles are exactly what I'm talking about," Wesley says, meaning my healed wounds and sickness.

"I understand. Which is why I passed this information to our friends at the Vatican."

"What?" Wes stands, alarm in his eyes.

"Sit down." Cisco remains unworried. "We cannot lie to them about the Monsignor's death."

"They'll come here and remove the gospel before we even—"

"Have faith they will see the miracles too."

"I'm not sure if I can." Wesley gestures toward the exit, toward the abbey. "It will divide the gap we're working hard at closing."

"You three are my flock. Not these Sinners."

"Really?" Wes's eyebrow raises. "That coming from a priest? And what about the nuns? Are they not your flock too?"

Cisco frowns and shakes his head. "You are bleeding the lines."

"I know why we were sent here," Wes says. "I know we color outside the lines. Maybe the Sinners aren't your flock yet, but they will be. Trust me. When the Vatican comes, they will take over the hunt for the relics."

"Does it matter who finds them, so long as they're used to defeat evil?"

"Of course it does. These women aren't the reprobates we were led to believe. We can't dismantle this organization. You've all seen the good they do here."

"Good?" Cisco's dark brows rise, and he glances at the sacristy that has become the Sin Bin. "These women have been sanctioned to sin for centuries. It's a little different than repenting afterward. It's permission to sin. Believe me when I say this is not a *good* life."

"But they're not *evil*, right?" I ask, my intense gaze on the priest. His sixth sense helped him advance to the position of exorcist in record time. He once told me I wasn't evil . . . despite my godless history. I believed him, but I need to know if he feels the same way about these women or if it was just something he told me to make me feel better.

Cisco's eyes dart to Dom, then back to me.

"No," he confesses. "I have not sensed true evil in one of them since the demonic possession. But all God's children are free to make choices, Ezekiel. Not all choices are good."

"You took a choice away from us," Wesley's eyes are darkly displeased. "We should have discussed what we wanted to do about our orders before contacting the Vatican."

"I am the exorcist in charge of this team. I do not need permission to speak with His Excellency," Cisco points out dryly. His tone sparks suspicious thoughts inside me. Cisco has never behaved like other priests. From his tattoos to his rushed time at the seminary to the way he loses his temper and storms off. He is ordained, yes. Watching him conduct an exorcism will prove that. He has faith, yes. Seeing him pray or offer Mass tells me that. And he is a good man beneath all that hardness. We spent six months together in Italy during the start of our team's relationship, and I witnessed him with his own parish.

He listened patiently, provided advice, and tirelessly helped the community, not once expecting anything in return. The parishioners trusted him. I've never doubted his loyalty to this team. We all come from dubious backgrounds, so a little misbehavior now and then was ignored.

But I realized something when I saw him under the crucifix wiping his stained hands with a cloth.

"You're one of them, aren't you?" I narrow my eyes. "You've been one of them all along."

No wonder he's always been such a domineering dick regarding our purpose for being here.

"What are you talking about?" Wes's gaze darts between us all.

A bitter laugh escapes me, and I shake my head before answering. "He's one of their spies."

From Dominic's exhale of relief, he knew about it too. The secret must have been killing him, despite having a priest conveniently absolve him of the lie.

"You're Entity?" Wes pales.

"There is no Entity," Cisco chides. "We are simply a trusted network of friends of the Vatican."

"Father Angelotti," Wes admonishes with a note of sarcasm in his tone. "You don't truly believe that's all they are, do you? There is nothing *simple* about spying and eradicating threats to the church."

"Enough," Dominic says. "We are not at war with each other."

"No, we are not." The priest levels his stare on us.

"How long do we have before they arrive?" Wesley presses.

"*Non lo so.*" Cisco shrugs.

"So we must have this conversation now." Wesley stands and buttons his crumpled jacket, his eyes blazing. "Will you stand with the Sinners, or continue with the original mission to dismantle them? I know what I choose."

My lips part, but no words come out. This is the moment I should stand with the people who saved my life, but all I can think of is how utterly confused I feel. Nothing in my life has made sense since Leila was Lei Ling. And now she is something I don't recognize, yet the darkness inside me craves. And that's wrong. She might be a Sinner here, but she's not pretending to be perfect. She let her wildcat out, and the only time I saw her scratch like she had hives was when she confronted me about not remembering her.

I can't go down and drag her with me. I have to be strong. Have to resist temptation.

Wes turns his glare to the others. "The gospel was clear. The saints must work with the sinners, and the sinners are the ones who will have the power to wield the holy relics. If you're doing this because your faith has been shaken by what's in the new scripture—"

Cisco stands, eyes blazing. "My faith is unbreakable, *mio amica*. What is in that gospel only strengthens it."

"So how can you reveal this secret to an organization that has proven they've tried to stifle it? Don't you understand the consequences?"

"*Si*. I cannot deny they lied . . . but it was long ago. Today, *this* organization of Sinners cannot be allowed to continue. Your relationship has clouded your judgment." Cisco's white collar glares in the light from the windows. "You know this to be true."

"Perhaps they can be saved," Dominic ventures quietly, looking at the scaled demon as he strokes the transparent frill down its back. "We all deserve forgiveness, no?"

"Saved?" I scoff. He wants them to repent. To be someone they're not. "They don't want to be *saved* in the way you think."

"They live in sin." Cisco frowns incredulously. "And they are not remorseful."

"I don't mean the murder part," I clarify. "I don't see any of them filled with joy over that. But the sex. The independence. The life here all goes hand in hand with their job."

"I agree," Wes says. "It's not so black and white. We need time."

I nod. "Not excusing it, but who among us can't say our hands are clean of blood."

Certainly not me. Not even Dom can make that claim. The miracle that pushed him into sainthood was a venerable resurrection after death during a battle to protect Romanian orphans from five dangerous traffickers. Dom fought them off with only his bare hands until he was the last one standing . . . but not without suffering internal bleeding. After being pronounced dead, he woke on the mortician's table about to have his chest sliced open . . . three days later.

"I'm in love with Thea," Wesley proclaims loudly, his face turning red with his passion. "She is good, kind, and smart. The Reverend Mother said the Sinners will have no more regular missions until we deal with Lilith. In the meantime, I refuse to throw them to the wolves."

As he stares at the arched gothic ceiling, Cisco mumbles a prayer, then audibly counts to five before responding.

"It was the right thing to do. The Vatican must know the second horseman is here. We are fighting a holy apocalypse. That is the *numero uno* important thing." He points at Wes and me. "Next, you must leave the abbey and have your tattoos fixed. Today or tomorrow."

"I can't leave," Wes replies, aghast. "I'm in the middle of translating—"

"We cannot have our team at half capacity," Cisco insists. "Not with *il demonio* running around. I want your tattoos fixed within the week—both of you."

"You must start trusting these women," Wes replies, but when he receives no response, he shakes his head and walks out.

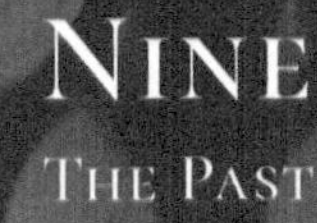

Nine

The Past

"Wait here," the boy said to the girl. "I'll find him."

"No," she cried and tugged his sweatshirt. "It will get you."

He stared into her teary eyes. "You will be safe out here until I get back. The demon doesn't want me, remember? It had a chance, and it walked on by. I will return with Snuggles."

"Promise?"

"Cross my heart and hope to die." He dragged his pointer finger over his heart twice. "Now you say the next part."

She pouted, fashioned her fingers into a gun, and pointed at his face. "Stick a bullet in your eye."

"Eat a horse manure pie," they said together and then made puking gestures.

She giggled. It was all he needed to hear. The world was empty without that sound.

He pushed her away and then jogged into the burning building.

He ran through the burning building, hunting for wildcat's stuffed toy.

Be like Doc Holliday, he chanted in his mind. *Be like Doc. He faced death without fear. Be like Doc.*

He found the toy kicked to the side of the upstairs corridor. It lay at an odd angle like its neck had snapped. Picking it up, he dusted it off and remembered when he'd first seen it years ago.

Nearby, air hissed from a vent repetitively. It sounded like sniffing. Flames licked up the walls, furiously growing brighter. The boy flinched and covered his mouth, trying not to inhale the smoke. His blood sang for him to escape, but something about this moment sent him falling into memory—the day his sister died.

Fire.

Smoke.

Sniffing. Sniffing.

The fiery-eyed demon reached for his sister, hissing the words, "*Snuggle time.*"

The teen gasped and looked down at Snuggles. One eye was missing, and the other was a button. Stitching down the middle looked like it had been on the receiving end of an autopsy. It flopped in his hands like a carcass.

Flames and fire had followed Wildcat wherever she lived. She would have been the same age as his sister. She'd had this toy since birth—it was the only thing with her when she was abandoned at the fire station.

What if the fiery-eyed demon had never been after his sister . . . but was after Wildcat?

What if Snuggles was the magnet this demon was drawn to? These fires would keep burning until one day, they consumed Wildcat as they had his baby sister.

His fist clenched around the toy, and he glanced down the corridor toward the exit—where the path to Wildcat was still clear and safe. He should leave the toy here, let the fire consume it. Or . . . he glanced in the opposite direction, to where the path was wrought with danger and flames . . .

When Doc Holliday's tuberculosis brought him perilously close to death, but his best friend—his *only* friend—Wyatt Earp was about to face the bad cowboy alone, Doc didn't give up. He didn't roll over. No. He pretended to be dying. Then he snuck out and killed the bad Cowboy, so Wyatt was safe.

Doc knew his life wasn't worth as much as Wyatt's . . . and he wanted to repay the man for giving him hope when no one else cared.

Everyone would think the boy had burned alive if he escaped now. But he could be like Doc. He could be crafty. He could use Snuggles to draw the demon out. He could be Lei Ling's huckleberry. He would kill the demon.

And if he couldn't, then the demon would kill him instead of her.

LEI LING STOOD outside the burning building long after the fire department arrived. She stood and waited for her huckleberry to come out.

"Come, child."

Someone grabbed her arm, but she snarled. She pushed all the burning emotion and fear from her gut and unleashed it on anyone nearby.

And she stood.

She waited.

She made a mental list of all the hospitals she'd call.

Then she crossed her heart and hoped to die.

He promised.

Ten

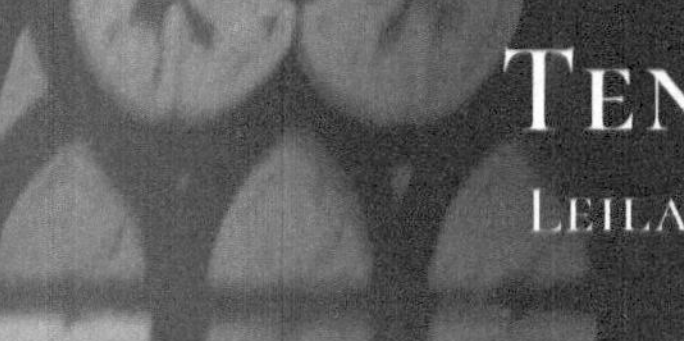

Leila

I slam my laptop lid shut. The old wooden table rattles, causing the brass lamp to wobble. From various points of the archives, glares are sent my way. Mercy and Tawny sit at a table monitoring news networks for signs of Asmodeus. Raven is with a book, probably doing the same thing I was doing . . . reading the same words repeatedly. I close my eyes and shake my head. We've been researching for days but have come up with nothing. This bookish stuff is not my forte. Plus, all I can think about is a certain brooding gunslinger walking around the abbey with an ex-demon fawning over him.

I keep replaying the days before the fire at the group home, trying to work out what I did or said to make him feel that faking his death was the only way out, but I keep coming up with more reasons to break my heart. I was in my final year of middle school, and he was about to graduate high school. He didn't do well with his grades, but neither did I—despite my trying. We were dreamers and preferred sports. Me, with a side of baking.

A few nights before the fire, he returned home late. Usually, he would stop by my room after school. But this one time, he never showed up and never turned up for dinner. Concerned about his lateness, I'd stolen dinner rolls and shoved them in my hoodie pocket before heading to the room he shared with other boys.

His door had been open, and I overheard an angry argument inside. Zeke sat calmly on his bed, his head resting against the wall, a butterfly knife flipping deftly in his hand. His attention was glued to the ginger-haired teen on another bed opposite him. Puck was about to age out of the system. He looked and sounded like a grizzly man.

From the day I arrived at the home, Puck had made it his personal business to make my life hell. I don't know what I did to earn that attitude, but as much as I despised him, I wouldn't have wished for the injuries he sported that day. For a moment, I fall back into the past, recalling the events as though they'd just happened.

PUCK'S EYES and lips were puffy, bloody, and swollen. Hate was unmistakable in his ice-blue eyes as he glared at Zeke and said, "You're going to fucking pay for this, Cohen."

"Good luck with that," Zeke drawled, unworried. "I won't pull my punches next time."

It was then I noticed Zeke's knuckles were bloody. But the rest of him seemed unscathed.

"Why do you even care?" Puck sneered. "Unless you're actually a pedo, and she's your little pleasure doll." He changed his tone to mocking. "Oooh, does Cohen want to make out with his little china doll? Maybe I should turn you in to the cops."

Zeke gave a cruel laugh. "Pedo. That's rich coming from you. Lei Ling is the only girl you haven't tried to shove your cock into, and you know it."

Ew. I scrunched up my nose. Why were boys so gross?

But then I registered my name was spoken and gasped. They were talking about me. I snuck closer to the door to see better. Even under the swollen face, Puck's dark intentions were clear. He didn't deny what Zeke accused him of. He was smiling.

"One of these days, Cohen, you won't be around to protect her."

"She can protect herself."

"She still sleeps with her fluffy toy. She ain't gonna do shit."

"You're sick."

"Maybe. But I'm right. She's growing up to be a juicy piece of ass, and you know what that means. Girls like that love it. They want it. They beg for it."

"You don't scare me."

He gestured to his face. "So this was for what, then?"

Zeke caught the knife. He pointed the blade at Puck. "That was your final warning."

"You gotta sleep sometime, Cohen. And when you do . . ."

My pulse skyrocketed, and I stormed into the room before I could stop myself.

"Did you threaten him?" I snarled at Puck, my fists clenched and ready to decimate.

Zeke grabbed me by the scruff before I made it halfway across the room. Puck's insane laughter followed us outside into the hall.

"Wildcat," Zeke said, irritation flashing in his eyes. "What are you doing here?"

"You didn't come to see me after school." I frowned and looked at my feet. "I was worried."

"I was caught up."

"Fighting Puck?"

"You don't need to worry about him. I'll find us a way out of here, even if I have to adopt you myself."

Warmth spread from my chest outward, then I remembered to reach into my pocket. "I brought you dinner."

Unfortunately, the bread rolls were squashed and crumbly. "Sorry. I'll make honey cakes tomorrow."

"It will still taste good." He bit a chunk out and made appreciative sounds as he ate. "And your cakes are the best I've ever tasted. Can't wait until tomorrow." I grinned with pride as he ruffled my hair. But then his mood grew serious as his hand slipped to tuck some hair behind my ear. He stared at me for a long, weird moment, suddenly scowled, and snatched his hand away. "I won't let anything happen to you. You trust me, right?"

"Yeah, of course."

"Good." He cleared his throat. "Now, off you go and do your bedtime checks."

MY "CHECKS" were nightly rounds around the group home to see if windows were closed. I couldn't leave any potential for stray sparks wafting in and setting the house on fire. At that age, I'd already had too many suspicious house fires blamed on me at other foster homes. I always received the blame, even if I was nowhere near the fire.

I still don't sleep well unless I've done my checks, although they've expanded from the group home to an enormous estate. Speaking of which . . . It's getting late. I glance at the arched window high in the archive. The sun will set in a few hours. I need to get in my workout and then start before dark.

Mercy notices me standing, whispers something to Tawny, then walks over to me.

"You finishing?" she asks, a pinch to her lips.

There is a wild, unhinged look in her eyes. Her usually glossy and wavy hair is frizzy and tied back. Despite no makeup, Mercy is a beauty beyond comparison. She's also one of our deadliest assassins and our team leader. Although Thea seems to be naturally taking over that latter role. I think it's leaving Mercy feeling rudderless, and from the look in her eyes, she wants to talk.

I tense and shift uncomfortably. Talking about feelings isn't really for me, but I guess with Thea busy, and Prue dead, Mercy's only other options are Tawny—the perpetual optimist, or Raven—the perpetual pessimist.

I nod. "Going to work out and do my rounds."

"Do you mind if I tag along?"

A churning in my gut says no, but I can't leave her here like this. And, if she's talking about herself, she won't ask about me. It's only a matter of time before they all figure out something is off between Zeke and me.

"What do you want to talk about?" I ask gruffly as we walk out.

She ties up her hair into a knot, sucks in a breath, and then unloads as soon as we're outside and walking in the brisk mountain air.

"I'm fucking horny, babe."

"What's new?" I intone.

She rounds on me with wild eyes. "I'm serious. I need to fuck."

I stop and raise my brow. "Mercy, you always need to fuck."

"But this is different."

I stare at her momentarily and debate whether I want to get into what's really bothering her. She bites her plump lip. I've never seen her so . . . the opposite of confident. Finally, I give in and ask, "Why is it different?"

She throws her hand toward the church in the distance. "They're here. Judging. I can't just skip into town and find a dick to sit on. I can't even do my usual video chat with a toy, and babe, self-love isn't cutting it."

"Why do you care what they think?"

"I don't. It's just . . . the priest wants me to confess, and I can't with him. He's too . . ." Darkness clouds her eyes, and she shakes her head. "Never mind. Let's run."

This is about the new priest? A few days ago, she was

flirting with him and flashing boob. Now she's ashamed? This isn't the Mercy I know. The Mercy I know can walk into a room of nuns and seduce one of them into lifting her skirt. The Mercy I know struts proudly around the abbey in lingerie, despite having cellulite on her wobbly bits. She makes those bits sexy. She can lure a devout married man into a private booth and then slice his carotid without blinking.

"Mercy." I grab her shoulder as she steps forward. "I know I'm not the best conversationalist, but if you, ah . . . need a person to unload on . . . then . . . um . . . I guess what I'm trying to say is . . ."

Her manicured brows lift hopefully. "You'll fuck me?"

"No!" I roll my eyes and start jogging. "*Jesus Christ*. I'm saying I'll listen if you need to talk."

"Aww, come on. Just a quickie to take the edge off."

Her steps crunch over the gravel behind me. She knows I'm not into women, so she's just testing my patience. After a few minutes, she blurts, "Can I fuck the Saint, then?"

"Nope."

"What about the priest?"

"Nope."

"What about the brooding one with pistols?"

I flatten my lips and speed up. She chases after me, saying, "He seems like he's up for it."

I run faster.

She pants behind me. "He's got a big dick too."

I don't engage. Keep running. Keep filling my lungs with air until we're burning through the scenery. Mercy doesn't shut up. Heaving breaths and footsteps punctuate her every word.

"I know because I saw him lifting weights the other day,

wearing a pair of those thin sweatpants that show everything in the crotch. I'm sure he was sporting a semi. You were there too . . . I think you were on the treadmill. But Jesus, Leila, I swear to God I saw the outline of his—"

I halt and spin so fast that she slams into me. I hold her at arm's length and glare.

"Stay away from him," I warn.

"Why?"

"He's . . ." I swallow my immediate response and instead snarl. "He's one of them. They're not to be trusted. Just go into the city and find someone."

Panting, chest heaving, her eyes go dark and sultry as she takes me in. "God, you're fucking hot when you get angry and sweaty."

It doesn't escape me that she's shifted into full antagonistic mode straight after I suggest she head into the city.

"I get it," I say. "You need to get laid, but it won't be with me. I can't help you if you don't tell me what's really happening. Are you afraid of going into the city?"

"Oh, like you're being honest about your feelings."

"Fine." I go to jog, but she grabs me by the shoulders and kisses me.

Full out, tongue shoved down my throat, cherry chapstick kiss. I'm so stunned that I freeze. Then I shove her off and glare. I want to smack her in the face. It's never cool to do that uninvited. But that helpless, rudderless look is still swirling in her wild eyes, and I can only exhale, shaking my head.

She throws up her hands. "See? I want to fuck everything. It's never been this bad."

"You're deflecting. And don't use me as your sex toy."

"I'm sorry." She pinches the bridge between her eyes.

"So why aren't you?" I swipe hair from my face. "Why aren't you heading into town and finding one of your regulars?"

She winces and glances down. Through the black yoga pants, a dark ring of blood soaks through on each thigh.

"Mercy, those cilices aren't meant to be used that much. You'll have no flesh left if you keep punishing yourself."

"They help me contain my demons," she mutters quietly.

"Well, they're not working. Take them off. We'll work out."

She shakes her head.

"You can't run with them on," I say. "You'll be cut to ribbons."

The cilices are barbed chains around her thighs and part of our instruments of penance—mortification of the flesh. It's an old religious custom that predates the Sisterhood, a way to purge sin. I never much got into it, but Mercy's blood drips down her legs.

Fucking Team Saint. They show up, and everything is a mess.

"Don't give them a single ounce of your shame, Mercy." I lift my chin. "Confess, or don't confess. Who gives a fuck what they think? They're all fuckheads who lie and cheat and are as bad as the next guy. We don't owe them anything."

"It's not that I think I owe them something, but that I want to give something and . . . I can't stop thinking about it. About *him*. He's a holy man who looks at me like I'm the scum off his boot. At first, I loved teasing him and making him blush. But then he started giving me these looks—like I'm disgusting. Like I'm so full of evil and sin that there's no saving me. And the worst part is that it affects me. I *want* his approval, and at the same time, I want to corrupt his goody-two-shoes soul and drag him to sex dungeon hell. What's wrong with me?"

I feel an odd sense of honor and pride that she opened her heart to me. Unlike myself, who bottles everything inside until I blow, she trusted me to share.

"There's nothing wrong with you," I point out.

"So why can't I stop thinking about things that I shouldn't?" She lowers her voice. "Do you think it's another demon? Is one of them trying to influence me?"

Movement in my periphery catches my eye. Zeke and Wes are outside the church near the lake.

"Blame Thea and Wes and that damn prophecy," I growl. "We have to work together. We're not used to it. We're not used to opening our hearts on missions. So it's messing with our heads. It's scary. That's all. But this is just another mission. It will eventually end. Until then, we have each other's backs."

She follows my gaze and then glances at me as though she knows exactly who I'm thinking of. But she doesn't push it. She slides her hands inside her yoga pants, unhooks the chain cilice on one thigh, and hands it to me. Red glistens on the barbed silver chain. The pain would be unbearable, but she's so used to it she barely flinches.

"Other one too." I hold out my palm.

She groans reluctantly and removes the second one. I shove both inside my yoga pants pocket, look her squarely in the eyes, and say, "You feel like you're going to do something stupid, call me. Okay?"

"Define stupid."

"Sneak into the priest's bed in the middle of the night, wearing only your panties."

She flattens her lips. "What else?"

"I think you get the picture."

"Fine. But the same goes for you," she replies.

"I'm sure I can resist climbing into the priest's bed."

"Babe." She claps her hand on my shoulder and gives me a serious look. "I'm not talking about the priest . . . or any of them. I meant, if you need me, I'm here."

My lips curve and I nod. "Alright. Enough chit-chat let's go. I'm about to work you so hard that you wish you never saw me."

Another groan slips out of her lips. "You say the sexiest things sometimes, babe."

I scoff. And then we're off again, continuing our jog around the estate.

ELEVEN

ZEKE

After Wesley storms out, I get up. "I'll speak with him."

"Then you come and see me," Cisco orders.

For confession. I don't want to, but I have to. Even if it's for our priest's sake because I know he's a man of routine. And he does care.

I jog to catch up with Wesley. His long legs are already making strides down the path to the abbey. "Wes."

He catches me in his periphery and shakes his head again. "How could they?"

"We probably should have told them earlier."

"It wouldn't have made a difference. You heard him—he's an agent of the Entity. What's worse is that they've been communicating with me as though I was their contact for this mission. Maybe it was Cisco all along. I don't know who to trust."

I fall into step beside him and put my hands in my pockets.

This whole situation is messed up. I don't even think our priest is confident he's doing the right thing.

"So, what now?" I ask.

"We keep hunting for the relics. That's all we can do."

"Will you tell the girls?"

"Of course I will. They deserve to be prepared for whatever the Vatican sends our way."

"You said there was something else Cisco and Dom needed to know."

Wesley pales and avoids eye contact. "I couldn't tell them. They're not ready. Cisco still wants to dismantle the Sisterhood. Dom thinks he can *save* them."

"So tell me."

His intelligent eyes dart over me as if he's actually putting me in the "people he can't trust" basket.

"There was more to the prophecy than us working together," he finally says, glancing back at the church. "Sinners of Saints, it said."

"Okay. What does that mean?"

"We thought it could mean a few things, but before Thea killed the demon Vepar, she confessed that I was the first to mend the cracks. The cracks are the divide between the genders. With the discovery of Mary's gospel, it proves a woman was in high regard of the Savior. This means women can be as involved in the church as men. Me being with Thea—us closing these cracks—is keeping the gates of hell shut. Lilith wants the gates open. She wants divide and friction. Each demonic horseman is foretold to split a relationship between a Sinner and a Saint apart."

"I don't understand."

"I'm only the first from our team fated to find love with a Sinner."

My lungs seize. "What?"

Leila's face flashes before my eyes.

He adjusts his spectacles. "I'm willing to stake my life on the fact that we all have had some kind of demonic experience in our childhood—something that involved death. Lilith's minions tried to kill me when I was a child . . . and for half my adult life. It was all to stop me from meeting Thea, but somehow, it's brought us all here."

"Are you saying it's my fault a demon killed my baby sister? Because I'm part of this prophecy?"

"I've lost people too," he points out. "We all have."

"Wes, come on. It's a bit of a stretch."

"I don't think so. Thea doesn't either. Look, I know you have secrets." His eyes narrow. "And that Leila's somehow involved, so is it too much of a stretch to think you shared something special with her that can be rekindled? I mean, I've seen how you look at her when you think she's not watching."

My heart lurches, begging me to confess and finally share this burden. But all I can manage is, "Aside from the fact one of those men in the church has taken a vow of celibacy, and the other could be a eunuch for all we know, Leila would rather murder me than love me."

"That celibacy vow was fashioned in a medieval institution based on scripture missing the vital truth in Mary's gospel. Jesus was *married* to her . . . literally in the biblical sense." He takes a breath, holds it, then exhales. "You know, priests weren't always celibate. Popes were married with children. This vow arose from the need to control funds entering and leaving the church. If priests brought in funds through their parish, and they could marry, then the church had to disperse those funds back to their families and sons. Do you understand where I'm going with this?"

My lips curve. "I understand you're a nerd. How you pulled that badass babe is beyond me."

He rolls his eyes, but I can see he's proud of Thea. And the fact she's with him. His eyes sparkle with emotion. I don't know what it is, but I know I want it. And I know it's when he's thinking of Thea.

Wes came into my life when I needed him most. I trust him more than any other person. A tiny kernel of hope flares in my chest. Maybe it's not the end for Leila and me. Maybe we can salvage what we had. My fingers roll across the charred bracelet in my right pocket.

How does one begin to make up for the kind of mistake I made?

"I'm not talking about a quick fix, Zeke. I'm talking about a lifelong love."

I think about Leila's avoidance of me, the unscrupulous tasks she's been asked to do, and the coldness in her eyes. I don't even know if any part of the girl I knew and loved still exists or if she's just a seductive killing machine with no morals.

"Do the other Sinners know about this?" I ask hesitantly. "Or is it just Thea?"

"Just Thea. Those women are as stubborn as Cisco and Dom. They've been hurt, used, and abused. We're far from convincing them we're a safe bet."

"But you believe I can make it work with Leila," I venture slowly.

"Thea and I can be dismissed as a one-off. But if two of us pair with Sinners, it will convince Cisco and Dom that building this bridge is key to stopping the apocalypse," he confirms.

"Are you trying to force the prophecy?" I narrow my eyes.

He chuckles. "I don't need to do that. I'm just saying, don't run from it."

"I don't know . . ."

"Can you at least try to have an open mind?"

I pull the bracelet out of my pocket and stare at the lake. I can't keep this all to myself for much longer.

"She was like a sister to me, Wes. For years, we were together in the group home where the rejects went. She was so eager to get out of there and find a home. I honestly didn't give a shit if anyone adopted me. All I cared about was keeping her safe. Occasionally, she was fostered out but always came back. What you said about demons in our pasts—I think one followed her. I worried it would get her like it did my sister so I left. The last I checked on her, I thought she was dead. Turns out, it was about the same time she came here."

"You still think of her as a sister?"

Sharp laughter barks out of me. "Have you *seen* her? She's . . . she's so . . ."

He sighs and casts a dreamy look at the lake. "Yeah, I know."

I tense. "What?"

"I feel the same way about Thea," he explains, still with a faint smile on his lips. "My heart stops, and my brain can't function around her."

Thea. Not Leila. Yeah, of course, he was talking about Thea. I shake my head and force my fingers to uncurl and relax.

"You get like that with Leila?" he asks warily. "Or is she still like a . . ."

"My dick gets hard when I'm within ten feet of her, so no. I don't think of her like a sister. Not in the slightest."

"Just say she's beautiful," Wes scoffs. "No need to be uncouth."

"I'm serious." I shove the bracelet back into my pocket and pull out a crumpled cigarette. "I can be walking down a hallway when suddenly my dick turns to fucking steel. Two seconds later, Leila walks around the corner. It's like a radar. I think my body knew who she was before my brain did. Admit it. You get the same."

"Maybe."

His confession sends us into a fit of laughter. Keeping these kinds of thoughts to myself has always been difficult, but if it wasn't for Wesley, I think I'd have gone insane. He gets it. He's not tied up in shame and angst by his lustful thoughts like the other two. We can have a joke without judgment. And the Monsignor . . . he was hilarious. Sometimes he joined in with the jokes.

My laughter dies out. The Monsignor was a good man. I'll miss him.

Wes glances at the church behind us with a frown. "I know we lied to them about the gospel, but Cisco is more connected to the higher-ups at the Vatican than we'd thought. Honestly, before Thea, I wouldn't have cared if they were coming to dismantle this organization. But now . . . it's not nameless people we're ruining. Nuns and women have risked their souls to save innocent people. The Entity won't care."

My upper lip curls at the implied threat. Even if Leila's changed since she was Lei Ling, even if she's a cold, heartless killer now, she's still my wildcat.

"Do you really think we're in danger?" I ask, lighting the end of my cigarette until it blazes. Because it won't just be the girls at risk. Wes and I are a liability now.

He plucks the cancer stick from my lips and stomps on it. "Absolutely. I've studied the history of the church, Zeke. They've got too much to lose. They'll send people here to investigate, and it won't be a friendly chat."

"How can you be so sure?"

"Because Cisco knows," Wes answers. "Why else would he send us away to get our tattoos fixed?"

I still. He's right. By all intents and purposes, we should be here at the abbey, working our asses off to find that relic and prepare for demon warfare. Maybe even invite a tattooist here to fix the spells on our bodies. But to leave . . .

"What do we do?"

"Simple. We find that second relic and use it to stop Asmodeus. He's the horseman of war. It's only a matter of time before he starts trouble, but if we have a way to stop him, no one can claim that finding the first relic was luck or a coincidence. It will be holy prophecy."

"Yeah, sure. Simple."

He gives me a deadly look. "If I catch you smoking again, I'll make Thea reverse the healing."

I blanch. "She can do that?"

"I guess we'll find out." He stares at me long and hard. "You've been given a second chance, Z. Don't blow it."

I put my lighter away and pick up the stomped butt. "You're right. I'll try."

"I wasn't just talking about the smoking."

"Yeah, I know," I answer quietly.

"Do you?" He narrows his eyes. "I mean, just look around us. Tell me what you see."

A beautiful lake. Mountains. An incredible estate. A church. Leila is still training with Mercy on a grassy spot near the back of the abbey. I take a deep breath and exhale. When I don't answer, Wesley continues. "I see a man who's suffered just as much as the rest of us, yet somehow is standing before me, healed from the brink of death and within fifty feet of a childhood friend he thought was dead. With everything going on in the world, God decided to give that miracle to *you*."

"Way to make me feel bad, Wes." I halfheartedly punch him in the shoulder.

"I'm trying to make you feel special. You were chosen, Zeke, and she needs you."

Feeling my cheeks heat, I nod and look at Leila practicing with a katana. I've never stopped loving her, but Wesley doesn't understand. She wants nothing to do with me. Miracles are a matter of perspective. If I can't get her to forgive me, then this could be my damnation. I guess God isn't done punishing me yet.

Twelve

Leila

My neck cracks as I stretch it side to side on my walk back to my room after training with Mercy. The workout was intense. I'm dripping with sweat and exhausted, but the sun is getting low. I have to get my rounds in before night falls.

I usually start and end in my room.

In every foster home I stayed at, something always burned. I look back on those nights and wonder if I had set the fires . . . had I sleepwalked or blacked out? Was I exactly what they said I was: a naughty, lying child?

But then Zeke told me his sister had been taken by a fire demon, and no one believed him either. Unfortunately, knowing this both comforted me and renewed my sense of fear. I didn't cause the fires, but something following me did. Something that couldn't quite reach me but never stopped trying.

One night, after Zeke and I finished playing our cowboy game, he noticed I couldn't sleep. I told him why, and he suggested maybe I was just having a string of bad luck, which had nothing to do with a demon. After all, he saw his demon with his own eyes. It was a real being. He explained how fires worked, so we systematically walked around the house and removed hazards, and I never took off my red string "evil eye" bracelet. I slept like a baby that night.

As I shove into my room, I absently rub my wrist and glance down. I've hardly thought about that bracelet for years. I lost it not long after he died. No, not lost it. I scratch my wrist again. I think I gave it to another foster child when she couldn't sleep. I gave her the bracelet because I felt guilty . . . so guilty. I didn't think I deserved it. Not long after that, the Sisterhood found me.

I still can't believe Zeke faked his death and walked out on me.

Pushing him out of my mind, I start my rounds by checking my room.

The small monastic cell is spotless and exactly how I left it, but I feel better knowing I've checked. Under the bed, inside the closet, and all the electric sockets. I check my window is closed but will test it one last time before I sleep too. Before leaving, I collect two essentials for the second phase of my rounds—my mini fire extinguisher and dagger.

The girls' rooms are next. No one is in, which makes it easy. Mercy must be showering. Tawny's room is a complete mess. I find at least two power boards facing upward instead of on the side. The empty sockets will collect dust over time, and before she knows it—*fire*. Her cot is unmade, her drawers are open, and her underwear and clothes hang out. But the window is closed, and no other fire hazards jump out at me.

When I'm done, I stand in the doorway. My fingers twitch as I stare at their closed doors, but the hallway is a battle line separating our side from Team Saint.

I should really check their rooms. Who knows what mess they leave them in or how many power boards face up and collect dust? All it takes is for one spark to fly through the window on a breeze, land in their mess, and the entire building will be on fire. Unlike the damp woods outside, everything in here is kindling.

The priest walks up the stairs and stops when he sees me. He says something in Italian or maybe English, but I can't hear because blood roars in my ears, drowning out all else. I need to check their rooms without rousing suspicion. But he's looking at me strangely.

I'll find a way another time.

As I head downstairs and out the front door, I can't stop the anxiety tightening my stomach. I haven't checked their rooms since they moved in. Maybe I should just tell them to close their windows at night. I'm sure Zeke would get a kick out of that.

Outside, I stop on the front steps and inhale the sweet air. I can almost taste the twilight coming. The air is cooler but not freezing. There's just enough of a dip in the atmosphere to invigorate me before it becomes uncomfortable.

I set off on my familiar path toward the walled garden. The walk around the estate is a few miles and can take up to an hour, depending on how thorough my check is. Chickens clucking grows louder as I near the hedges and limestone walls. The metal gate creaks open as I enter. I have to admit, being surrounded by vegetables, herbs, and even poisonous plants is my favorite part of doing my rounds.

I sweep the place with my eyes, looking for anything unusual. There are no dry patches of grass or kindling and no strange demonic behavior. The chickens look happy. The birds chirp. Further down in the garden, three nuns tend to a vegetable patch.

While logically, I don't think the garden catching fire would risk the abbey, I still like to check. Embers from a roaring fire can travel for twenty-five miles on the wind. It's better to be safe than sorry.

Once inside the wrought-iron gate, I take a step but then still at a sound echoing behind me. *Footsteps?* My hand tightens on the gate. I strain my hearing and search behind me but see nothing. I'm probably just jumpy because I haven't completed my checks thoroughly since Team Saint arrived. The priest getting in my way unsettled me. It's like I need to check their rooms even more desperately now.

Exhaling, I concentrate on the task at hand.

The entire walled garden covers about three acres and is sectioned by paths and manicured hedges. A greenhouse sits at the back next to the chicken coop. I'd be here all day if I swept every corner for hazards. Every cell in my body wants to, but I'm already pushing the edges of sanity with this daily habit.

I scratch my neck. *For fuck's sake.* A rash is breaking out.

The nuns stop raking and plucking out weeds. They smile at me, wave, then dip their chins and touch their hands to their hearts. At first, I don't understand what they're trying to say, but then realize they're thanking me for keeping them safe. Asmodeus did a number on this place. Fear glimmers behind the gratitude in their eyes, and for once, I'm glad for what I've become at the Sisterhood. Sometimes it's hard to rationalize the violence, but seeing the faces of people I'm saving hits me squarely in the chest. I return a hesitant wave and smile.

"You need help?" I gesture to the wheelbarrow half full of weeds and then glance at the sky. The sun is a burning orange ball sinking behind the trees. They shouldn't be out here after dark.

A nun with blue eyes and white hair nods, her smile stretching. The badge on her habit tells me her name is Sister Agnes. I think she's also good with mechanics. A scratch on her cheek is covered in disinfectant. She probably received it during Asmodeus's chaos-induced episode. The nuns tried to kill each other. I check the others and note they all have battle scars.

It's no use telling them to finish up soon. They seem to have their hearts set on weeding this plot, and to be honest, physical work and routine will be good for them. I start plucking out the weeds in the bed, helping them as best I can. The jostled dill releases a delicious fragrance, and my mouth waters. With every weed pulled, I fall into a comfortable silence with the others. Before I know it, we're done, and I'm waving goodbye to them.

I'm still smiling as I round the coop to check on the compost pile. Rustling deep in the stinky mess sends me on high alert. A dagger is in my hand, ready to fly at whatever is hiding in the offcuts of food and grass, but when a dark and iridescently scaled head pops out of the pile, I put it away.

Jinx. Goddamn ex-demon is getting into all sorts of mischief. I shoo her with my hand, but she dives back into the pile and rolls around in the waste like it's catnip to a cat.

I shake my head, ready to continue, but then smell smoke. Panic seizes my mind. Fire.

No. It's not a fire. Relax.

Calm down.

I'm sure there's a perfectly sane explanation. I'm out here every night checking, and I have never smelled smoke.

The Sisters are putting away their tools. I don't want to alarm them, so I move with slow, quiet precision despite my heart pounding in my chest. The mini fire extinguisher is in one hand, and a dagger in the other, as I creep around the coop to a sheltered alcove filled with dead leaves and gardening refuse.

Zeke leans casually against the hutch, hands in his pockets, puffing on a cigarette. He watches ash drop onto leaves and catch fire before stomping on them. With his old colt pistols holstered on his narrow hips, he's the epitome of a modern-day cowboy, brooding over his thoughts, face hidden by shadows. He spots me and his lips curve on one side.

"Hey," he says, voice deep and intimate in this private space.

I'm gobsmacked. I don't know what to think. What the fuck?

"Are you spying on me?" I gape.

"Still doing your nightly checks?"

Outrage turns my vision red. How dare he think he has the right to slot himself back into my life so familiarly? I spray the extinguisher in his face . . . well, at his cigarette, narrowly missing his face.

"What the hell, wildcat?" He swats the air and coughs.

I stomp on his cigarette as it lands. Satisfaction blooms in my chest when his expression morphs from surprise into guilt and contrition. If only it didn't make his face seem more youthful. I don't want to be reminded of what we meant to each other in the past.

"You see me checking for hazards," I growl, "and you know exactly why I do it. Then you do this?"

Neither of us concedes the lock we have on each other's eyes. Who the fuck is this guy anymore?

Then he lowers his gaze and sighs.

"Yeah, I know." His tone is self-deprecating, and he grips the back of his neck. "Wes said the same thing. But, fuck, it's hard to quit."

I see the guns. I see the self-indulgent habit. I see the devil-may-care attitude still flickering in his eyes despite what he says. I'm disgusted. He's a grown man, yet he's still behaving like he's the only person in the world.

"I think this obsession with Doc Holliday is a little too much, don't you?" I say.

His mouth opens, closes, then opens again, but nothing comes out. I take his hand and slam the dead cigarette into it, then shake my head and turn to leave. "I don't need your help, Zeke. And I don't need you following me."

"Lei Ling, I was dying." His deep voice punctuates the silence between clucking chickens.

Hearing my old name on his lips freezes my heart and steps. *Dying?*

Every line in my body is rock hard as I let that word sink in. My eyes burn, and I focus on the Sisters at the tool shed to stop the tears. But he keeps talking, and I can't move. I'm rooted to the spot with no thoughts, only the inescapable feeling that

I'm falling down a deep hole I won't know how to climb out of.

"I got sick. Real sick. It started as emphysema—damage from smoke inhalation." He laughs bitterly. "And not the cigarette kind. I spent years investigating demonic fire activity, and then I developed tumors. It was then I took up smoking. I was ready to die, but then Wes found out about you Sinners, and the prophecy, and we came here. He hoped a Sinner would lead him to the healing relic and he could save my life." There's shuffling sounds behind me like he's nervously dragging his feet through the dirt. "Cisco and Dom didn't know what Wes and I had planned. They came here to dismantle the Sisterhood, but I wanted you to know it wasn't why I—"

I whirl to face him. "Why are you telling me? I don't give a shit. You could be lying in a gutter for all I care."

"Wildcat . . ." The hurt flashing in his hazel eyes is like a dagger to my chest. But I wrap up that wound and bandage it hard.

"Stop calling me that." I poke him in the chest, and he winces. "You lost the right to call me that when you made me think I killed you. *Me*—a thirteen-year-old girl, thought her stupid, selfish need to have her stupid, stuffed snuggle toy caused the only person she ever cared about to run into a burning building and die." I choke on my words, hating how emotional I sound. Hating how I'm the first one to bring it up, and it's been a week since I confronted him about not knowing me. It takes a moment to force the feeling from my voice, to remember I'm the fucking boss bitch in this situation. "Clearly, you're alive and well. I should put a bullet in your eye, but I want *nothing* to do with you so—"

"Look out!" He tackles me as a *whirr* brushes my ear.

The wind knocks out of me as we land hard on the ground. I gasp, trying to catch my breath. Zeke's hard and warm body is on top of mine, shielding me, his eyes full of concern and panic. For me. For my safety. It takes a moment for me to realize what's happened. A gardening scythe is stuck in the wooden hutch above us, wobbling like it's just been embedded hard. A furious nun glares at me with bloodshot blue eyes.

Oh shit.

Sister Agnes is infected with Asmodeus's war sickness again.

THIRTEEN

ZEKE

She's safe.

She's safe. I repeat the words as I cover her body with mine. Leila is unharmed and breathing beneath me. Her skin is warm and soft. Her heart pounds against mine as our chests press together. God, she smells so good. I'd forgotten this smell. Passionfruit and vanilla. It brings me back to sitting on a couch with her at midnight, watching *Tombstone* from beneath a blanket, hiding from the drunk matron because it was way past our bedtime. This smell, coupled with the sensation of her soft body blooming into womanhood, gave me the hardest boner I've ever had in my life. I freaked and pushed her away because she was way too young. It confused the hell out of me.

But now . . . now this smell reminds me of home.

I cup her face and brush her cheek with my thumb. "You good?"

"Yeah," she croaks.

I roll to my feet, grab my Colt, and mark the center of the evil nun's head as she tugs the scythe from the wooden hutch with feral, animalistic snarls.

"No!" Leila body slams me to the side.

Bang!

My shot goes wide, hitting the greenhouse pane and shattering glass.

"Leila," I growl. "What are you doing?"

"She's not possessed. Don't shoot her."

"She tried to chop off your head."

My wildcat's eyes flash with defiance as she stands between the nun and me, her dagger pointed at my face. A grin curves my lips. Still the same fucking moxie. I shake my head, then holster the pistol.

"Fine." I point at the snarling nun. "But when she gets that out of the wood, it's coming for your head."

"Get Thea." She sheaths her dagger into an ankle strap. "Tell her to bring the staff."

"I'm not leaving you—"

"Go!" She shoves me.

I stand my ground and fold my arms. "No."

She clenches her jaw and looks about to explode with a lecture, but then walks to Sister Agnes. I startle and hover my hand over my pistol, ready to shoot no matter what Leila wants.

"Hey, Sister," she says softly. "It's me, Leila."

The nun switches her focus from the scythe to Leila and attacks.

One second, Leila stands before the nun. The next, she has

the nun in a chokehold, effortlessly cutting her airway and bringing the Sister down as gently as possible.

I've never seen her in action like this—Leila is lethal. Magnificent. But she's not cold. Not like I feared. As Sister Agnes loses consciousness, Leila coos soft words in her ear, saying things about how she will keep her safe and fix this.

Jinx slithers out of the compost with a mess of dirt and carrot peel on her head. The sunset makes her usual iridescent scales seem warm. Big liquid-black eyes blink up at me and she makes her dolphin sounds. I crouch and flick the carrot off her head.

"Hey girl, do me a favor and run and tell Thea we're coming."

The ex-demon yips and then darts along the garden path like an oil streak on fire.

As the light winks out from Sister Agnes's eyes, I scoop her into my arms. Leila's eyes on me are flames against my skin as we walk back to the abbey. My first instinct had been to kill this innocent woman, but Leila's was to save her.

"Up here," Thea shouts from the top of the staircase as we enter the abbey.

I carry the unconscious nun upstairs to the archives, where Thea instructs me to lay her on a table cleared of books and papers. The Reverend Mother sits at the table, her eyes alarmed. Wesley, Raven, and Tawny stand around, listening as Leila explains what happened.

The archives are massive, taking up an entire floor of the monolith abbey. I stand back a few steps, lean on a bookcase and fold my arms. I'm still unsettled that I almost royally fucked up, not Leila—the "Sinner." Jinx darts from beneath the table to curl around my legs.

I drop to give her a quick pat. "Good girl."

She preens under my attention and then shoots back to Wes, scampering up his body and settling around his neck. He stands behind Thea as she listens intently to the story. When Leila is done, The Reverend Mother plants her gnarled hands on the table and tries to leverage herself up to standing.

I rush to her side to help her stand. I swear she's getting older by the day. She smiles briefly at me and leans heavily on my hand and her cane.

"Thank you, child." To the other Sinners, she says, "Raven, Tawny, check on the nuns. I'll be right behind you."

"Got it." They dash away.

We watch as Thea presses her angelic staff to the fallen nun's sternum. The wooden length glows a warm color as it sweeps over her body. I remember that feeling seeping into me when Thea healed me. It was like seeing God. Pure, heavenly, rapturous joy obliterated every bad thing in my body. But it didn't last. The instant the healing was over, all my doubts crept in and stayed.

The Reverend Mother clutches the rosary beads at her belt and slides her watery gaze to me. "This war sickness is taking longer than we thought to clear. We must stop Asmodeus. Will you help us, Mr. Cohen?"

"Of course."

"Good." She pats me on the arm. "I'm glad to hear that. Thea and Wesley can explain what we need you to do."

My eyes narrow. That sounds awfully like they've been talking about me. But after what Wes revealed earlier, I shouldn't be surprised.

The Reverend Mother leaves us, hobbling downstairs, her cane slamming heavily with each step.

I shuffle closer to the table. Wesley stands next to me as Leila pins the sister down. Thea's magic is making her convulse. It's not a pretty sight, this healing. It was never this bad for me. But here—it's ugly.

Thudding on the stairs announces the arrival of my missing team members. Dom and Cisco stride into the room, their eyes hard and focused. Their concern gives me hope. Despite what Wes fears about Cisco siding with the Vatican, I see the compassion in his eyes and hope it rules over his loyalty to the people signing our paychecks.

"Again?" Cisco asks, frowning as Mercy squeezes past him to get closer to the nun.

Her long copper hair drips all down her pink silk robe, sticking it to her skin. Must have come straight from the shower.

Wes replies over Mercy's head to our priest. "The cycle keeps repeating. Thea can't leave this sanctuary until the nuns are all completely healed."

"Or Asmodeus is dead," I add. We assume.

The wooden staff flares brightly, then fades as Sister Agnes's eyes flutter open.

"Did it happen again?" Her voice trembles, and she wipes her pale face with clammy hands.

Mercy squeezes Agnes's hand. "Yes, love, but you're okay now."

"No one got hurt," Leila says as Raven rejoins the group.

"Everyone else is fine," Raven confirms.

"Hear that?" Mercy pats Agnes's hand. "Nothing to worry about. I'll take you back to your room."

"Oh, my!" Sister Agnes tries to slide off the table but stumbles.

Leila and I simultaneously reach for her, but Raven tugs us away. "You two need to stay. I had a vision that involves you." She looks to Dom, frowns, then slides her gaze to Cisco. "Father, if you can help Mercy bring Sister Agnes to her room, I think she'll like that."

"Of course," he replies. His tone is dry toward them, but then he takes Agnes's other side and says warmly, "I'll stay as long as you need, Sister."

"I've got you first," Mercy insists, a narrowed glance at the priest.

"Oh, it's really not necessary—" Her eyes widen, and tears form. "I'm *talking* . . . I . . . Lord forgive me, I've broken my vow again."

"The Lord will understand." Cisco's smooth voice leaves no room for confusion. "You take the time you need, *Sorella*."

Mercy and Cisco escort the trembling woman downstairs. Dom, Wes, and I are left with Leila, Raven, and Thea. I glance warily at Raven and find she's already staring at me with an indecipherable look. A shiver runs down my spine, and I resist the urge to draw my weapon like a security blanket. I have the sense this short Latino woman with dark, rainbow-tipped hair is a chameleon.

Watch your back around her, my instincts scream.

"This can't go on." Leila paces alongside the table and restlessly flips her dagger.

"I agree." Thea returns to the table and collects books and papers from the floor.

Wesley helps, and they arrange the papers into something only they understand.

When Thea meets Raven's eyes, I catch a kernel of excitement before she carefully shutters it.

"We found something . . ." she says. "And Raven's vision backs it up."

"Should I call everyone back?" Leila takes a step toward the exit.

"No. The Rev knows," Thea says.

"Francisco?" Dom rumbles.

Wes shakes his head. "We'll let Father know after he's finished with Sister Agnes."

Thea slides her finger across the lost gospel's discolored parchment. She clears her throat and reads Mary Magdalene's words.

"Lo, a vision hath come upon me, Mary Magdalene,
after a blessed communion with our Savior and the
Holy Spirit that dwelleth within me—"

Leila snorts.

"Be serious," Thea warns, but a smile tugs her lips. I'm not sure what they're referring to and then Leila gives a derisive reply.

"How can you not chuckle at *blessed* communion with her savior? The Holy Spirit inside her?"

I chuckle. "She fucked him. I get it."

Dom mumbles some kind of prayer for my soul. Leila shoots me daggers—as if I have the gall to laugh at her joke—but I brush it off with a smirk. I kind of like this side of Leila. It's not the first time she's made inappropriate comments. Wes told me he caught her making rude hand gestures to Thea once in his class. This makes me think that at least some of me rubbed off on her during our childhood. Fun Leila is still in there somewhere.

"Continue, Thea." Wesley taps the table.

"Okay . . . where was I . . ."

> *For a trial hath been ordained by the Lord our God,*
> *a test that shall be undertaken by sinners and*
> *saints alike. That which was the tool of the greatest*
> *sin in passion shall be forged by saintly fire into a*
> *chamber of forgiveness against the greatest of*
> *sinners.*

She turns a page and points at another passage of ink on parchment. "There is a passage we can't quite translate properly. We're working on it. But then here she recounts a conversation about a prophecy with another Apostle . . ."

> *And I saw a rider, with a mouth of flames*
> *and a heart full of vengeance, riding forth upon*
> *a black steed. His name was War, and he*

sought to spread his flames and burn all in his path."

But then a voice spoke to me, saying, "Do not be afraid. For like all who repent, he who rides upon the black steed shall be forgiven, for he shall take unto himself the helmet and bridle of passion."

Peter said to me, "Surely you do not speak of forgiving a dark one such as this?"

And I replied to him, "These objects hold a deeper significance, for they represent the dual nature of man, the gentle and the fierce, the sinner and the saint. It is not until he takes this gift unto himself that war becomes peace, forgiveness becomes absolution, and the final crack is closed."

And I knew then that even the darkest of sinners would be given a test, a trial of temptation and revelation, a means to sink or swim.

"It sounds like gibberish to me," I grumble, but nevertheless, a chill runs down my spine.

Thea lifts her gaze. "It's clearly about Asmodeus. It talks about forgiving him, which is weird. But it also mentions two important objects—a bridle and a helmet."

"You think one is the relic?" Leila hardens her stance.

Thea nods. "Here, where it talks about a 'tool of the greatest sin,' I think she's referring to the nails used to crucify Jesus. And here, where she says a helmet and bridle of passion—she must be talking about *The Passion* . . . the final moments of Jesus's life before he was crucified . . . and here, it says—"

"All I need to know is that you're sure," Leila returns.

Thea looks at Wes, who nods for her to continue. "We translated this last night. Wes pointed out that an early Roman emperor named Constantine was said to have used the nails of the cross to forge a warrior's helmet and a horse's bridle. We're pretty sure that's the first bet."

"Okay," Leila says. "Tell me where to go, and I'll bring them home."

Thea slumps. "Constantine's helmet and bridle were lost."

"Okay," Leila replies. "You said first bet. What's the second?"

Wesley scratches his head. "Venerated Holy Nails are held in nine different European places of worship. If we can't find the helmet and bridle, then maybe we can forge our own weapon made from holy nails."

"Nine different claims?"

Thea nods. "That we know of."

"So we should get anyone not hunting the helmet and bridle to take a location and check."

"The nails are mostly in Italy." Wes looks at Dom. "Can you go with a Sinner to each of the locations and authenticate?"

"*Si.*" He nods and frowns. "I have seen one such place already. But how do I, how you say, authenticate?"

Wes suggests, "A Sinner with the *sight* will likely be able to see if the object is truly holy or not."

The *sight*, meaning the supernatural gift these women received after first uniting the two halves of Mary's gospel. To us, a demonic possession looks indistinguishable from a regular person. But they see the demon's true face.

Dom nods thoughtfully.

"I'll go with you," Leila offers.

My brows raise. She's definitely busting to get out of here —away from me.

"No," Thea replies curtly. "We have another job for you." Her gaze shifts to me. "And you."

Leila shakes her head. "I'm not working with him. I'll go with Dom."

"Mercy is already going with Dom," Thea returns, her dark brows lowering. "Unless you have a valid reason not to travel with Zeke, the assignment I have for you is more important."

"Who died and made you our leader?" Leila's eyes flash. She stabs her dagger into the wooden table. It remains upright, hilt wobbling.

"Look, I don't have to go." I raise my palms in surrender. The last thing I want to do is cause a division.

Raven grabs the dagger and points it at me. "You're going."

Fuck, she's scary. "Okay. I'm going."

To Leila, she says, "You don't have a choice."

When Leila folds her arms, I realize how wrong I was. Raven's not the scariest. It's my wildcat. Ice-cold death bleeds from her posture. She has a look that shrinks my balls . . . and I've stared down some of the vilest, most brutal bastards around. I'm reminded of how swiftly and confidently she took down Sister Agnes, and I wonder about what else she's done for this messed-up organization. How much of her soul has been sacrificed?

Her eyes narrow. "What aren't you telling me? Is this a part of your vision?"

My gaze darts between the Sinners, and when Raven and

Thea share a meaningful look that Wes passes onto me, my pulse spikes with a realization. *Leila still doesn't know.* She doesn't know that a Sinner is fated to be with one of my team. Neither does Dom, going by the confusion in his expression. I rub my temples. I don't want to be part of another lie. But I'm also not the person with the right to reveal everything.

If these people think it's important to keep Leila in the dark about the truth, then I could mess everything up by blurting it out.

Thea holds Leila's hard gaze as she grinds out, "You're needed because we have a lead on an antiquities collector bragging about a new rare helmet acquisition that sounds eerily like Constantine's helmet. And he has a thing for being dominated by brunettes with long legs."

"Send her," Leila growls, tossing her hand in Raven's direction.

"She's technically black haired, and her visions give her unpredictable migraines. Besides, Madam Mina is our best."

Raven's bleak eyes soften on Leila. "I don't trust myself on a mission at the moment."

"Fine," Leila concedes but then points at me. "But I'm not working with him."

Thea doesn't miss a beat. "Zeke is needed because he has connections with the arms dealer running a private high roller poker game where this collector will be. He can swindle you a couple of invitations."

"I can?" Wait. What? My old . . . My eyes widen. "But I haven't been in touch with those men for decades. And as these poker games are usually organized weeks in advance, I don't see how I'll get an invitation. We didn't leave on good terms. And wait just a goddamned minute—" I gesture at Leila but keep my eyes on Thea. "What do you mean he has a thing for being domineered by brunettes with long legs? And who is Madam Mina?"

"Madam Mina is Leila's BDSM persona," Raven states tiredly, rubbing her temples.

"What do you expect Leila to do?"

The Sinners look at me like I'm stupid.

"I'll do what needs to be done, Zeke." Leila stands up straighter. "I don't run from my responsibilities."

Her words are a punch in the gut. The thought of Leila sexually dominating a disgusting, morally obtuse man makes my blood curdle. Surely that's not what she intends to do. Surely they're just talking about other ways Leila can domineer. But as I take in my surroundings, I remember who we're dealing with and why Team Saint was sent to dismantle them. I run out of excuses.

My gaze flicks to Leila, and I start to sweat.

"Love," Wes pleads quietly with Thea.

"Wes, I said my body is yours. But if this mission requires a brunette with long legs who can seduce a man into revealing his dirty laundry, would you rather it be Leila or me?"

His jaw clicks shut. They stare at each other momentarily, then he replies, "You know my feelings about that."

"I could always torture this collector," Leila offers. "It would save us time."

Her steady gaze makes my heart palpitate. She said the word torture like one speaks about Tuesday. It's nothing to her but another day of the week. I refuse to let her fall further into this shell of a person when she's only like this because of my mistake.

So I'll have to go with her every step of the way. If I'm to walk back into that city, I'll likely have to get my hands dirty and return to being the godless man I longed to leave behind.

If I'm to walk back into that city, denying my itchy trigger finger will no longer be a problem.

"I'll go. I'll do what needs to be done." I level my stare at them.

I'll keep Leila safe.

FOURTEEN

SOMEWHERE OFF THE INTERSTATE

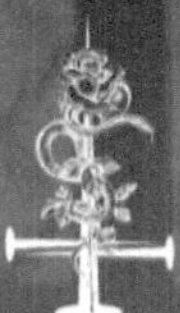

Mary Sue pulled another glass from the rack beneath the bar and cursed under her breath. Dirty. Again. This one had a raspberry-colored lipstick mark. Being a dive bar in the middle of nowhere shouldn't mean they couldn't clean their dishes.

"Goddamned busboy needs to do his job properly," she mumbled, using her apron to remove the stain.

"Today, sugar!"

She scowled at the line of sweaty, beefcake bikers waiting to be served down the bar. The glare of the backlit window light made it hard to see their faces. The smell of sour hops and cigarette smoke made her feel sick. Music and conversation made her feel deaf. One of these days, one winning Powerball, and she was out of here. She dropped her scowl and smiled tightly at the line, then finished pouring her beer from the tap.

"Here you go, Joe." She handed the old regular his beer.

Joe had a long beard and patchy hair. He was the logger

down at Old Grogan's Mill and there from sunup to sundown but was now retired. His back ached as much as Mary Sue's.

"Now, darlin'." Joe smacked his gummy mouth as he dropped cash onto the bar. "Don't you be paying them no mind, you hear? They're just fixin' to drink since they been out ridin' all night."

"Used to be a time they'd be fixin' to drink cos of a hard day's work. I don't think these fellas know how to tie their own damn bootstraps. Don't you worry about me, Joe. I can handle myself."

"'Course you can, darlin'."

"And my twelve-gauge is here for all the other times. But, heck. Sure is busy today."

"Ain't that the truth. Must be almost a full house. Say, where's that handsome fella of yours? He should be out here helping."

"Pete's on delivery. Tried to squeeze in a last one before it's too late. Didn't think the bar would get packed so early."

"Hey, lady!"

"Talk later, Joe."

Mary Sue straightened her shoulders and strode down the length of the bar to meet the waiting customers. One wore a leather jacket with the colors of the local motorcycle gang. He was a big red-haired brute who chewed tobacco like it was made from the Lord's own personal stash. Two of his buddies wore plain T-shirts and stained jeans but had gang colors on their bandanas. More stragglers leaned on the bar and smoked cheap cigars. All look like they'd walked straight off the cocaine boat with that wired look in their eyes.

"Who's next?" she asked as the bell over the door rang.

The smell of fresh pine wafted in.

Not another customer. Any more, and they'd be sardines in a can.

Big Red tossed a crumpled bill onto the bar, signaling he was next in line, no matter who stood there first. A whistled tune floated over their heads. It was jaunty yet simple. And it caught the attention of everyone in the room. But Mary Sue didn't have time to pay attention. Too many customers.

Suppose I can't complain. Money is money, she thought.

"Who's next?" she asked again, ignoring Big Red's tossed cash. Money was money, but the least they could do was look her in the eye, ask nicely, and hand it to her like a decent human being.

"That would be me." A deep, cultured voice cut through the din. It traveled over the heads of the bikers and sent shivers skating down Mary Sue's spine.

"Wait your turn, asshole," Big Red grumbled without turning. He flicked ash from his cigar onto the bar, then clicked his fingers at Mary Sue and pointed at the dropped cash. Before he could get another word out, blood dribbled from his eyes. Then his nose. And his ears. When Big Red flopped to the floor, Mary Sue saw a tall dark-haired—and obscenely handsome—man behind him. Dressed in an expensive-looking business suit, he whistled his jaunty tune like he had no care in the world. Or he was a loony.

Definitely not a local.

Big Red's biker friends aimed guns at the newcomer, but their eyes bled too. *What in the Lord's name?*

One by one, they fell like dominos. The whistling newcomer stepped over their twitching bodies to get closer to the bar. Somewhere, in a far-off place in her mind, Mary Sue knew she should be terrified. But she couldn't muster the fear. It was frozen in a faraway place that screamed for her to run. All she could think about was this handsome stranger's face and how she would do anything to please him.

"Are you the descendent of Sarah, Daughter of Raguel?"

"Beg your pardon?" She blinked.

"Sweetheart, repetition is tedious."

"I . . . I don't know who you're talking about." She just wanted to please him. To answer correctly.

He cocked his head, studying her. Then he leaned across the bar countertop and inhaled deeply. His upper lip curled in a snarl, and he straightened back up with a vicious flash in his dark eyes. "I smell her blood in you. She imprisoned me for millennia. And you, my dear, are her spawn. I won't stop until you're all eradicated from this earth. But first, you're going to tell me who helped her."

"Sarah from the laundromat?" Mary Sue felt warm liquid ooze down her legs.

"Not to worry," he drawled. "Your blood will remember."

"Wh-what?"

His eyes turned wholly black—completely soulless—and Mary Sue finally had the sense to scream.

Fifteen

Leila

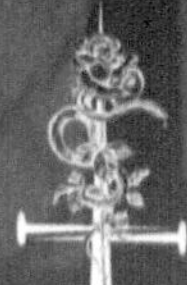

"Enjoy the ride, bitch," Thea says as I pass her cell door in the hallway, a sugar cookie wedged between my teeth.

I'm dressed in my black skin-tight Sinner uniform, carrying a duffel bag of clinking supplies in one hand and a sheathed katana in the other. It's been a day since they surprised me with the new mission.

I might have cooled down a little, did a little baking this morning, but I'm still too pissed off to respond. It's her fault I have to spend days alone with the one man that makes me blind with rage.

Scratch that. Maybe I have something. I shove the cookie into my lips, chew the mouthful, then flip her the bird over my shoulder, using my sword as a giant middle finger. Her laughter makes me lose a little of my defiance and I smile, despite myself.

"Call me when you get there." She shuts the door to her room, and I hear a feminine giggle followed by a masculine rumble of appreciation. I suppose she deserves to take a break. She's been pulling all-nighters with Wes in the archives.

But I've been railroaded into this mission with Zeke. I can't really blame Thea for taking the lead. She has the relic and the knowledge. Mercy is distracted, and Raven is having migraines. If I know her, it's probably worse than she's letting on.

We spent the day reviewing what Thea knows about our mark and the relic in more detail. I'd intended on drilling Raven about her visions, but she stumbled out the night before, looking like she was about to die from pain. I haven't seen her since. Half our team left this morning for Italy. Without their input, the rest of us could only run through possible scenarios for how this mission could turn to shit.

When the others left, Thea and I brainstormed what I might have to do to get the collector to talk about his mythical helmet. Madam Mina is an effective dominatrix persona. I haven't been on a mission as her that didn't get results. Sometimes I think I should just become her. It would be a helluva lot easier living my life by BDSM rules.

While we brainstormed, Tawny sent a dossier of the mark while mid-air on her plane across the Atlantic. She'd hacked into highly classified police files that tied this collector to trafficking rings in Romania. All the women he helped kidnap were brunettes.

He has a standing membership to five sex clubs worldwide, an Only Fans subscription to a Dom specializing in spanking and denigration, and a nameless benefactor who donates five million Euros annually to procure rare antiquities for his private collection. With all the extracurricular activities, I wonder how much of his business is authentic.

Over the hour I talked with Thea, it became glaringly obvious that Zeke, Dom, and I were the last to know about this new information from the gospel.

Wesley and Thea are lying about something. I'm sure the Rev knows too, but I can't find her anywhere. She hates lying, which is why she made herself scarce at the mission briefing. But why lie?

Maybe Raven's vision was something I wouldn't like. Maybe they're sending me to my death. Or Zeke's. He mentioned his old contacts would kill him if he showed his face. And what the fuck? How does he know an arms dealer? What exactly was he doing with his life since the group home fire?

Zeke has dark secrets from his past, and I don't like the icky feeling in my chest from knowing this. Instead of spending the past few weeks fuming over his reappearance, I should have shoved my feelings deep down and acted like a Sinner. I should have pushed aside all emotion and just *got on with it*—hunting demons and finding these relics are more important than my feelings.

The man in question waits on the front porch, facing the wrought-iron gate in the distance. He absently flicks the flint on his lighter, but at least he's not smoking.

I've caught him unguarded as he stares at the setting sun. The golden light accentuates his brown hair's uneven texture. It's as though he cut it himself in the mirror with blunt scissors found at the bottom of the bathroom cabinet. I did a better job when I was nine and playing his Wild West barber. I'd trimmed his hair and then combed olive oil through it to emulate Val Kilmer's greasy style when he played Doc Holliday in the movie. I even glued freshly cut hair onto Zeke's prepubescent upper lip to give him a mustache. Not that he needs the help now. His five o'clock shadow is already thick and dark. The scruff only adds to his sex appeal.

Torn jeans mold lovingly to his toned buttocks. When he flattened me in the garden, the hard muscles of his abdomen contracted against mine. There wasn't an ounce of fat on him. My cheeks heat at the memory. I felt everything—even his steady heartbeat thudding rhythmically against my breast. He'd looked concerned, but that heartbeat had soared.

My gaze slides to how Zeke's shoulders and biceps stretch the leather of his jacket. He's strong. I've caught him a few times in the gym with Dom, but he tends to stick to the weights. Cardio would have been difficult with his illness and smoking habit. I could probably outrun him in a pinch if I needed to. I'm sure he won't keep up.

But he pinned me down easily.

Zeke *saved* me. A lethal blade came at my head, and he shielded me with his body. Then he cupped my face and asked if I was okay. His hazel eyes blazed with panic, but when I said I was good, that panic turned to steel. He almost killed Sister Agnes . . . I think to protect me.

And was he following me as I completed my fire-hazard checks?

No.

Why would he do that when he . . . No, it doesn't make sense. He must have been hiding out in the garden to have a cigarette without being harassed by his team. Saving me was what anyone would have done in that situation. And even if he was trying to weasel his way back into my life, I have no room for him.

"We need a car," he says without facing me.

"I booked an Uber." I drop my bag. Weapons inside clanked.

He slides an amused gaze my way before tucking his lighter into his jeans pocket.

"So you just cab it or walk everywhere?" Dark brows raise. "That has to be costly."

"It's cheaper and more reliable."

He scoffs. "I find that hard to believe. There has to be another reason. I thought this place was meant to be secret. Why invite strangers to your doorstep?"

"Obviously, it's part of the cover," I reply dryly. "The more people who think this is an average Benedictine Abbey, the less likely they'll suspect us of being deadly assassins."

"So what was with Thea turning up with a severed hand?"

My teeth grind. "People assume what they want. He likely thought she was in costume."

"That's dumb, and I think you're lying." He grumbles under his breath about how *he* would do things but then points out, "Raven has a motorcycle."

"She won't let anyone borrow it."

His eyes narrow. "So you all head into town by taxi every time you need groceries?"

"Fine," I admit. Fucker is persistent. "We have an old pickup truck and a project car some of the sisters work on to learn about mechanics."

"It's in that shed there, isn't it?" Clearly pleased with himself, he points to the old wooden barn down an offshoot from the main driveway. It's almost hidden behind bushes and trees. He wouldn't know what's inside unless he's broken in . . . or—he jingles as he jogs down the steps and strides toward it. *Keys in his pocket.* Sister Agnes is one of the mechanics. Maybe he checked in on her, and she gave him the keys.

I can't imagine Thea handing them over. Sinners are too set in our ways, and taking a cab or a share ride is usually how we do things. I jog after him and catch him unlocking the padlock at the barn doors.

"It won't matter." I slam my palm on the door as he tries to open it. "We don't use it on missions for a good reason. The car links the crime back to us if we're caught."

"Switch the plates." He tugs the door hard, knocking me out of the way as he walks in.

Damn it. The dust and straw he kicked up bloom in my face. I wave to clear the air and then follow him inside. He drags a white tarp from our black vintage Mustang and gives a loud wolf whistle of appreciation.

Great. Now he's eye fucking the thing. He'll never let this go.

I fold my arms. "Where will we find fake license plates at this late notice?"

He flashes me a disarming grin. "I know a guy."

"Sure you do," I mumble. "You know arms dealers . . . why not a chop shop?"

Curiously, my words make him falter as he opens the driver's side door. But he swiftly recovers and inhales deeply as the smell of polished leather fills the air.

"Ahhh." He releases a breathy, deep, and lust-filled growl. "Nothing beats this smell. Except a woman's—"

"Don't say it." I hold up my hand, and his grin widens to something mischievous. Even when he was a teen, he was a lewd son-of-a-bitch. I had no idea what he meant back then when he said things like a *woman's kitty* or her *savory delights*. That's what I liked about him; I was basically his kid sister, but he never treated me with kid gloves. I was just me—normal me. Not the fire starter. Not the weird spitfire no one wanted to adopt. Just me.

My lip twitches with the need to smile, a fact he picks up on as hazel eyes lock with mine. His amusement falters as he reads my face. He's no longer a teenager spouting incomprehensible rude shit. He's a man with experience and desires who recognizes that the woman before him is amused because she's thinking the same lewd things as him.

A strange feeling bounces between us, and I can't put my finger on it. Whatever is happening right now has to be shut down.

I blurt out the first thing I think of. "Raven told you to take the car, didn't she?"

I take immense pleasure in the guilt splashing over his facial features. While I couldn't have a one-on-one with her because of her migraine, I know how she works. If she couldn't say it to him, then she would have told someone to tell him when the time was right.

"How did you—?" he starts. "Never mind."

He slides into the driver's seat and caresses the steering wheel. Another low, sexually loaded groan rumbles from his lips. I shouldn't like the way the deep timbre warms my blood, or the way he slouches in a very male way that draws the eye to his hips . . . but I do.

I caught him once sitting like that in the student common area at school. He was on a couch with a male friend. A cheerleader stood before Zeke, giggling and tapping her pom-pom on his nose. He darted his hand forward and flicked up her skirt.

How annoying, I'd thought. *He deserves a smack in the head for being rude to her.*

But the cheerleader loved it. She sat on his lap. How naive I was. He's always been a player. I guess I was just another in his game.

"Get in," he says, still gazing lovingly at the steering wheel.

"But I booked an Uber."

"Cancel it."

"Zeke, we don't—"

"One thing." His two words hurl me into the past. I'm spiraling so fast that I feel dizzy.

"No." I fold my arms, steadying myself. "I'm not playing that game anymore. Get out of the car. Let's go."

"*One thing,* kitty cat," he repeats, then gives me a challenging stare. "Tell me one thing you'd change if you can go back in time. I'm not getting out of the car until you do."

I cover my face with my hand and take a deep breath. For fuck's sake. I drop my hand and say in all seriousness, "I'd go back and stop you from cutting your own hair. It looks ridiculous. Happy?"

He roars with laughter, and I hate it. I hate how his voice is so rich and familiar despite the decades that separated us. I hate how his joy melts the stiffness in my body. I hate how I want to curl into his arms like that cheerleader had.

He wipes tears from his eyes and then goes silent, still

staring ahead through the windshield into a dark corner of the barn. His knuckles turn white on the wheel, and he mumbles, "I'd have left Snuggles to burn."

My breath hitches. This is the first time he's voluntarily acknowledged the fire since I confronted him a week ago.

Why? I want to ask. Why did you go? Why didn't you stay? Why break my heart? Why, why, why? But he's already shifted his attention to testing the dials on the car radio and I'm too stubborn to admit I'm hurting.

Some truths are better left buried.

"Come on, Leila," he pleads. "You know that driving ourselves to the city will be more comfortable and convenient than an Uber. Arriving in a sexy car like this will strengthen my cover if I'm to get back in the good books with my old crew. I promise to drive carefully." He makes some kind of weird sign of the cross, then kisses his fingers and salutes with a scout's honor. "I promise and kinky swear and all that shit."

"I think you mean pinky swear."

"Do I?"

"You're an idiot." I scowl.

"You used to laugh at my jokes before." He turns the key in the ignition, and the engine roars to life. "Aw, hell yeah. Listen to that baby purr."

He pumps the gas a few times until the ground quakes from the roaring engine. Then he puts it in reverse, places his arm across the backrest, and stares at me. I must have a few brain cells missing because I give a long-suffering sigh and mumble, "At least if we're driving, I can bring more weapons."

"That's my girl."

"Go to hell," I return.

"You first."

Those words. My lungs seize as I tumble further into our past, to where the thrill of acting like a villain was a drug so illicit that I still remember it with crystal clarity. We were in the courtyard, acting out the opening scene from *Tombstone.* My stuffed toys were the victims before the church. I was the bad cowboy shooting my way through town, putting holes in everyone from the old to the newlyweds. I don't remember much about that game except those words and the thrill of being naughty, of shooting people just because I could.

But now . . . as I watch Zeke in the car, looking at me, waiting for me to move so he can reverse, I'm struck by a second part of that memory.

Before we started to play, I'd broken out in hives from the stress of keeping to the group home rules. I always made my bed perfectly. I always brushed my hair and teeth. I did my homework. I'd learned to hold shut my smart mouth. I did everything possible to be the perfect little girl someone would want to adopt, but no one did. My reputation for setting fires had spread to other homes. Every social worker in town knew about me.

They'd branded me a misfit despite my behavior. The realization that I'd never be good enough, that my reputation was inescapable, had caused the rash. My skin bled from scratching. Zeke had been annoyed—but not annoyed at me. He was defensive. Frustrated. He'd said, "Where's my wildcat gone?" And then, "Let's do something naughty just because it's fun."

They already thought I was a pyromaniac, and the thought of getting into more trouble made my hives worse. Zeke suggested we reenact the *Tombstone* opening scene with us being the bad guys. No one would actually get hurt, and I could let off steam.

Back then, I didn't think much of our age gap. He was my best friend, and that was it. But now I see that five years between children is a lot, and I wonder . . . how many of our games were just him entertaining me, giving me something to enjoy? How much of our time together was he protecting me?

Zeke's frown deepens as I stare at him. He opens his mouth. He's going to say something about the fire. I can see it in his eyes. Hot, prickling panic engulfs me.

"I need more weapons," I blurt. "Meet back here in an hour."

I spin and walk back to the abbey, rubbing the center of my sternum, trying to calm my rabbiting heart as I finally realize it's not just him I should be angry at for not talking over the past week. I'm afraid of learning why he left me.

Sixteen

Zeke

Killing an hour should be easy, but since I'm trying to quit smoking, I find myself walking on the edge of a razor blade, ready to tip into insanity at any moment. I'm already packed. Can't smoke. We've already touched base with old city contacts and have planned our movements for when we arrive.

If I stand around waiting for Leila, I'll go nuts wondering where this next week will take us. Will I crumble and fall into old habits? Will Leila hate me? Will we reconcile? Will I come out of this alive? The questions toss around my mind on repeat. Ultimately, I decide to find Cisco and confess as he asked me to, hoping it will alleviate some of the unrest in my soul.

Wes might not trust him at the moment, and to be honest, I'm not sure I do either, but I can always count on him being a good priest. I need the council and know he'll keep whatever I reveal to himself.

Half expecting not to find him after the morning we had, I'm surprised he's kneeling on the punishing pew inside the Sin Bin, wearing his purple and black confessional sacramental vestments and white collar. His head is bowed, eyes and brows drawn as he murmurs his prayers.

This morning, he seemed out of sorts when we were brainstorming in the archives. I know he took confession from the Sinners who left for Italy and put it down to that. But maybe it has something to do with his conflicted loyalties and the Vatican.

Candles behind him give the room a soft ambiance. Not wanting to interrupt, I quickly peek to see if a Sinner occupies the wooden confessional next to him. The booth is a beautifully carved antique with three doors. The outside doors are solid, but the middle door reminds me of a swinging saloon door. A light globe in that center cavity is not on, which usually means the priest is not giving the sacrament of reconciliation.

Maybe Cisco is about to start, or he's finished for the day. Either way, I'm not sure what to do. He seems pretty deep in prayer. Maybe it's best I find something else to do.

At least I killed a few minutes walking here.

"I thought you had forgotten." Cisco's smooth Italian voice echoes through the church.

I can see why they keep the Sinners in this private room rather than out in the public confessional. Anyone walking in would hear all the sordid details of their often illegal sins.

When I don't respond, Cisco opens an eye, takes in my expression and then opens the other. He makes the sign of the cross and says in Latin, "*Nel nome del Padre, e del Figlio, e dello Spirito Santo. Amen.*"

He presses his threaded fingers to his forehead and frowns so deeply I think he'll strain himself, but then sighs and stands. He wipes his palms down his robes, settling the wrinkles, avoiding my gaze.

It's been a while since I checked in on him or Dom properly. These past few weeks have not been good for our friendships. I see now how self-involved I had been with my illness.

Over the years, we've all spent time in close quarters, living in shared houses and learning all sorts of secrets about each other. One thing I've learned about Cisco is that he prays when he's conflicted.

"Are you all right?" I ask, not sure if I should broach the subject, but fuck it, today's a day for taking risks.

He nods, but I don't believe him. His lips are pinched ever so slightly at the side. It's a worry. Who does the priest confess to when he needs guidance? Cisco gestures for me to enter the confessional.

"In there?" I grimace.

"*Sì,*" he replies and widens the door to the room, propping it open with a wooden peg. "I think it is good we treat Sinners and everyone else the same, no?"

"It's probably a good idea." Treating people like they're bad only removes the barrier to doing bad things. Although, I can't really picture one of the nuns in there, hiding out in the dark closet, knowing a wall of deadly weapons waits just outside.

Maybe I can move them to the workout area where the other weapons are. It will help alleviate any awkwardness the nuns might feel in the confessional. I think these weapons have been blessed, but to be effective against demonic possession, they need sigils carved into the surfaces. Leila is the weapons expert. She needs to learn how to do this.

I'm also Team Saint's weapons expert. Technically, it's my job to teach her.

Cisco takes in my intense stare and says, "We don't have to go in there."

"I just thought I should carve sigils into the blessed weapons. The Sinners need the extra protection they afford." Wes started teaching them about the geomancy techniques that form the basis for most of our occult spells, but we've all been distracted. And I've avoided facing Leila.

The priest's eyes take me in for a fraction longer than normal.

He nods. "This is a good idea."

"I should confess first."

"I can close the doors for privacy."

I watch him walk to the double entrance doors. His black robes swish gently, but his stride is confident and sure. Always is. He reminds me of myself in this part. Our pasts have trained us to walk with one eye on danger and our muscles coiled to strike. Although it's been years since he used his body as a weapon, he still keeps himself fighting fit. Being the exorcist means he battles beings with supernatural strength and often for long periods of time.

Definitely fitter than me, despite my daily trips to the gym. My fingers absently reach for the lighter in my pocket. Fuck's sake. I drag my hand back to my thigh and tap. *Don't think about having a smoke. Don't do it.*

The sound of the big wooden doors closing is like thunder,

and I face forward to the sanctuary and altar. The crucifix looks down at me. Blood drips from the wooden effigy's thorny head in red streaks. Pretty macabre, but it suits the hidden teeth of this place.

Cisco sits on the pew next to me. When his brown eyes meet mine, I see tiredness and hesitate. Adding to his conflict is the last thing I want, but if I head off on this trip with Leila, knowing I'm already on a slippery slope toward a place I don't like, I might do something stupid like go completely off the rails and say fuck everything.

I've done it before when I thought she'd died. What if something happens again?

"Bless me Father," I sigh, "for I have sinned. It's been . . . fuck knows how long since my last confession."

"*Quattro settimane.*" Cisco's eyes crinkle as he holds up four fingers. The tattoo of a cross covers a jagged scar on his ring finger.

"Of course, you'd be counting." I chuckle.

"One of us must, no?"

We share a small smile.

"Go on," he prompts.

"Well, I guess you know about the lie Wes and I told to come here." I hold my breath. Leila's face flashes in my mind. Usually, she's scowling, but after today in the barn, she's smiling at me. "You know I lived in a group home when I was young."

He nods.

"Well, for most of that time, I knew Leila."

"The Sinner?" His brows knit together. "The angry one?"

I smile. "Yeah."

He nods, indicating I should continue.

"She was family to me." I lean forward and brace my elbows on my knees. "She reminded me of my sister, although I'd never had a chance to meet her. Not really. For about half a decade, I protected and sheltered Leila. I looked out for her well-being. Well, as best I could, being a teenager myself." I rub my knuckles where the scars used to be. Thea's healing erased them. "We were in the home for rejects. No one wanted to adopt me because of my reputation—I liked to fight. And the story of my sister's death followed me everywhere. They all thought a bad kid like me obviously killed my sister. Leila faced similar prejudice. Everywhere she went, fires started."

"She did not start them?"

I shake my head. "They blamed her, but she told me something evil followed her."

"You saw this evil?"

"No. But I believed her. The same thing happened with my sister."

Silence answers me. I glance at the priest and find his eyes filled with pain. But the moment he catches me looking, he puts on his clerical mask, hiding the evidence just as Thea's healing erased my scars.

"And your sin?" he prompts.

"I lied to her. There was a big fire at the home. I promised I was going into a burning building to rescue her favorite toy, and that I'd be back. But I realized something when I got in there. The toy was called Snuggles. The demon that killed my sister said something about snuggling as he set them both on fire. It made me fear the same demon was after Leila too. It even made me think that the demon was after Leila all along and not my sister. I thought that if I left then and there, everyone would think I had died in the fire. I'd be free to hunt down the demon and . . . get away with doing things I couldn't if I was alive."

"She thought you were dead?"

I nod, then rub my eyes. "She thought it was her fault too."

"Did you know she would blame herself?"

"Honestly, I could only think about protecting her at the time." I shake my head. "The thought of losing her after I lost my sister was too much."

Cisco is silent for so long I'm afraid to look at him. He already thinks I'm a piece of shit for what we did to him and Dom. Now this.

"Ezekiel." The tone of his voice gives me nothing. I can't meet his gaze. "I had a sister once."

I look up. The pain in his eyes is a wound reopened.

"You did?"

He nods. The pain recedes momentarily, and a wistful smile tugs at his lips. "She was a beautiful, bright and talented ballerina. She was going to be a star."

I almost don't want to ask. "What happened?"

He rubs his lips, lost in his memories. Then the pain is back, obliterating all else.

"She drowned. I was jealous of the attention Mama and Papa gave her. I teased her about how she must float in the storm if she wanted to become the best prima ballerina. I showed her how easy it was. But you see, I was almost a grown man. Fifteen and with strong muscles. The waves were nothing to me, but I did not know she was not eating her food. The dancing had made her thin and brittle like a stick.

She could not fight the ocean and I was not as strong as I believed."

"It was an accident."

"*Si*, but my jealousy was not." He rubs his fingers over the Bible sitting on his lap. He traces the grooves of the embossed letters M.A. and says, "Maria Angelotti was *mio picolla angelo*." He swallows hard. "You asked me once how I became mafioso. I thought, if I had sent an angel to her death, then I must be a devil, no? And this was why I could sniff out my own kind."

"I'm so sorry."

He gives me a sad smile. "Gratzie. But I am telling you this because you must know your story is not unique. We are all tempted by many evils, especially in our youth. The Lord forgives as long as you feel in here"—he points to my heart—"you were wrong and do not wish to do it again."

"But that's the problem," I reply darkly. "I'm not sorry I left to keep her safe. I'm sorry I hurt her, yes, and I'm sorry she became a cold-hearted killer because I left her behind. But for all I know, keeping that stuffed toy was what stopped the fires following her."

"How do you feel your deception made her feel?"

"Shitty, of course. She feels shitty. I feel shitty. She wouldn't be here if it weren't for me."

"So your penance is to make amends with her."

Easier said than done.

"As for your lie to us, your penance is twelve Hail Marys."

"That's it?"

"You are not planning on lying to us again, I hope?"

"No."

Nerves tickle my spine.

He makes the sign of the cross before my face and prays for my absolution in Latin. I've heard it too many times.

"But . . ." I start after he's done.

"You have more?"

"No, it's just . . . about me heading into the city."

"You are getting your tattoos fixed as well?"

I nod, but I want to talk about what I might have to do if pushed to my limits.

A long, tired breath shoots from his lips. He stands and tugs out his white Roman collar. "I need a beer. Walk back with me."

After he divests himself of the robes, he returns with his black shirt open at the collar. He flicks the lights off and closes the doors as we leave. With his hands in his pockets, we start the short walk back down the winding lakeside path.

"So," he says, "you will attend Leila on a visit to the city to speak with a man who is boasting about a helmet of importance."

I nod.

"But you will have to connect with old acquaintances."

Again, I nod. He knows exactly who I need to contact and what I might have to do. For a split second, he's no longer the priest but the mafioso with disheveled hair and finger tattoos. I imagine he walked like this with many of his crew, discussing the ins and outs of a speedy and fast execution. Maybe he's not the right person to talk me down from the itchy trigger finger ledge.

"We've seen the miracles the archangel's relic can perform," he points out. "Something like this must not be allowed to remain in the hands of evil. We agree with these Sinners on this front."

Every time he uses that word to describe them, I bristle. But his point is clear. Do what I must to bring the relic back.

"This trip is a good chance to do your penance," he adds.

Telling him about the prophecy is on the tip of my tongue. But Wesley is a helluva lot smarter than me, and if he thinks Cisco isn't ready to hear about how he's fated to break his vows with one of these *sinning* women, then I should probably keep that to myself.

I pull the lighter out of my pocket and flick the flint.

"You are worried about the trip, no?"

"Yeah." I smother the lighter and crush it in my fist. "I don't know if I'm strong enough to crawl back out of that dark place again."

He stops and faces me. The hazy twilight makes his facial expression hard to read. At first, I think he's concerned. Then I see it's anger.

"This is not a good place for you, Ezekiel," he agrees. "But you are strong. You have come back before. You will do so again."

Hearing my full name reminds me of the verse Asmodeus painted on the wall in blood. "Do you think that message on the wall was meant for me?"

"Why do you say that?"

I hesitate. "The number after it seemed personal. It's a reference to all the . . . people I've killed."

His eyes narrow on me. "No. I think this demon has his own path of vengeance. It is a coincidence. Perhaps just another message to confuse us. But you changed the subject."

"Yeah, I did."

We continue walking. He says nothing, just waits for me to speak.

"It's bad enough I can't quit smoking, but seeing Lei Ling —Leila—I realize I never stopped wanting to keep her safe . . . even from herself, if I have to. When I was that bad person, it was because I thought I'd lost her. I thought I'd failed. I had nothing to live for."

He slides me a look. We're almost back at the abbey now. I head for the stairs, but Cisco stops me.

"You are not the same man," he reiterates.

"But what if I'm worse now that I have something to lose again?"

"No."

"How can you be so sure?"

"Because love makes you better. This I know."

"You sound like you're speaking from experience."

He stares into the distance but gives me nothing.

"Do you miss it?" I ask brashly, curiously. "The sex?"

His lips curve on one side, and for a brief moment, I think Wes has nothing to worry about him and this fate of ours, but then his smile drops.

"There is no pleasure," he replies, "worth more than my service to the Lord. My penance is *molto lungo*. But you, my friend. You are not a boring old exorcist like me."

"Old." I scoff. He barely has a wrinkle, is fitter than me, and barely a gray hair at his temples. He can't be older than forty. Maybe younger. "Hardly."

"Old, as in, my time for these indulgences of the flesh is long past."

"Right," I drawl, unconvinced. "But for the record, you're as bad at changing the subject as me."

He gives a hearty laugh and claps me on the back. "Come. I must drink."

"I can see why."

"Stop."

I hear the smile in his voice. We head inside the abbey, and I feel like one of the weights on my shoulders has been lifted. Many remain, but at least I'm not worried about how my feelings for Leila might evolve and affect this team. He said love makes us better. He must mean he'll be happy for me.

But as we walk into the abbey, Cisco's cell phone rings. He takes the call, speaking in Italian before making his excuse to leave—forgoing his beer.

Suddenly, there's nothing in the way of me tracking down Leila.

Seventeen

Leila

"All right," I say as I open Raven's door. "Lay it on me." She's reclined on her bed with a cold compress against her forehead. I hesitate. Maybe I should leave. But maybe she needs help.

"You okay?"

She peels the cloth from her head. Her pupils are two pinpricks of pain.

"Migraine," she mutters, then reapplies the compress.

"Sorry." I want to ask if she needs a drink or one of the sugar cookies I baked this morning, but something holds me back. She doesn't look like she wants company. I should make this visit quick. "What did you see in the vision?"

Her breathing falls silent. It's too much of a tell to ignore. Something about my question unsettles her.

"You actually had a vision, right?" I ask. She could have lied about it . . . or Thea could have lied.

"Yes."

"So what aren't you telling me? Am I going to die? Get tortured? Assaulted? Possessed?"

"It's nothing you need to worry about. It's my future I'm worried about."

I rub my eyes. "Are *you* going to die?"

"Jesus-fuck, Leila. Why so morbid?"

My lips clamp shut.

She sits and fumbles for her cigarette packet, but when I glare at her, she puts it back down. "I haven't seen your death or mine."

"So what can you tell me—just lay it on me."

"I saw a poker game where you were dressed like a Dom. I saw a man who looked like Rick Moranis wearing an emperor's helmet. You stood on his face while he looked like he wanted to own you. I saw a car. And I saw flowers and . . . Dracula. I know that's weird, but it is what it is." She frowns, looks at her feet, and shakes her head. "I'll let you know if I understand any of it. Also, FYI, Rick Moranis is the antiquities collector and . . ." She frowns. "The helmet he wore was definitely Constantine's—an emperor known to be one of the worst in history, especially toward women."

"Anything else?"

"Yeah. Tell your cowboy that when it's time to negotiate with old friends, just tell the truth."

"Zeke?"

"And tell him gods don't worry about the rats they step on while protecting the innocent."

"Okay. That's weird."

She sighs and sits back down. Taking it as a dismissal, I move to leave. Raven's hand suddenly snakes around my wrist.

I gasp and glance back. Her eyes are white—clouds cover the irises. She's having a vision right now.

Her voice comes out deep and wrong as she says, *"They're coming to tear us apart. We win one, we lose one, we can't trust our own."* Her eyes return to normal and she stares at me for a minute, confused. Then she blinks and clears her throat. "Go and get the blessed weapons from the Sin Bin. You'll need them."

Raven lets go of me and then winces. "Headache," she grumbles.

"Maybe ask Thea to—"

"No. The moment we start abusing that relic, it will stop working."

"You saw this in the vision?"

"It's common sense." She hunts around her bedside table until she finds her pills and takes one.

I'm not sure I believe her, but hand her a half-empty bottle of water I find sitting on the floor.

"Raven. What did you mean? Who's coming to tear us apart?"

"What?" She takes a swig of the water.

"You just had a vision. You said, 'They're coming to tear us apart. We win one, we lose one, we can't trust our own.'"

"I said that?"

"Your voice was creepy and deep."

"Huh." She leans back on the bed and closes her eyes, then shoos me out. "Go get the weapons."

"You have to tell Thea."

"I will," she murmurs. Two seconds later, she's asleep.

Frowning, I give her room a quick sweep to remove fire

hazards. If I'm not here, she might do something stupid like fall asleep with a cigarette burning. With a last final thought, I take her entire cigarette packet and toss it in the trash on my way to the church.

Can't trust our own.

I WALK DOWN the church aisle toward the Sin-Bin but stop at the sound of clinking metal within. Who's here?

After Raven's strange warning, I tense. Whoever is inside, even one of our own, can't be trusted. With my senses on high alert, I push the Sin Bin's door open and find Zeke plucking blades from the rack on the wall.

"What are you doing?" I narrow my eyes.

He glances at me with guilt, like I've caught him stealing. Then he rubs his neck and blushes. "I wanted to surprise you."

"With our own weapons?"

"I'm carving spells on them."

I lift my brows, instantly curious. "What kind of spells?"

"The kind that give you extra supernatural protection." He points at a short claw dagger. "The basic ones repel evil on contact. The symbols are small and easy to remember. I have them on my bullet casings."

"What happens when you shoot a demon?"

"I've never shot a demon," he replies, frowning. "But I've shot demon-possessed people. Usually, the demon is exorcised."

"At the expense of the host."

He nods.

"Maybe you can show me more on the ride." Guilt stabs me. I should have learned this stuff over the past few weeks.

Zeke gives me a hopeful look, stands, and steps toward me. That sense of panic I felt in the barn returns as he slides his hand into his pocket like he's hunting for something . . . something he wants to show me. But before he can, I lose the battle with my fear and run out.

I SPEND the three-hour drive to the city attached to my earphones and a podcast. It was a tough choice between Nigella Lawson on baking or Martha Stewart. These shows are a guilty passion despite having no place in my life. It probably stemmed from my childhood when my baked goods brought joy . . . especially to the scowling gunslinger at the wheel beside me.

He wants to talk about us, I know it. It's in the very air we breathe. But I can't. I'm worried I won't like his reasons. Or I'm worried I will, but after Raven's warning, I could be setting myself up for more heartache and betrayal.

So I will just get this job done and then get out.

A Sinner knows how to flip weaknesses into strengths. My old teacher's voice is loud in my mind. The nun knew so much about seduction and assassinating that I'd always wondered if she used to be a Sinner. *One must adapt in a pinch,* she would say. *Use what the Good Lord has given you and twist it to your advantage.*

I'd much rather break into the target's house, tie him up,

and waterboard him until he gives us the necessary information. Infiltrating a poker game seems like a waste of time. The others are already in Italy, making the pilgrimage to each Holy Nail site.

I get that this Rick Moranis guy wore Constantine's helmet in Raven's vision, but this trip could still be for nothing.

"Leila." Zeke's voice is loud enough to break through my podcast.

The app on my cell phone suddenly becomes fascinating. I swipe through multiple episodes until I hear my name again, and Zeke tugs my earphones out. Reality rushes in.

Country music on the radio. The roar of the engine. The soft *click click* as something on the road hits a tire. Zeke's breathing beside me. His smell.

"Leila," he says, voice soft. "Can we talk?"

Shit.

I take a deep breath and count the woodland trees as they pass. The sun has set, and we're in the middle of nowhere. We dawdled too much at the abbey, packing more weapons and speaking with Raven. It was worth it. But now we'll arrive around midnight in the city.

"I reached out to old contacts," he says, "and I'm good to meet them when we arrive. So it's best to find a motel where I can drop you off while I run the errands before the game."

I exhale with relief. He's not going to push for a deep and meaningful conversation.

He pauses. "It's weird that Raven knew all this. Right?"

"She's usually right. You get used to it." That reminds me. "She told me to tell you a few things—tell the truth when you're negotiating with old friends, and that gods don't worry about the rats they step on while protecting the innocent."

"What does that mean?"

"You'll probably know when the time comes."

I lift the earphones to my ears.

"Wait." His gaze hardens on the road. A tendon ticks in his scruff-covered jaw. "What sort of things did you do as a Sinner?"

"Pardon?"

"Tell me about your life with the Sisterhood."

I blink, shocked. I expected the big questions but not this. Somehow, it irritates me. And then I'm irritated that I'm irritated. He made my guard drop for a split second, and I'm not prepared. My emotions are all over the place.

"Tell me why you have contacts with dodgy arms dealers," I shoot back. Then because my brain can't stop my mouth, I finally let out the real question I'm afraid to ask. "Tell me why you left me."

In the time it takes him to open and shut his mouth, that fear is clawing back into my brain, taking charge of my words. A cruel laugh slips out of me, and I shake my head, using the bitterness in my voice to create distance between us. "You want to know about my life but don't even have the balls to tell me why you ruined it."

"Is that what you think I did?" The words hiss from his lips. He darts a cold look at me, and I almost gasp at the animosity vibrating off him. His presence was already stifling in this car, but now it's suffocating. "You think I *ruined* your life?"

"You faked your death! You knew I would blame myself,

but you did it anyway. Do you know what kind of complex a young girl gets when she thinks she's a bad luck charm? That she's evil? I spent years here sweating the guilt out of my system —decades reconditioning myself into believing I have control over my choices."

"And do you?" he asks dryly. "Have control?"

"It's sure as shit better than what I had before." I gesture at him. "Clearly, you felt the need to change, too, because you're not covered in burn scars or anything. You weren't *missing* after the fire or in a hospital with amnesia, covered in third-degree burns. I honestly can't see another reason for you leaving the way you did other than you were done with an annoying little girl hanging off your every word. I should shove a horse manure pie down your throat."

I face the window and concentrate on breathing slowly and steadily. *Don't let him see your struggle. Don't give him the satisfaction.*

"You thought I was in the hospital?"

"On a good day, Zeke. On a good day, I fantasized you were in the hospital, just waiting for me to find and claim you. I called around. But every other day, I grieved for you."

He exhales slowly. I hear the remorse in his sigh and see it in his body language, but still, he doesn't apologize.

"Are you going to tell me what happened?" I ask.

"How long was it until the Sisterhood came for you?"

I roll my eyes and shake my head. Typical. Changing the subject the moment I get too deep.

"Did the fires follow you?" he presses.

Honestly, I don't understand him.

"Leila, the reason I left is because—"

Weird shrieks blare from the radio speakers, making us wince. Between white noise and country music, it sounds like a banshee is trapped in our car radio. Instrument lights flicker. The dial rotates between stations. On. Its. Own.

"What the fuck?" I tap the instrument panel, desperately trying not to pay attention to the back of my neck prickling with alarm.

"Probably faulty wiring," Zeke grumbles. "It happens in these old cars."

"But it's . . ." I try to hold the dial, but it spins in my fingers like an invisible hand fights me for control. Zeke has a go but can't get a grip. I glance up. A dark figure stands in the middle of the road, backlit by embers and mist.

"Look out!" I yank the steering wheel.

We veer to the side. Tires screech. Zeke takes over, expertly steering into the drift. We fishtail across the road, burning rubber, bumping over fallen twigs and branches. I jerk side to side, then forward as the car stops inches from hitting a tree. The seatbelt burnt my shoulder. My heart pounds so hard that I press my hand to it as if I can stop the organ from bursting from my chest. But another hand is already there—Zeke's large palm is splayed against my sternum, holding me to the seat, acting like my personal airbag.

His wild eyes dart over my body. "You hurt?"

I shake my head.

He unbuckles and leans across me to open the glove compartment and retrieve his Colt. "Wait here."

I scoff and lean into the back seat to retrieve my sword.

"I'm serious." He checks the rounds in the chamber—five bullets engraved with holy symbols—and then closes it.

I open the car door and step out, searching the darkness, straining my senses for danger. The whisper of my katana escaping its wooden *saya* is loud in the empty night. In Japan, they believe your sword carries your soul. Right now, mine is vibrating with the need to slay, eager but full of tension.

No insects chirp in the woodland trees. It's too quiet. Goosebumps ripple across my skin as I scour our surroundings, but the Mustang's headlights are too bright, blinding us to what's ahead on the road.

"I swear I saw someone," I mumble.

"I saw it too."

I briefly lean back into the car, place my knee on the seat and toss the *saya* into the back. The headlights wink out, pitching us into complete darkness. Somewhere, an owl hoots.

"Leila?"

"I'm here." I crawl back out of the car, straighten, and face the woods. A man with rotting flesh awaits me. Black holes for eyes. Bugs crawling across exposed tendons. Demon.

"Possessed!" I shout and duck, narrowly missing clawed hands as they fling past my head and hit the car roof.

With an upward strike, my blade sinks in beneath his ribs. A gun fires. The force of the bullet whips the possessed man's head back. Zeke unloads his remaining four bullets into the man's heart. Black smoke billows from the demon-possessed's mouth. Once it's all out, the corpse drops.

I yank my sword out and prepare for more danger, but after a few breaths of silence, I don't think anyone else is coming. The demonic presence is gone.

Zeke jogs to my side of the car, already reloading his gun. He takes one look at me and then searches the darkness around us. While he does that, I crouch to inspect the fallen man now that my eyes have adjusted to the dark.

"He's a biker," I note. "Has an MC logo on the leather jacket."

Dark veins spider out from the wound on his forehead—possibly an effect of the spell attached to Zeke's bullets. I definitely need to finish carving that into all the weapons when we get to the motel.

"What's a biker doing out in the middle of nowhere?" I ask, straightening.

"Not sure," Zeke answers, eyes locked onto something in the distance. "But I think someone in that bar can tell us. I'll check it out."

I follow his gaze and gasp. "You mean the bar that's on fire?"

The embers and mist I saw behind the man on the road were actually fire and smoke.

Fire.

A lot of it.

Sweat breaks out on my upper lip, my neck, everywhere. It prickles over my body and quickens my breathing. The ground moves beneath my feet, and I use the katana to steady myself.

"There might be survivors." Zeke holsters his gun. "Wait here. I'll be right back."

Wait here. I'll be right back.

Blood roars in my ears. I start panting.

Promise?

Every cell in my body is split between the past and the present. Like a zombie, I watch Zeke jog toward the bar and become consumed by smoke. It's like I'm in my very own horror movie with my eyelids taped open and my hands strapped to an execution chair. I can't press pause.

Stop, I try to shout.

Stop.

The fire will burn him alive.

Eighteen

The Past

The boy, who was now a man, stared at his latest effort stitching up the snuggle toy's chest cavity. The old thing was losing stuffing. He'd tried to reinforce the seam the girl had stitched in the home, but it didn't work for him as it did for her. She was so good at fixing things. Good at baking, too, even for one so young.

He missed her cookies.

He missed her smile.

The smell of her fruity shampoo.

The way she sighed softly when she enveloped him with her arms.

But most of all, he missed how her face screwed up when she remembered her defiance and let it out.

He sighed and put the floppy toy down, hating how it judged him with its one-button eye. It had been a year since he left his wildcat. A year since he made her think he was dead, but he was no closer to finding the fire demon today than he was then.

This toy had remained a toy.

Looking around at the tiny damp room he squatted in, he was glad she couldn't see him like this. She would be horrified. There was mold in the air. No electricity. Half-eaten packets of deli food overrun by ants. Even his cell phone screen was cracked and in need of repair. He had to charge it at the local McDonalds every morning.

Perhaps he made a mistake. Perhaps he should have spent this time away working a decent job, saving money, and building a respectable home to apologize for his mistake and adopt his wildcat.

But he wanted her to see him as a god, as her hero, a protector. Someone she could always feel safe around. Right now, he looked like a fool. He couldn't go back until he was sure he was a man worth being around. Less like Doc Holliday and more like Wyatt Earp.

What would she look like now? Would her hair be longer, her lips plumper, her face more angular as she turned into a woman? A blush hit his cheeks as he remembered how his body had started to react at seeing these changes. Then how he'd cocked it up and pushed her away. He scrubbed his face, still angry at himself. He shouldn't have taken out his confusion on her.

He could have just calmly told her they were too old for such cuddles. She would have understood.

His cell phone lit up with a notification. He'd set up Google Alerts for house fires in the area his wildcat now lived in. He'd also set up alerts for her name . . . to monitor her safety no matter where she was. But those had never activated.

Frowning, he picked up his phone and read. With each passing second, dread grew like weeds in his chest, suffocating his heart. *No.*

Local Orphan Girl Dies in House Fire.

The boy, who was now a man, fled out the door and was on a bus, using the last of his money to buy a ticket. He didn't stop until he arrived at the right neighborhood, two hours away, and stood in the shadows of the night, watching as the last remaining firefighters finished securing the hazardous area. It seemed they were done.

All bodies had been taken to the morgue.

Nothing was left but charred walls, coal, ash, and debris.

Nothing was left.

Smoke threatened to make him cough, giving away his position. But he had to get inside the house. Had to see for himself. Lifting his shirt to cover his nose and mouth, he slipped passed the officials and crept into the creaking and groaning house. He cared little for his safety, only for the few feet ahead lit up by his cell flashlight.

He went from room to room, scouring every inch, not knowing what he was searching for until he found it. A charred red string stuck out of the rubble beneath the black remains of a bed. *It's not it. It's not hers.* With his throat closing up, he flicked away coal and tugged the string out. A sob burst from his lips when he saw what dangled from the end of the string— a white bead with the evil eye painted on it.

His wildcat was dead.

Nineteen

Zeke

The bar isn't on fire, only the trash cans outside.

As I warily approach, I take in the row of Harleys and Ducatis filling the parking lot along with pickup trucks and old beat-up cars. The red blinking fluorescent sign on the tin roof reads *The Last Stop*.

A slice of foreboding settles in my gut. But I force myself to walk up the rickety wooden porch steps and stop at the frosted glass door. Music filters through. It's Kenny Rogers . . . "The Gambler."

Taking a breath, I scan the front of the bar one last time. As far as I can see in the darkness, no dead bodies or demon-possessed people are outside. Maybe nothing is wrong after all. Maybe we were randomly attacked.

Still, I hover my finger over the trigger, and the gun is cocked as I open the door, step in, and slip on something wet. I grip the doorknob, stopping myself from ending up on my ass.

The smell of death assaults my nose with an eye-watering

stench. I've smelled decay in my life but this . . . I don't know what it is about this, but it's worse. Like a hot oven of infestation. I'm too nervous to look inside, so I stand there in the doorway, gathering my courage.

The jukebox skips and then starts the song from the start. After a moment of standing in the doorway and breathing fresh air, I brave another look inside.

Blood and death are everywhere. Bodies. So many bodies . . . if you could still call them that. They're pulpy red messes on the floor, on the bar, flopped over tables and beneath them. Some corpses are frozen in rigor mortis, grasping broken bottles and wooden stakes made from table legs.

Was this a bar fight to the death?

Then I see the bloody footprints leading from the puddles at the bar toward me at the door. Two sets.

Whooshing outside jolts me into alertness. I twirl and aim my gun, but it's only Leila using her mini extinguisher on the trashcan fires. I quickly step outside, shut the door, holster my pistol, and use my body to hide the splashed blood on the frosted window.

Leila tosses her spent can when the fire is out and stalks up the steps with a murderous expression. She stops before me and punches me in the face.

Blinding pain radiates along my jaw. Stars burst behind my eyes. *Holy fuck*, I'm calling her Slugger from now on. Jesus Christ, that was some hit. I work my jaw, testing it. It's gonna be sore for a while, but I've had worse. I think she held back. *Jesus Christ*, I always knew she held back, but this is better than anything I envisioned.

My wildcat is strong.

"What was that for?" I rub my jaw.

She points in my face. "You're fucking clueless. You know that? You just ran toward a fire without any preparation or forethought."

She's trembling—not anger. It's fear. Panic. Her plump bottom lip wobbles. Her eyes are large and liquid. Her skin is colorless. I've never seen her so distraught. Not since . . . not since . . .

Promise? Her little voice cuts through the night.

Cross my heart.

Guilt hits me hard as I realize what's happened. She still runs her nightly checks for fire hazards. She carries an extinguisher around. She growled at me for smoking near dead grass. She's still afraid of fire, and I just ran toward it like the day I left her.

"I'm so sorry." I raise my palms.

"You could have been . . ." She gestures to the smoking trash. "I thought it was . . ."

"Hey." I pull her gently into my embrace. "I'm sorry. I wasn't thinking. I'm safe."

She stiffens in my arms and then punches my chest. "I don't care if you're safe. I hate you."

I tighten my embrace, squashing her, hoping my warmth will ground her.

"You don't mean that, wildcat," I murmur against her hair, loving that smell again. "Darlin', you don't hate me. And I don't hate you."

I can't let her go. Her fruity shampoo is there, eliminating the smoke. She feels too good in my arms, and I think she feels the same because she's not pushing me away. She's also not hugging back.

"Just tell me why." Her voice is small and muffled against my front. She's ice in my arms. "I'm ready now."

I glance at the bar door. Behind it is nothing but death. Suddenly, I feel like I'm swimming in a swamp. There's no up. No down. Just never-ending viscous mud everywhere I turn. No matter what I've done, we keep returning to this shit. I've wasted most of my life trying to keep it from her. Even when I feared she was dead, even when I was a god in a godless city, a part of me hadn't stopped hunting the demon . . . just in case.

All it got me was loneliness and time away from the one person who mattered anything to me.

"If I tell you . . ." I sigh. "If I tell you everything, *then* you'll hate me."

She'll know all of it was for nothing.

She pulls back, and the ice melts from her eyes.

"Zeke," she whispers. "What did you do?"

My thumb swipes a strand of hair from her flawless skin. She's so fucking beautiful it pains me to look at her. The Reverend Mother said something about Beatific Vision, or was it people gazing upon God's true face and going insane from being unable to handle the divine sight? That's the edge I feel whenever I look at Leila—like my body can't handle how stunning she is or how much she means to me.

I try to look away as though my eyes will burn, but I'm stuck because, without that fire, I'm cold. How did I ever have the strength to walk away from her?

What did I do?

"Not enough," I answer.

It physically hurts to disengage from our embrace. I step

back and look where the Mustang is a black shadow amongst the gray haze. Cisco wanted me to make amends with Leila. I tried to tell her everything before we left, but she kept freaking out. It's either talk now or face the blood and death inside that bar.

I don't think we're in danger. Everything is dead in there. So we have time. If I don't confess to her now, who knows when she'll be ready to listen again?

My voice sounds foreign as I let it all out.

"When I found Snuggles in the group home fire, I realized something about the demon who killed my sister. It hissed the words *'snuggle time'* when it killed her. I don't think the fire demon had ever been after my sister." I meet her shocked gaze. "It was after you—the one who was followed by fire all her life."

"Me? How?"

"You looked similar. Were of the same age. We were close by. With what we now know about you Sinners being targeted, it had to be you."

Her shock contorts into agony. "You *blamed* me?"

"No." I reach for her, but she slaps me away. "*Fuck*, I can't get anything right."

"Oh, I think you did." Her emotion disappears until her face is a cool mask of indifference. It saps the beauty right out of her and breaks my heart.

I scrub my hand through my hair. "I left with the toy because as long as it was near you, the demon would keep coming for you. I thought Snuggles was some kind of beacon for demonic activity. It's the only thing that made sense. So I left and took the toy. I had this grand plan for it to come after me so I could kill it."

"But . . ."

The shame heats my face. "I failed to kill it, Leila. It never came for me. I waited and waited. I spent all my free time and money learning about demonology and the occult. A year after I left you, I received an alert for a house fire. A local orphan girl had died." I pull out the charred red string from my pocket, curl my fist around it, and then show it to her. "I found this in the rubble."

"The Sisterhood," she whispers, mesmerized by the bracelet. She touches it. "I forgot about this until recently. I gave it to another foster kid—I thought your death was my fault. Thought I didn't deserve the protection."

My throat clogs, and I force myself to breathe. "I thought you were dead, Leila. That's why I didn't recognize you. Even knowing Leila is so similar to Lei Ling . . . I just never guessed I would be so lucky. I did some very bad things after I thought you had died." I slide her an empty look. "Eventually, I found Wes . . . or he found me. He helped me escape the country. Together we figured out which demon killed my sister . . . and you. Flauros was its name. I saw its real form once—do you remember?"

"You said it looked like a man that was a cat, and it had glowing red eyes."

I nod. "We tried to summon it, but it never came."

"I've never seen it. Do you think it gave up?"

"Maybe. But also, Wes said that if I saw its true form, it came through physically into this realm. That kind of transference takes a *lot* of power. The gates of hell are closed. The cracks weren't big enough for demons to just slip through. He thinks if, by the time it found you, all it could do was light fires nearby, then it likely had little power left. It's probably still back in hell, stuck there until it's strong enough to escape again. Maybe that last fire with the girl and the bracelet was the last of its strength." I exhale and close my eyes. "It's like everything I ever sacrificed was for nothing."

"And then you got sick."

I nod, brace myself on the porch railing, and hang my heavy head. I thought I would feel lighter if I confessed everything. But it doesn't change the fact that because of me, Leila is now an assassin—a woman who uses her body to get close to slimy men. She lost that spark in her eyes because I wasn't good enough. Because I made mistakes.

"I was supposed to be your huckleberry, but I fucked up." My voice is rough. I look into her eyes. They're not full of hate. There's something else I can't grasp. Something warmer than the cold.

"Zeke," she says. "The only fuck up is that you cared for me."

Every cell in my body rebels against her words. "What?"

"I'm the problem. Thea made it clear that we, the Sinners, are fated to wield the relics. *We* are the targets. Anyone close to us is a target too."

"I'll *never* regret fighting for you." I bluster, trying to find the right words. "I just regret I did it wrong."

"You had nothing but hell because of me. And now you're back here with demons and death." She gestures at the bar door and winces. "I know you're trying to hide it, but I can smell the blood from here."

"Leila." My tone is hard and commanding, my movements steady and sure. I take her chin and lift her gaze to mine. "I'm going to say this once, so listen up. You are not my hell. You are my heaven."

She inhales sharply, knowing what I mean. She has to. The hours of watching that stupid *Tombstone* movie have to count for something. There's a scene when the flirty actress asks Wyatt Earp what his idea of heaven is. It takes him the entire movie to find his way to her . . . his heaven.

Her gaze darts over my face, and then she does something I've only dreamed of. She puts her palms on my chest, lifts up on her toes, and presses her soft lips to mine. A dam of yearning breaks in my body. My groan is long, deep, and shuddering. I'm in agony. From my head to my heart to my toes. I only want to kiss her back but restrain myself. *Don't scare her away. Let her lead.* Her lips are on mine for two eternal seconds. But then she lowers with an unreadable expression and a soft sigh.

What was that?

My lungs heave. I can't think.

She kissed me. She doesn't hate me. Her hands are still on my chest, but what the fuck was that? It was almost a sisterly thank you. A chaste placation. Something you give a family member because you're obligated to.

It occurs to me I've never told her I want anything else. I've held it all back. Even Puck knew why I beat him within an inch of his life after he taunted me about why I kept a pretty young girl around. I whaled on him because his taunt held a kernel of truth somewhere in all the lies. I couldn't understand or name the longing in my soul back then, but it was always there. She was mine. *Is* mine. We belong together.

Her eyes slide to the door. "We have to go in."

No. I refuse to let her see that mess.

And I refuse to let that be our first kiss. She deserves a moment so hot it's seared into her brain forever. She deserves to have someone stare at her longingly from across the room. She deserves to feel wanted. Precious. If there's one lesson drilled into my thick skull, it's that this doomsday shit will never stop interfering with our lives. Why wait another second to let her know how I feel? Why not shoot two birds with one bullet?

Leila steps toward the door, and it's like the ground has opened up beneath us. All I can think is that I'll lose her again, so I yank her back. She slams against me. Breath bursts from her lips. My fingers tangle in her hair and tug down so her face tilts up, and we're looking into each other's wild eyes.

Slowly, I lower my lips but stop and check her eyes again. Satisfaction ignites my blood as her pupils darken with desire. She licks her lips and releases a breathy moan.

Good . . . she doesn't think of me as family either.

Our lips collide. I claim every inch of her mouth with hungry, beastly tongue strokes. Her moans become needy breathless whimpers. I deepen the kiss until her body melts against mine.

She grabs me by the shirt and kisses me back.

How I've dreamed of this moment. Every sleepless night since I arrived at the abbey was spent thinking about her across the hall, imagining how I would melt her icy armor—even before I realized who she was to me. I think my body knew. It craved her like a drug.

And now I'm hooked.

She tugs me closer—as if there is still space between us. She knows exactly how to use her tongue. It duels with mine, teases and taunts, battles and submits. Every erotic slide shoots obsession into my veins. The world, our responsibilities, everything falls away. I groan into her mouth and bend her backward with my ferocity. Fuck, she's so perfect—*ow*.

Pain pierces my bottom lip. With a gasp, I pull back and test my throbbing lip with my finger. *Blood*. "You bit me."

Twenty

I shove Zeke off me and turn away. He's too handsome with all that brooding entitlement and scruff that I know I'll lose my resolve if I look back. I'll kiss him again, but I'm *angry*. So fucking angry that I don't know what to do with it all.

He can't go dropping a bomb like that here and now. It's confusing the hell out of me. I need to think. To figure out what's happening in my body when he touches me. What's happening in my soul when he tells me he only ever wanted to protect me.

Bastard.

"Why did you bite me?"

"I'll keep biting if you kiss me again."

"Promise?" His deep, velvety purr sends shivers down my spine.

I should hate that word. It's given me nothing but grief. But instead, I glance at him and wish I hadn't. Wicked mischief glimmers in his eyes. He's back to how he looked at me before remembering who I was—with carnal desire. His tongue swipes blood from his lower lip in a slow, sexy, deliberate move.

"Stop it." *Stop making me want you.*

"No," he replies curtly. "I'm a straight shooter, kitty cat. I made a mistake leaving you. Thought I lost you for good. Thought I was dying without knowing what your lips would taste like."

"Gross. I was a child."

He chuckles. "I didn't even know what I wanted back then, only that I was obsessed with you. The fantasies came later . . . even when I thought you were dead."

"Sure," I counter dryly. The crusty, cheap bracelet is still in my fist. "I was so memorable that you forgot what I looked like."

"I didn't forget," he replies, brow furrowing. "I told you. I thought you were dead. I didn't expect you to be alive and to have grown into such a beautiful woman. Now that you're back in my life, I won't stop showing you we're supposed to be together."

When I don't reply, he steps back and raises his palms. "One thing, darlin'."

One thing? My mind scrambles to recall what he said to me in the shed from the car.

I'd have left Snuggles to burn.

I lock eyes with him.

"I'm going to do everything I can to turn back time," he promises.

I wish I could trust him. I wish that word meant something to me anymore.

"You can't," I breathe and drop the bracelet. "The damage is done. Good luck charms don't work. Time travel doesn't exist. Promises break. We're different people now."

Hurt flashes in his eyes, but I don't allow another word. I turn and stride to the door.

Alarmed, he reaches for me. "Leila, don't."

I palm the door hard enough to fling it open. The bell smacks tonelessly as my boots slap on something wet. Blood and dead bodies are everywhere. At least fifty, maybe a hundred people of all shapes and sizes litter the room. No children as far as I can see. The lights are on. The jukebox plays something on repeat. The beer tap is pulled down, but nothing comes from the nozzle. The keg must be drained dry. Broken glass is everywhere.

My eyes sweep the place again, taking in each body. Some still clutch a weapon, whether a broken bottle, gun, or kitchen knife. I sense the same tainted feeling in the room as I did at the abbey.

"This is like what happened when Asmodeus infected the nuns." I step into the room and try not to breathe the miasma too deeply. "This is the carnage we'd have found if we were a few minutes later and Thea didn't have the staff."

Writing on the mirrored wall behind the bar catches my eye. I almost missed the message written in blood. Ezekiel 9: 5-6.

"Definitely Asmodeus," I whisper with a shudder.

Zeke's gun is out and cocked as he reads the message like it will jump out and hit him in the face.

"Does that mean something to you?" I ask, my brow lifting.

He shakes his head a little too fast.

"You think it's a coincidence he quoted Ezekiel twice?" I pull out my cell phone, take a picture of the words, and send it to Thea. She doesn't answer immediately, and I'm impatient. I try to recall my Bible studies but never could retain much of it. With a frown, I realize the range on my cell is poor. *Damn it.*

"Do you know what verse that is?" I ask Zeke.

He looks at me like I've grown two heads. "I don't read the Bible. Oh, wait. I do have one in my bag."

While he returns to the Mustang, I stand in the open doorway and infuse my lungs with fresh air. Through the shadows down the road, I see him rifling through his bag in the back seat. It's so dark out there. Owls still hoot in the woods. Clouds pass the moon. A trickle of apprehension sharpens my gaze, and I search for signs of the enemy.

Zeke drives the car into the lot and then brings me my katana and a small beat-up Bible.

"Looks pretty well used for someone who never reads it," I note.

"I don't." He smirks as he thumbs through page after page of handwritten notes. I catch lists, diagrams, and crude demonic sketches. This must be his demonology notebook. I want to read it like his diary, to find out if anything he said to me was true, but I flick through to Ezekiel's gospel. It's Old Testament and closer to the start, which means plenty of scribbling over the words. Hopefully, the verse we want is still legible through the notes. I run my finger down the page as I scan.

"Here." I tap between a handwritten list of ghost hunters

Zeke must have been investigating and a list in another language. Is that Romanian?

Zeke's presence is warm and calming at my back as he reads over my shoulder. "The Lord commands: kill without showing pity or compassion. Slaughter old men, young men and maidens, women and children."

"That's pretty dark." I turn the page. "What was the verse Asmodeus wrote on the wall next to the Monsignor?"

"Ezekiel 18:4."

I glance at him, surprised he remembered.

But he's focused on the new verse and reads. "All lives are mine; the life of the parent and the life of the child belong to me. Only the one who sins will die."

"So Asmodeus started out saying only the sinners will die, but now wants revenge on everyone. Great."

"He's mad," Zeke says.

"He's War."

The sound of something metal and heavy drops behind the office door at the end of the bar. It's open a crack. I creep toward it, readying my sword. Zeke grips my shoulder, trying to stop me, but I shake him off, annoyed. *Christ.* If he keeps doing this protector thing, I'll lose it.

When I don't stop, I hear his pistol cock and his footsteps shuffle behind me. Hasn't anyone taught that man to creep quietly?

A trail of bloody footsteps leads behind the bar. I try not to contaminate them as I follow and discover a woman's corpse on the floor. Going by her apron, she's the barmaid. Blood covers her from head to toe. It's hard to see what her hair color is. I harden my heart, gesture for Zeke to back me up, then open the office door.

Shuffling.

I take stock of the long, narrow room. Desk. Security screen. Papers strewn about. Further down, it seems to be a storeroom with kegs stacked against a wall. Perhaps more space behind there. Another shuffle whips my head to my right. Below the desk, a boot retracts behind the chair. I crouch and find a terrified middle-aged man. He hugs his knees and squeezes his eyes shut. The floor is sticky and smells like urine and excrement.

"It's okay." I hide my sword behind my back. "I'm not going to hurt you."

He opens his red-rimmed eyes.

"But I might." Zeke keeps his gun pointed at the man.

"Put it away," I growl. "He's not infected like the others."

"How can you be sure?"

"I just am." I search the man's face. There's no sign of chaos or war in his eyes. Nothing like what I see in the nuns when they lost control.

Zeke keeps his gun out, and I flatten my lips. He doesn't trust me either.

I turn back to the man and ask, "You weren't infected, were you?"

When he looks at me oddly, I clarify, "Did you feel the uncontrollable urge to fight and argue with anyone? Like the people out there?"

"I was out on a late delivery."

"And when you returned, what did you see?" I don't think

he'd be hiding in here unless he saw something. "Or did you hear something?"

"I don't know." He shakes his head. "I don't know what it was."

"I think you saw a demon," I tell him.

"It was a monster. A beast. It had three heads and a dragon's body. Wings and red eyes."

He saw Asmodeus's true form. *Jesus.* This will haunt him forever. "You saw a powerful demon. There was nothing you could do to stop this. Hiding was the only way you'd survive."

He covers his face and sobs. I should probably comfort him or something. Zeke puts his pistol away. I reach out to, I don't know what, but settle for patting the man awkwardly. Zeke grunts impatiently and nudges me away.

"Come on, buddy," he says gently to the man. "Let's get you out of there. At least sit on the chair here, and I'll get you a drink. Is there someone we can call for you?"

I stand back and watch Zeke coax this man out of shock and wonder how he retained all that affection and compassion after the life we've had. I don't want to touch, speak to, or deal with strangers. At first, I thought this reaction of mine was simply because I thought other people were dumb. After learning all I had about the world, how to manipulate the human psyche and to kill, there wasn't much a stranger could offer me. Even sex became dull. It was nothing new. Only an equation that needed solving. A plus B equals O.

I watch Zeke as he gets on one knee, looks into the man's eyes, and speaks softly with compassion. I care for the nuns at the abbey and my girls, but it's so foreign to me with strangers. He's a natural, and I'm a little jealous. I used to be like this.

While he works his empath magic, I try and wrap my brain around what we should be doing next. If the cops get a whiff of us here, we'll be people of interest in their investigation. Ideally, we should eradicate all traces of our visit.

I should probably kill this man. We'd probably be doing him a favor, to be honest.

But as soon as my mind goes there, my eyes tell me I'm wrong. Zeke brings a glass of water to him—Pete, his name is— and then collects a jacket hanging on a hook behind the door. He tugs it over Pete's shoulders to keep him warm.

The jukebox skips and starts playing *The Gambler* again.

"That's weird." I step back into the bar and scan for anything unusual. It looks the same. A bloody, pulpy mess. I turn back to Pete. "How long ago did this happen?"

Pete looks at me, confused. "I . . . I don't know."

"Has that song been on repeat the entire time?"

He nods. "It's all I heard."

I wonder how many people are missing from the bar. A demon attacked us outside, but he could have been there to scare people away. Then again, maybe he was meant to infect more people with the war sickness.

Zeke points at a small television on the crowded desk. "Is that CCTV Pete? Mind if we take a look?"

Pete stares into his glass of water.

I join Zeke at the security station. It's not the latest technology but has a hard drive containing about a week's worth of data. I use the computer mouse to click on the most recent file and bring up the first video.

My eyes widen at the bloody scene. "This was time-stamped a day ago. Look, the bodies were already there."

"Go back further," Zeke murmurs, leaning in beside me.

We systematically go back in time until we find a video with movement. The day starts off with the usual people milling about the bar. It was two days ago. Before I watch any further, I glance at Pete. I'm surprised his body hasn't shut down already. Zeke must be thinking the same thing because he murmurs quietly into my ear, "We'll make an anonymous call to the authorities when we leave."

I nod and scan the CCTV footage until we reach the moment blood starts spraying. I rewind a little and hit play. Sound filters in, and I quickly press pause. Shit. I didn't expect this older system to have audio functionality.

"Pete shouldn't hear," I mumble to Zeke.

"I'll take him outside. He should be there when help arrives anyway." Zeke rubs the back of his neck and then says quietly for my ears only. "We can't be here when they do. I'm not supposed to be in the country. I had warrants out for my arrest when I left. The Vatican said they'd sort it out, but I never confirmed."

"You telling me they could arrest you?" The words feel hollow in my mouth.

He nods.

My brow furrows. He's a wanted man. An outlaw.

While I've had the Hildegard Sisterhood covering my tracks for my misdeeds, Zeke was alone until he found Wesley. With Team Saint, he managed to stay clear of prison, but now we've forced him to reacquaint himself with old contacts. I hope this mission is worth it.

I don't know what Zeke and I are to each other anymore, but I know that if we're separated again before I figure it out,

I'll never forgive myself. We'll have to leave here and erase evidence we were here. Then I'll get Tawny to check the police records and confirm if the Vatican actually followed through with its promise to clear Zeke's records.

"You got a back entrance, Pete?" I ask.

No answer.

Zeke ventures further into the narrow office space where kegs and other supplies are stored.

"Found it," he shouts from somewhere behind the kegs. A door creaks open. A breeze filters in.

After Zeke returns and guides Pete out, I sit on the office chair and hit play. The sooner we get this information, the sooner we can leave.

Loud music and chatter fill the air. It almost makes the conversation inaudible. The security camera is over the office door. It captures the length of the bar and most of the room— all the way to the wall at the back where patrons surround the glowing jukebox. Above the crowd at the bar, the front door opens and then closes. A dark head cuts through the crowd like a shark's fin in water.

Twenty-One

I wipe my taloned hands on the barmaid's apron, stand, and admire my handy work. The woman makes high-pitched squeaks and twitches, but I have what I need. Her blood courses through my veins.

I shut my eyes and focus on her whirling ancestral information flooding my consciousness—there are generations of it . . . at least thirty. So much more time has passed while I was in my stony prison than I realized.

Millions of Sarah's descendants are now alive. It will be nigh on impossible to track them all down. My only option would be to wipe out the entire world.

I smile. Why not? A little chaos is always fun.

My nose crinkles as a sudden whiff of sulfur arises from somewhere. My eyes open in time to see the barmaid convulse. The human body is so pitiful and without dignity in the end. No matter who they are, how much influence or money they hold, they all piss their pants and emit all sorts of stink.

Disgusting. I dust my hands and get ready to leave, but then her head twists toward me as if she still maintains control of her motor functions, despite half of her brain leaking onto the terracotta floor.

"Asmodeus," the deep, husky female voice hisses.

A chill enters my bloodstream. Beneath the barmaid's unremarkable visage, I glimpse the face of a sinfully beautiful woman with olive skin and red hair.

"Lilith," I purr. "To what do I owe the honor of a visit from Your Highness?"

"To congratulate you on your escape, of course."

Unlikely. I stare at her and wonder what the real reason is. Why now? After all these centuries, why finally reach out when she refused to answer any of my dark prayers? She left me to rot in that prison. I should kill her, just as I intend to kill this world. But now I'm curious.

"I must admit," I drawl. "I'm a little disappointed there was no welcoming committee."

"Well, as you can see, it's rather difficult to come topside these days."

My lips curve on one side. So it is as I suspected. The gates of Hell are still shut too tightly for anyone else to enter this realm. I may have been captive in a stone prison, but it seems that most of my brethren are also locked away.

"What do you want?" My tone darkens with the knowledge of my advantage. "If you're asking for help crossing to this side, I'm afraid you'll have to wait . . . perhaps as long as you made me wait."

"Oh, come now, Azzy. You're not angry about that still, are you? As you can see, I've been rather locked up too."

My growl is a low rumble I don't think she can hear. We've always had a precarious relationship. I scratch her back, and she scratches mine. I tempt her into original sin, and she . . . my memory blurs as I try to recall how she retaliated.

"How did you get out?" she asks, interrupting my thoughts.

I bite my forked tongue and weigh whether to reveal the truth. It's not like she can use the same method without Raphael's staff. I settle on, "I simply appeared here on this plane after your darling Leviathan took my place in the prison. Speaking of that . . . you wouldn't happen to know why these Sinner people believe Leviathan was the Horseman of Pestilence, would you? Or that I'm War?"

Preposterous. Why in damnation would I ever be denigrated by such a label?

The smell of rancor bleeds through her host. "It's because you *are* a horseman. The apocalypse has started."

Laughter roars from my mouth before I can stop it. I laugh so hard that tears spring to my eyes. "Darling," I chide. "I think the *actual* horsemen will beg to differ."

"They are . . . indisposed."

I still. "And Lucifer?"

The barmaid's blue lips stretch into the parody of a self-satisfied smile.

"Oh, you naughty queen," I say, silently impressed. "You've gone and locked them up, haven't you? Or killed them."

Her shoulder lifts on one side. "They reigned for too long. Always gloating, never doing."

"And now you reign, I suppose."

"For eons," she confirms. "Since you were imprisoned."

My eyes narrow. What a coincidence. I try to recall details of the circumstances leading up to my downfall. There was Sarah. There were her seven husbands. There was my anger and hatred . . . and there was . . . Lilith, spurring me onward.

She and I were always competitors. The fact I had to be imprisoned for her to gain leadership grates. Just imagine where I would be now, what power I would hold, if I'd evaded Raphael's wrath. If I'd let go of my obsession with Sarah. My fingers twitch at my side. If Lilith crosses into this realm, she'll be a thorn in my side.

"The seal is still holding the gates of hell closed," I point out.

"Not for long. The cracks are growing. Soon, we will all be out of our cages."

My eyes narrow. *All* out of their cages?

"Who else is here?" I ask. "Abbadon? Balthazar?"

"In the flesh like you? I'm afraid the answer is rather abysmal." She pouts.

Lies pour off her tongue like wine. Surely there are others like me in this realm. I glance over my shoulder. Most of the bar patrons are now dead or dying, lying at odd angles with torn throats and glass sticking crudely out of soft flesh. Near the door, three large men—bikers apparently, they're called—wait for my instructions. They will serve well as vessels for my legion to possess. They watch me with screaming eyes, waiting. It reminds me all too much of my own entrapment not that long ago.

Suddenly, the suit I conjured feels tight on my body . . . like stone rubbing against the flesh. *I'm not there. I'm out.*

"You"—I point at a big red-haired chap—"play some music. This party is becoming rather boring."

The man ambles toward the jukebox and hits a few buttons until something comes on. I close my eyes and listen. While in my cramped, stony prison, I astral traveled to this plane on occasion. It took years to amass enough power through ritualistic sacrifice. But as the years went on, people stopped worshipping me. Possessing a vessel was occasionally possible, but only for short periods. It tired me out, and I often skipped complete centuries before visiting this realm again. Culture has changed so much.

The twang of a guitar blares on the speaker.

"No," I bark and gesture to my man. "Next one. This is too, I don't know, stupid."

Honestly. Some of the things these people are entertained with these days. It boggles the mind. They've lost touch with the very essence of life. But they're also easier to manipulate. So much easier.

We cycle through another three songs before a deep, rumbling male timbre draws me in with a tale of gambling, sex, substances, and death.

"Yes." I smile. "This one."

It's been so long since I had fun. The song reminds me of the last time I had the strength to visit this plane and indulged in violence, hedonism, and lawless revenge. Utterly delicious.

"Asmodeus," Lilith hisses.

I clench my jaw and face her. "You're interrupting my fun."

"I don't have long."

"You're mistaken if you think you can order me around."

The barmaid's brows lower. "I care not what you do for

revenge. You will wreak havoc enough to destroy millions and herald the next horseman by simply being yourself. Pestilence cocked everything up."

"I'm not your horseman," I snarl.

I feel her patience waning from here. But, unlike me, she holds in her dissatisfaction.

"What do you want, Lilith?"

"Merely to warn you."

"I see." I've heard this song and dance before. She sidled up to the princes of hell, trying to curry favor with each of us, but then fucked Lucifer and told him all our secrets. She didn't get this far without stepping on a few cloven hooves.

"The Sinners have found a way to stop you," she says.

"Bah." I wave my hand. "The only prison capable of holding me is occupied."

"They are more cunning than Tobit," she warns. "How will you exact your revenge when you are dead?"

Tobit? My mind scrambles. Oh, yes. Tobit was Sarah's father. It was he who weaseled his way into Raphael's grace. He convinced the archangel to work against me.

But how did Lilith know? The more I try to recall that time, the more it evades me. And for some reason, my mind slips further into my past—to when I was an angel. When I had a soul. Like Lucifer, I had been unsatisfied with the Almighty's treatment of his creations. I wanted to enjoy them . . . and the more I played with them, the more my soul emptied. Until finally . . . fog.

"Azzy? Did you hear me? How will you do anything if you're dead?"

Dead? She plays a dangerous game, trying to manipulate

me. The song skips and the ceiling lights flicker from the power of my wrath. I don't need Lilith's help. She has a way of always being there when shit turns sour.

I'll eventually discover what kind of threat these Sinners are on my own.

But imprisonment has made me cautious. It's taught me to listen.

"If you're leading me on," I say, "I will personally come down there and annihilate you myself."

"A long time has passed, Asmodeus. I'm not the weakling I used to be." Her tone gives me pause. Then it lifts again like a vapid, brainless female. "Besides, if you come here, you'll be stuck with us until the seals break. You wouldn't want that, now would you?"

"No, we wouldn't want that," I mock and then check my talons. "So, what is it then? This all-powerful weapon that will supposedly kill me?"

"You know the drill."

I clench my teeth. "What do you want in return?"

"A favor."

"A favor," I repeat, my eyebrows lifting. "I don't think information is on par with a personal favor from yours truly."

"Information to prevent you from dying is worth *more* than a favor."

I suppose cutting short my fun now would be a travesty.

"And the parameters of your favor?"

"To bring one of my own into one of your strapping vessels there. I need someone topside. That's all."

Her minions are no match for me. "So long as the demon does as I tell him, fine. You have a deal *if* your information proves to be true. Tell me everything you know," I say, crouching low enough to hear her whispered words. When she's done, I reach into the barmaid's chest and crush her whimpering heart. Then I straighten and let my demon out.

In the mirror behind the bar, black draconic wings unfold from my reflection's shoulder blades. Goat's horns sprout from my head, a serpent's tail from my rear, and flames drip from my mouth. A metal lance materializes in my taloned hand, and I grin, baring monstrous fangs.

Twenty-Two

Leila

I sit back on the chair and stare blankly at the CCTV screen. What the fuck was that?

"Shit." Zeke mumbles behind me, frowning at the screen. I was so enthralled with the video footage that I hadn't realized he returned. "That was Lilith, right?"

"That's what he called her." My mind is awhirl with what we witnessed. "And Asmodeus didn't seem too happy to see her."

"Trouble in the ranks?"

"I don't think they're actually working together." I frown as I recall how they spoke to each other and the unsaid tension written between the lines. "And she didn't tell him about the cracks being the Sinners and the Saints working together. I mean, isn't that what Wes said was happening? When he and Thea had a fight, the cracks on the seals grew big enough for that demon Vepar to come through to our realm fully. Now that we're working together, we haven't had a big demonic sighting like that since."

He nods. "You think she's up to something?"

"I don't know, but it's also odd that he had no idea he was her Horseman of War."

"What did she say at the end?" Zeke asks.

I find a cloth and start wiping everywhere I've touched to eliminate fingerprints.

"I couldn't hear that part. She whispered it . . . but Lilith knows we're looking for a weapon to kill Asmodeus. It was probably where to look. The fact she warned him means we're on the right track."

"We or the others?"

"Whoever it is, there's now a race to find the relic."

Zeke picks up the urgency in my tone.

"Let's go, then." He moves toward the back exit. "I've already called the cops."

Before I leave, I erase any footage of Zeke and myself. I delete everything from Asmodeus' demonic transformation to the part when Lilith arrived. On second thought, what's the point in allowing any of this footage to be seen? It will only sow chaos. I hit delete on all the files and then spill water over the hard drive until the electrical wires fry. I give a last wipe down and then collect my katana as I walk out.

Zeke waits at the back door with narrowed eyes. "All good?"

My boot hits the dirt outside and sticks. I gasp, glancing down. "Blood."

"What do you mean?"

"I mean, we've left bloody footprints everywhere."

"A million other footprints are in there, too," he points out.

"But Pete saw us." Dread drops like a stone in my gut, and I stare through the darkness along the bar's external wall to the parking lot. Pete most likely waits for help to arrive on the porch steps. Adrenaline pumps through my system as the only likely scenario to fix this circles in my mind.

"Shit." Zeke scrubs his face. "I'm sure we can figure something out."

But we don't have time. He called the police. I walk past him toward the front porch.

"Leila?" Zeke jogs to catch up. "What are you doing?"

"He's a loose end, Zeke. And the first lesson I learned at the Sisterhood was loose ends need to be cut."

He pulls me to face him. "You're actually considering killing him?"

"We can't afford to have police chasing us down. You sat him on the porch, where he probably read our license plate. We deleted the only evidence proving our innocence. Coupled with our faces, names, and bloody footprints in the bar, if he snitches, then the authorities will be on our doorstep before the night's end."

He looks at me as though I'm a monster. "My God, they've done a number on you."

"Don't judge me," I return. "You're a killer too."

"But I have remorse," he spits. "I don't kill innocents, and I regret every ounce of blood I spilled."

His words steal my ability to breathe.

"No one deserves it, Zeke. But sometimes it's a mercy," I whisper.

Distant sirens bleed into the night. My adrenaline spikes and I reach for my katana, ready to swallow my humanity and cut a loose end, but before I can unsheathe the blade, Zeke swears and grabs something behind me. The smell of kerosine scourges the air.

"Then we'll burn it down," he growls. "Get Pete to a safe distance."

My feet are frozen to the spot. The only thing running through my mind is the word *fire*.

"Go," he shouts.

Hating that I'm useless when this infernal beast rears its ugly head, I swallow my pride and continue to the front porch. I must look frightened because Pete starts whimpering when I round the corner with my hand still on the sword. He's standing at the railing, ready to bolt.

I hold up my palms as I climb the steps. "We need to get you moved closer to the road. The bar is on fire."

"On fire?" He gapes, glancing over my shoulder.

The smell of smoke reaches us. I should be used to it by now, with all the fires I've seen in my life, but it still makes my insides watery at the thought of what comes after that smoke.

The distant clouds flash blue and red—signaling the police are almost here. I help Pete down the porch steps just as Zeke jogs back around the corner. I don't know what to tell Pete, but Zeke gets down on his knees and speaks softly with the man for a moment. We quietly say farewell and leave him for the authorities to find. Then we get in the car and leave.

Zeke drives with laser focus, his eyes straight ahead and his hand gripping the wheel. In the small cabin, there's nowhere to hide from his disapproval of me. I can feel it like the flames of the fire we left.

I scratch my inner wrist. Two seconds later, the itch is back, and I scratch again. *Fuck's sake.* I'm getting hives. Zeke's hand whips out to grab my hand before I cut my flesh into ribbons. I shake him off but turn my glare toward the darkness outside. I don't even know why I'm so irritated. It's not like I have to defend my actions to Zeke.

He thinks I have no remorse. I snort to myself. Zeke glances over and then scowls at the road. I *have* remorse. I have it in spades. But sometimes, we Sinners must draw a line in the sand.

I close my eyes and see the bloody corpses littered over the bar, their dead soulless eyes, staring blankly. That's the line. That's the part we must never forget so that we do what's necessary to save others.

We can't hesitate in the face of evil. If we get the chance, we must go in for the kill.

I turn to look behind us through the rear window. The glow of blazing orange is now distinct and reminds me of my nightmares.

"I'm sorry," Zeke murmurs, still with his eyes on the road. "I didn't mean to make you feel like shit. I just don't like seeing you lose your humanity over this." Then he mumbles, "You've already lost so much."

I face the front and stare ahead. "You need to prepare yourself, Zeke. Before this is over, we'll lose a whole lot more. Asmodeus transformed into a winged beast I've never seen before. And if he couldn't care less about Lilith, the Mother of all Demons, then we have to consider he's more powerful than her."

His knuckles whiten on the wheel. "I get it. If we hesitate, we're all dead."

Twenty-Three

Leila

Looking into the small motel bathroom mirror, I put the finishing touches on my makeup. Menial and repetitive tasks let my thoughts turn to things I usually try to avoid. Zeke is out there, doing whatever he needs to do to reconnect with his old gang. After we arrived in the middle of the night, I slept on the bed, and he slept on the couch.

Seeing the death in that bar has done a number on both of us. It's made it more real somehow. I didn't kill Pete, and so far, we haven't been chased down by the police, but we burned down the bar. We burned it to free ourselves to find this relic and fight.

I start to ask myself, do the ends justify the means? At what point are we the villains?

When I woke, he was gone.

It's funny, years of suffering denigration and judgment from the Sisterhood hasn't affected me as Zeke's disappointment did. He says he understands now, that our mission might have consequences we won't like. I know I shouldn't care what he thinks, but a part of me still yearns for his approval. It wants to be that sweet person who made him smile when she shoved a cookie down his throat.

I should have gone with him. Should have tracked him down and made sure he was safe. That's what Leila the Sinner would have done. The mission comes first. But Lei Ling can't face another minute, knowing her iron heart is unsteady. First Zeke, then the fires, then Pete—I'm losing confidence in my decisions. Stupid to dwell on this now. I'm a hop, skip, and jump away from pretending to be someone else. I should be using this time to disassociate, and channel Madam Mina, but each slide of my eyeliner doesn't hide my own eyes behind it.

It's now seven o'clock, and we're due at this poker game in an hour. Zeke was missing for most of the day. He texted me and said our invitations are sorted and that he has a few errands to run before he returns.

Frustration flays my nerves. My mind travels in circles, thinking about everything Zeke confessed. And I get it. He left me because he tried to protect me. He went about it in a way I wouldn't recommend, but I only know that because I'm an adult now. He was seventeen. When I was seventeen, I was being led by the Sisterhood from mission to mission. Having already completed my training in the Art of War, poisons, how to seduce and kill . . . I had no opinions for myself. I didn't know how. That took time. That took my Sinner sisters and countless tiny moments of bonding.

Sometimes we sat around a fire pit in the walled garden and talked all night. It was never about work but about the world outside. We talked about how we didn't fit into it anymore. Somehow, those conversations morphed into unspoken bonds.

The girls and I might shout at each other, fight, and keep secrets, but we're sisters. You don't choose your family, but you can keep the ones you find if you're lucky enough.

After sweeping a layer of dark, smokey eyeshadow over my eyelids, I step back to study myself in the mirror. My black patent leather corset cinches my waist so tight that my breasts virtually spill over the top. The corset stops above my belly button. My red lace thong sits high on my hip bones. I'll put a tight black skirt on in a minute, and that little red flag will flash above the waistband, luring in any male with a pulse.

With my eyes made up so dramatically and my hair cut short into a bob, I look nothing as I did when a child. It's no wonder Zeke didn't recognize me. My face has sharpened into a pixie shape. For all intents and purposes, I *should* look like the girl he knew, but there is nothing familiar about the cold, soulless eyes blinking back at me.

I try smiling, but I don't feel it. The woman in the mirror is a doll. A puppet. A madam about to dominate the answers out of our target.

I wouldn't recognize me either.

The front door opens and then shuts. I should probably grab a robe, but as I glance through the open bathroom door, I see Zeke frozen by the bed, looking at me. He has a new black eye. It must be windy outside because his hair is messy. My gaze darts over his body and I look for evidence he's been in a fight, but his knuckles are clean. Which means that black eye is from someone hurting him.

Anger simmers in my blood. It's one thing for me to bite

his lip, but another for someone else to hurt him. I roughly open the lid on my mascara and scowl at my reflection.

"What happened?" I ask tonelessly as I swipe my lashes with the wand.

All the while I'm seething inside, hoping I get to lay my hands on the person who hurt him. The last time I saw him beat up was that night in his room with Puck. He'd fought to protect my honor, but I'm finally old enough and bad enough to do the same for him.

He clears his throat and drops his garment bag onto the bed. He steps closer. That's not my pulse quickening. I'm just here, unaffected, getting ready for another gig. I'm about to be a cold-hearted dominatrix. I shouldn't be panting beneath my corset.

"It's sorted," he says gruffly, resting at the door. "We're invited to the poker game. Andrei won't kill me."

"He just gave you a black eye?" I ask. "Seems a bit light for a betrayal that cost him enough money to want you dead."

That's the story I've gathered from his little reveals. In the periphery of my reflection, Zeke leans against the doorframe and watches me until my skin buzzes with awareness and heat.

"I gave him something he's always wanted." His voice is a little too rough for me to consider him unaffected by my attire. Stupid. I should have closed the door and dealt with this later. I can't let my hormones distract me before a mission.

Wait. *Something he's always wanted?* The mascara wand pauses near my eye. "What did you give him?"

"The Mustang."

"*What!*" I whirl and find him unapologetic. "That's why

you took the car. And you think I'm immoral. You stole from nuns."

"Relax," he purrs and slips off his leather jacket before heading to the shower and turning on the faucet. When he's satisfied with the temperature, he drops the curtain and faces me. "They knew."

It takes every ounce of self-control to stop my jaw from dropping. *Don't get shitty. Don't get shitty.* It's not like everyone is making plans behind my back. It's not like you have no control over your life anymore. I'm sure they had a reason for not telling me. I yank the lid off the black eyeliner and sharpen the pencil with harsh, jerky movements.

I don't need to apply more eyeliner, but what the hell, it's the only thing keeping me sane at the moment. Zeke tugs off his shirt in the mirror behind me with stiff movements. His deeply tanned skin is peppered with fresh tattoos. The black is a beacon, begging for attention. I drop the eyeliner and find a smudge tool in my makeup bag. When I face the mirror again, Zeke is in the shower, tugging the frosted plastic curtain closed.

The outline of his body is visible as he washes. I lean on the counter and force my pulse to calm the fuck down. He's only baiting me, testing to see if I react to this intimacy. To be honest, maybe that's what I'm doing too. Something changed between us at the bar, and I'm confused. But he's clearly not giving up, despite me biting his lip.

A smile tugs at my lips. Such a Zeke thing to do. He never backed down from a challenge. My smile drops when I remember that he usually finds a way to win, even when he loses.

Butterflies swarm in my lower stomach at what letting him

win might entail. I pick up the mascara wand with trembling fingers and apply dark goop to my lashes. Then I put on the false lashes, but it takes too long. The tricky sons-of-bitches always slip. The faucet turns off.

The curtain slides open, and a tanned, muscular arm reaches out to collect the white towel hanging on a hook beside the shower.

Why am I looking?

Lipstick.

Zeke steps out of the shower. I meet his piercing hazel gaze in the mirror as he moves behind me and checks his hair with a swipe of fingers. A veiled smugness covers his expression. He knows exactly how appealing his body is. I thought I could pretend I don't give a shit, but apparently, my body never got the memo.

My tight nipples rub the patent corset. Heat pools between my thighs. I can't breathe properly or look in one place for long.

Even with a black eye, he's the definition of masculinity. Steam has brightened his complexion. Dark, wet hair drips onto his shoulders, running rivulets down the hard slabs of muscle that make up his torso.

He has just enough hair on his chest and lower abdomen that I could scrape my nails through it . . . if I wanted. Veins in his body have popped from the heat. They line his abdomen and disappear beneath the tiny white towel wrapped around his narrow waist. My gaze bounces back up to follow a vein, but then I notice purple blotches beneath the occult tattoos on his side.

I put the lipstick down and touch him gently. He sucks in a sharp breath.

"They beat you up?" Shadows cloud my vision. "Did you do what Raven said? Tell the truth?"

His lips flatten, proving he heard, but then he reaches around me to collect a disposable shaver from the vanity. The heat of his freshly showered body flares against my face, amplifying the scent of man and soap.

I step back as he nudges his way into the small space before the mirror. Now that I see his back, I notice more tattoos have been re-inked. The skin is raised and raw in many places.

He squirts shaving cream into his palm. "Had to get those fixed, or they won't work. Cisco's orders."

"Shouldn't you keep the new ink dry?" I grimace, gesturing at the shower. "It had to hurt getting inked over those bruises. Why didn't you wait?"

Why didn't you tell me you were getting beat up?

He catches my expression. "You worried about me, kitty cat?"

I clear my throat. "You're not operating at full capacity."

"My trigger finger is fine."

He dabs foam around his scruffy jaw but can't hide his pain. His eyes pinch when he lifts his hand. He's trying to act tough, probably thinking he can hide it from me, but I see it all. I have a good mind to watch his little charade, but he can't hide the pain when he runs the razor under the faucet and flinches from leaning forward. He might have a fractured rib.

Macho idiot.

"Give it to me." I take the razor and slot myself between him and the mirror. Leaning my butt on the counter, I inspect his jaw and work out where I need to begin. Once the optimal path is identified, I tilt his head and shave. He doesn't flinch, which means he either trusts me or is too afraid to move.

After a few raspy swipes, I fall into a soothing rhythm. My mind calms, and I lose myself in the moment. There's something so domestic about this act; for some weird reason, it reminds me of baking. It's repetitive and therapeutic. When he eventually speaks, I almost jolt. Thankfully, the razor is running under the water and not pressed against his skin.

"A man could get used to this," he says softly.

"Being waited on hand and foot by a woman in lingerie? Of course, he can."

His eyes sparkle. "I mean watching you fuss over me."

"Hm."

"But the corset and thong are a nice touch." He snaps my underwear.

I glare at him, which turns his grin into something disarming.

He must sense my frustration because he drops a hand on the counter, leans close to my ear, and whispers . . . nothing.

He simply holds there for a few seconds and then inhales deeply through his nose. I think he intended to say something witty. To keep the banter going. But he can't control his reaction to me either. His body hardens everywhere. The air thickens with tension.

"I never believed in God . . ." he rasps deeply, "until he put you in my world." His voice surrounds me, burning through every cell in my body. "And now that he brought me back to you, I believe in miracles."

"Stop," I whisper.

"Why?"

"Because I have a job to do. A relic to find."

The roar of his silence stabs me between the ribs. And then I hear his two sharp intakes of breath. The heat leaves my face. I open my eyes, and he's wiping his jaw with a towel, looking at me with pain in his eyes.

This time it hits me hard. That pain isn't from his injuries. It's from me. He just said all those wonderful things, and I . . . Good God, this is *Zeke*. The guy who was always there for me, who wants to be that person again.

As he pats his face, my gaze sweeps down his bruised and tattooed body.

"You're too skinny," I mumble, poking his pecs. I thought he was more muscular, but on closer inspection, I think it was more of an illusion his clothes created. Or my wishful thinking. He's definitely toned, but I feel like that illness has left scars we can't see. "Remind me to get some proper food into you when we return to the abbey."

His brows draw together, and some of that hurt leaves his eyes. I know I will regret this, but seeing that pain dissipate is addicting. I reach into my makeup bag and pull out a vial of ointment. He watches me curiously as I dab some onto my finger and then apply it to his freshly inked tattoos.

I start at the back, circle gently over the raised welts, then trace my finger around to his front.

"What's this one do?" I ask, finding an interesting sigil.

"Protection spell." Goosebumps ripple across his flesh, and his breathing becomes ragged. "Paint it on doors to stop demons entering."

"Does it work on your body too?" I circle the sigil again. "Didn't Wes use blood to activate some of his spells?"

"I put it there so I don't forget." His eyes crinkle. "Not as smart as Wes."

"What about this one?" I slide my finger to another series of interconnected black lines over the ridges of his abdomen.

He sucks in a breath and holds it. "Transfers the blessing from a sanctified object to another."

The bulge beneath his towel grows. But he doesn't move. He's a rock of fortitude as I explore every hot, velvety surface I can get my finger on. I'm not even using the ointment anymore. It's just the tip of my finger tracing around his torso, pretending to study the tattoos, but I'm really remembering, and relearning parts of him I'd forgotten existed.

There's a small little birthmark just above his nipple. I teased him about it when we went to the local water park. It's in the shape of a love heart. As I repeat my circle around it, I glance up.

He watches me with hooded eyes. A strand of wet hair has fallen from his forehead and drips onto his cheek. But he's not interested in the water running down his jaw. He steps back and drops his gaze to the juncture between my thighs.

"My turn to touch you."

Twenty-Four

His eyes haven't left my panties. Humor flees his expression as he realizes something I've known for a while. I'm wet. Soaked. The red lace is dark and saturated at the core.

My cheeks heat. I don't know why. I've never been ashamed of my body. But I've also never been this aroused before. It's like every ounce of awareness of my body is there between my legs. I squirm under his attention and start closing my thighs.

"Don't you fucking dare, kitty cat," he growls and meets my eyes. "It's my turn to touch you. It's only fair."

I don't like this game. Maybe he sees the panic in my eyes because he doesn't drop to his knees as I fear. As I need. *Jesus*, I don't know what I want.

He touches me with his fingertips, trailing them all over my body, learning my shape, eliciting goosebumps in his wake. I squeeze my eyes shut as if I can hide from this moment.

"Open your eyes, Leila." His voice is a dark whisper near my ear. His breath is hot and damp on my cheek. "Watch me touch you."

God help me, but I do as he says. I watch as he swipes his fingertip down my throat, circles the hollow at my collarbone, and traces along the corset's top. He groans as he cups my breast through the leather.

"Fucking perfect." Reverence bleeds into his tone as he circles the hard bud of my nipple with his thumb. The patent leather isn't as thick as it seems. Every swipe around tugs the leather down and gives my trapped breast the freedom it needs.

My dusky nipple pops out, scraping along the seam. Sensation shoots straight to my pussy, flooding me with desire. My breath hitches. I resist the urge to press his hand there, to relieve the aching heaviness begging for attention. When he pinches my nipple, my lashes flutter and I whimper.

"Keep watching," he breathes.

"Why?"

"So you can see this is what's real." His palms slide over my breasts, my hips. He swivels his thumbs inward when he hits my thighs, teasing closer toward the line of my thong. "This reaction your body is having is from my touch. Listen to it, not whatever the fuck is in your head telling you that we don't belong together."

To prove his point, the next swipe of his thumb presses deep into the juncture between my thighs. I gasp as sensation builds in me. We're approaching a point of no return. His touching game is far more erotic than mine was. But I can't stop watching what he does to me.

He brushes over the lace with his thumb, rubs my clit, and revels in my moan as I rock into his touch, chasing more.

"You love this," he rasps. "Admit it."

Lipstick.

"We have a job to do."

I swallow the lump in my throat and lift the red stick toward my mouth. Storm clouds come over Zeke's expression. His eyes scream outrage. How dare I pretend I'm not affected? He captures my wrist before I can paint the red, cups the back of my head, and holds me still. We stare at each other for a long, hot minute. A standoff between old friends and new enemies. But we aren't really anymore. We're neither.

One thing that's for certain is this magnetic pull between us. It's always been there.

He takes my mouth in a hot, plundering kiss that tells me he's hurting in more ways than one. I'm left dazed and breathless when he pulls back and returns to wiping the last of the shaving cream from his jaw.

"Why did you do that?" My words barely have the power to form.

"So you remember me when you're doing your *job* tonight." He snarls at my corset, then hands me back the lipstick.

Dismissed.

Sort of.

It's my fault, but this isn't the reaction I wanted. I don't know what I wanted, only that I wanted to keep playing this game. A switch flips inside me. Defiance so strong and pure hurtles through my system, turning everything hot, obliterating the last line of resistance surrounding my heart. I knock him backward. He thinks I'm going to fight. I can see it in his eyes.

He doesn't expect me to switch our positions until his back is to the mirror, his ass planted on the vanity. My eyes lock with his, and I yank his towel from his hips, springing his thick, hard erection free.

"What are you doing?" he snaps, as if I'm annoying him now.

"Giving you something to remember while I'm doing my job."

His breath shoots from his lips as I take him in hand, but he doesn't break eye contact. It's strange how one can read emotions in eyes. The actual organs never change. They remain two orbs framed by long lashes. One minute, I think I read a challenge. But the next, I see his submission. Finally, something deeper bounces between us that is open, raw, and vulnerable. It's then I realize I'm staring at my emotions reflected back at me.

We want this. Deeply. But we're afraid.

With each stroke of his cock, my pulse quickens, and my breath turns ragged. His hand works into my hair and clenches hard until my scalp burns.

"Suck me, Leila." His words are a plea, a prayer. "I want to feel the inside of your pretty little mouth."

How can I say no to the raw need in his voice? I slide to my knees and open my mouth but don't move. A wicked part of me likes seeing him work for it. I mean, he did leave me. He did make me feel like his death was my fault. He can't be let off that easy, right?

He cups the back of my head and glides past my teeth.

When his cock hits the back of my tongue, his strangled groan is sweeter than honey. I taste salty precum, moan, and then continue to blow him with barely restrained fervor.

"Jesus—fuck," he gasps, his fingers flexing in my hair. "Slow down. Fuck. No—do that. Do exactly that."

He throws his head back, scowls at the ceiling, and breathes through flared nostrils. There's nothing like the view of a man in the throes of passion, flexing and tense, trying to make his body last. He winces as he tries to hold back his desire, to prolong the experience. But when his brows lift in the middle, and his eyes flutter closed, I feel that wickedness in my heart again.

I scrape my nails down his thighs and pull off his cock long enough to say, "Look at me, Zeke."

The darkness in his gaze hits me like a jolt. His lips curve on one side, and he says, "You little teasing wildcat."

I lick my lips and pretend to rise, but he forces himself back through my lips and starts fucking my mouth. My body melts from the need in his eyes, in every line of his body as he pumps into me desperately, saying between ragged pants, "You have me in such a . . . *fuck* . . . I can't resist you . . . *goddammit* . . . I'm a slut for you . . . I want to do this every fucking—" He sucks in a breath, rolls his eyes back in bliss, and unloads down my throat with a low groan of satisfaction.

He watches me with awe as I swallow. Awe and then fear. Fear and then panic. He pulls me up to my feet, a wild look in his eyes. His lips part. Close. Part again.

Paranoia wraps barbed vines around my throat. Is that shame? Is he . . . regretting this?

"What the fuck, Zeke?" I mumble, wiping my mouth.

He grips my face between his hands and shakes my head gently, his jaw hard, his eyes volcanic. He is a man disheveled in every sense. He still can't speak. I'm about to lose my shit. I'm about to pretend like this was nothing to me. But then he blurts, "Leila, I fucking love you."

"Wh-what?" I splutter.

"I love you."

"It was a blow job, Zeke."

"It was the best fucking one of my life."

I push at his chest, irritated. My eyes burn with unshed tears. I don't know why.

Yes, I do.

It's not the first time a man has proclaimed his love to me after an act like that. It's not real. It's the high of the orgasm. It's my job.

He tugs me back.

"Don't you fucking do that," he snarls.

"What?" My voice is cold again.

"Don't belittle my feelings, Leila."

I force him away and step back. "They're just like every other man whose cock I've had in my mouth."

My words create the small reprieve I crave. But not the distance. He stalks back toward me, eyes hard and determined. Then he pinches my jaw and makes me look up. Danger flashes. Violence. Jealousy.

"Mention another man's cock in your mouth again, and I swear to God I'll . . ."

"What?" I whisper.

"I'll hunt them all down and put a bullet between their eyes."

I gasp at the promise in his words. He'll do it.

He once left to protect me, but now he'll kill to possess me. The thought makes my hormones surge, and I bite my bottom lip to stop him from seeing my reaction. Too late. He cups me between the legs, presses the heel of his palm into my clit until I whimper, and snarls, "Don't even ask what I'll do to another man who puts his cock down here."

I go weak at the knees, grip his shoulders, and moan, "You don't own me."

He yanks my thong aside, drives two fingers deep into my core, and flicks his thumb over my clit until I pant and turn feverish all over.

"Don't break my heart, Wildcat."

My eyes clash with his. The possessive fire is gone. He's now pleading with me. Begging. I can't say no. I don't want to. What the fuck is happening?

He must read the helplessness on my face because his expression softens, and he dips to kiss my neck. He saves me from confronting these feelings bursting in my chest.

I cling to him as my body submits to his touch.

"Come for me, baby," he murmurs against my skin. "Come for me now, or I'm kneeling and using my tongue."

The thought of him between my thighs pushes me off the edge. I implode. Explode. Break apart and float. I see stars. I see the time on my cell phone sitting on the vanity. Shit. We're late.

Twenty-Five

Zeke

I forgot how dark this port city gets at night. It's miserable, dishonorable, and addictive. It's not a city with vigilantes or good cops. This is the one God forgot. The one the moon ignored. And without a glimmer of light, darkness festers in the open.

I walk next to Leila on the dark city street and silently stew over how incredible she looks. Every drop of makeup and care in her presentation isn't for me but for some braggart collector with a gambling problem. She'll strut into that room on her killer stilettos, and every man will drool.

And I'll desperately try to keep my itchy trigger finger from moving.

Her full dominatrix outfit is intoxicating. She's classy and tempting at the same time. Shiny black patent leather sticks to her skin like glue, except for the flash of midriff and the red thong straps curving over her hips. The eye is drawn there like a magnet. She also has a bullwhip attached to her hip, sharp stiletto heels that can be used as daggers, a ring she said is filled with poison, and two metal hairpins twisted into two little buns on top of her head.

Every time she steps, a long delectable leg flashes through a slit in the skirt, and I think about my hand sliding up that thigh. I think of the moans she gave me. The sweet, utter surrender. Then I think of how I want to taste her next, to sink my dick into her.

Fuck.

The tease is doing more to heat my blood than a short dress would have. The woman knows what she's doing. I tug my tie for the millionth time since we left the motel. This damned designer suit is too tight.

Out here in the dirty street, Leila is impervious to the lewd looks from passersby. Whenever I catch a filthy stare, I flip open my jacket and reveal one of my guns. There was a time this wild country was my playground, but it wasn't really godless. Not with me here. Today's visit with Andrei could have gone in a different direction.

Despite the heat Leila and I shared in the bathroom, the coldness in her eyes is back. It grew the moment she realized we were late. I don't know how to stop it from completely consuming her.

I can see why the Sisterhood plucked her from the group home. She's everything anyone would want in a seductive assassin. Cold, detached, all business. No wildcat in sight. It fucking kills me that this has become her life. That I failed to protect her.

Sometimes it feels like life is a never-ending cycle of bad luck. Death. Grief. Violence. Illness. More violence. More death. I start to wonder if I'm someone's sick joke. Am I a toy at the whim of a bratty god with nothing to do but torture me? Then I remember the tiny specs of joy in it, the laughter and sheer bliss from spending time with Leila, and I think . . . I'm the luckiest man in the world. God gave me all the shit so that I understand what good feels like. He's testing me so that when I find it again, I'll do everything in my power to hold onto it.

I've been given the most precious gift twice. I won't squander it.

I glance at her walking next to me. Her chin is up. Her spine is straight. She refused to bring a coat, insisting that it would mess with her cover. She sashays along the cracked sidewalk like it's a catwalk in Milan. But her expression is stern, her eyes reveal death, and her mind is a steel trap of fortitude, preparing herself for a task that will have no happy ending.

I assume. She won't tell me. But I can put two and two together.

"Down here." I gesture toward the driveway of a five-star hotel.

A valet collects keys from drivers of Lamborghinis and Bugattis. The fanciest of cars are lined up at the front of the hotel.

Leila's clicking heels stop. She angles her head up at the high-rise twinkling in the black night, then back at me. "I thought you said it was an underground poker game. I expected some dark basement somewhere."

I try to hide my smile. "It is an underground game, meaning it's not legal. Don't tell me the stone-cold assassin has never been to an illegal high roller poker game before?"

"Gambling is more Raven's wheelhouse. I'm called in

when a deft touch with weapons is needed." She taps the hairpins.

My brow furrows. "Exactly how many weapons do you have on you right now?"

Her only answer is a sly smile.

"So you can't play poker?"

"I can get by."

I scrub the back of my neck. "I guess it's a good thing I told them you're just my good luck charm."

"What?"

"Figured you never were good at math."

She gasps. "I was better at it than you!"

"No, you weren't." I put my hands in my pockets and start walking. "You were much better in the kitchen . . . baking cookies."

"Asshole. I'll remember you said that next time I bake." She scowls at me and rushes to keep up but still looks perfectly high class. "Besides, I don't need math to be good at cards."

"If you want to count them, you do."

"Whatever." She blows air with derision. "I know how to read people. That's better than counting cards."

Moments before we arrive at the rotating glass doors, I take her gently by the arm. Pain flares in my ribs, reminding me I'm still hurt. It's not as bad as I let on in the bathroom. I wanted her closer to me, so I lied about it.

Something dark exists inside me. Something so black it blocks out all the light . . . just like this city. The awareness of this darkness started the night my sister died—when I hesitated before screaming for help. Holding Leila now, seeing how good she looks and knowing the minefield we're about to walk into

—bad doesn't begin to describe the lengths I'll go to keep her safe. And mine.

It strikes me that I've been worried she's changed too much to fall in love with me. I blamed that for her not saying it back to me in the bathroom. I keep remembering the sweet, innocent girl and wonder where she's gone. She has the same shampoo, still likes to bake, and going by her Dom name—Madam Mina—she's still weirdly obsessed with Dracula. Mina was Dracula's wife . . . or something. But everything else about her is different. It's me who's changed. I hid all this darkness from her from the start. I wrapped her in cotton wool. Now I have to prepare her for a glimpse of that darkness—the reason my trigger finger gets itchy.

Leila's brows pucker as she waits for me to talk.

I ask, "Do you remember when Wyatt asked Doc why a bad man like Johnny Ringo does the things he does?"

"Maybe. I haven't watched *Tombstone* in a long time."

She's lying. She knows the words better than the Lord's prayer. I check the rounds in my pistol, then re-holster it, and I make a show of doing it so everyone sees I have no fear. The valets pale. A couple waiting for a taxi steps away. Leila gapes at me as though I've gone mad as I continue. "And Doc said, a man like that has a great big hole right in the middle of himself. And he can never kill enough, steal, or inflict enough pain to ever fill it."

"I don't like where this is going." She flattens her lips.

"And then Wyatt asked, *What does he want?*" I draw my second pistol and check the rounds. "And what did Doc say to that?"

"He said a man like that wants revenge."

"For what?"

"For being born."

"That's right." I'm so proud she remembers, but then I grow somber as my next words bring memories I'd rather forget. "That was the kind of man I became without you. The last glimmer of light in my world was gone. All that was left was darkness. And when we head in there, that's who I'll be."

"What really happened with Andrei?" She cocks her head. "What did he ask you to do?"

My lips curve on one side. "Always so clever, kitty cat. You can read people better than anyone I know."

I found Andrei in his office at the docks, already dressed in a navy suit for the game. Two of his goons followed me into the office, took the keys to the car, then patted me down.

"He's clean," the first guard says and then stands by the door.

Andrei sits behind a desk and brushes lint from his shoulders. "You have the nerve to come here, Sifon."

Calling me a snitch. That's rich coming from him. He's the one who told the authorities I wasn't dead in the house fire, and I was the one to blame for a missing dockworker. When my only option had been to leave town, I told one of our arms buyers Andrei was skimming. He deserved the problems that came with it.

"I'm looking for two invitations to tonight's poker game."

Andrei blinks. Then roars with laughter.

"I heard you were involved in the game," I continue, unperturbed. "I see your money laundering habits haven't changed. Bit risky, don't you think? Using the same old tired scheme?"

Andrei's eyes go dead at the insult. "We have plenty of police under our protection now. We think of everything, unlike you."

I could enter an argument and tell him all the ways he's wrong, but honestly, I don't give a shit. I just want the invitations.

"If that car isn't enough to buy my way in, then what do you want?" I ask. "There has to be something, otherwise you would have killed me on sight."

"Always direct and to the point."

"Am I wrong?"

His eyes fill with dark thoughts. I feel them in the air. "Why do you want to go to my game?"

"A man attending has information on an artifact I'm looking for."

"Why not follow him home? Why do this at my game?"

"You might be surprised to know this, but I'm not trying to cause trouble. I didn't have to come here with the money or to let you know I was here, but I'm trying to do things a little differently. No violence. No trouble."

He snorts. "The God of Guns has turned over a new leaf. I do not believe it."

"I'll be out of your city by the night's end. You won't even remember I was here."

Andrei's distrust sizzles, but he seems to be accepting my explanation.

"I want nothing from you," Andrei says, "but I will allow you to come for old times' sake. On one condition."

Of course there is. "What?"

"I can't let you go without looking like you have paid for the trouble you caused me when you left this city. Take a beating from me and still walk out, then you can go."

I exhale. "Fine. Do what you need."

He stands, opens his jacket again, and pulls a hotel key for what I'm guessing is the poker game room. I see a flash of his firearm holstered. Glock. He puts the key card on the desk and motions for his men to hold me down.

Submitting goes against every cell in my body. Fear and defiance rises. I want to fight back and defend myself, to make sure I get back to Leila. I hear Cisco's voice in my mind: *Love makes you better.* I chant it in my head on repeat, willing myself to take the beating, to breathe through the pain he inflicts. Hit after hit to my midsection is swallowed until panic sets in.

What if he doesn't stop? What if I misjudged everything?

I remember Raven's warning. She knew we'd be at this game. I can't get there if I'm dead . . . right? So this has to end with me walking out of the office. As long as I keep telling the truth.

Andrei's next strike doesn't land. He stands back and frowns. "You truly do not want to stay in this city?"

I spit out blood. "It's the last thing I want."

"Why?"

"I . . ." Tell the truth. "There's a woman I'm dedicated to. I'll go where she goes, and we're only here for the collector."

"Ah. A woman." Andrei massages his hands. "You risk her life by telling me she exists."

I sigh. "I just want to talk to this man and then leave."

"Okay," he says, surprising me. "I will give you the key, but I change my mind, and now there are two conditions. You will bid against Petrov over there any time he bets. This way, we can inflate the pot and we have less trouble later with the money."

"That's it?"

He flashes me a dangerous grin. "Of course, we will kill your woman if you fail to do as you are told."

My trigger finger twitches. I glance at his Glock, and the urge to grab it almost takes hold of me. But I push it down and nod. Even if he changes his mind by the night's end, it doesn't matter. I'll have my Colts with me. If he threatens Leila, I won't hesitate next time.

"What did Andrei want then?" Leila asks.

"He wants me to inflate the bets. I guess it's so they can launder the money faster."

"That's all?"

"He threatened you if I didn't do my job."

"Okay." She exhales. "It's good I know danger might come from other places tonight."

"I'll kill him if he tries to make good on his threat."

"No, you won't."

I lean toward her and speak very clearly so there's no mistaking my intentions. "In a heartbeat."

"So would I," she snaps, eyes flashing. "I mean . . . we're partners. So . . . yeah. I've got your back."

She quickly looks away.

A slow grin forms on my lips, and suddenly, I'm not worried in the slightest that she didn't say I love you back to me.

"Just admit it." I put my hands on her hips.

"Admit what?"

"That I'm still your huckleberry."

She pushes me away, but not before I glimpse the smile in her eyes. It's the light this godless place needs. That I need.

A burst of laughter somewhere near the hotel draws my

attention to a richly dressed couple entering the lobby. The reality of the night closes in with all that festering darkness. The next time I look at Leila, I see the makeup, the dress, and the narrative she's created.

The light winks out.

"You don't have to do this," I murmur.

"Do what?"

I touch the corset. "If you go in there, throw away these clothes, and just be Leila, I'll back you up. If you choose to say fuck everything and we escape to a deserted island, I'll still be there. Whatever you want, wildcat."

Her breath hitches, and warmth floods her bright eyes. She looks at me like she did in the bathroom—like I'm her man. Then she gives me a fond pat on the chest, kisses my cheek, and says, "Let's get this over and done with so you can throw away my clothes."

Twenty-Six

Leila

As we approach the elevator for the penthouse, I think about the part of the gospel where Mary talked about matter. It went something like:

All nature, all formations, all creatures exist in and with one another, and they will be resolved again into their own roots.

I didn't quite understand the old-world language, but Thea explained that it's like what our physicists today say about matter. She thought it was rather remarkable that Mary, a woman in a time when they were meant to be uneducated, had understood better than the other apostles. Matter can't be destroyed but can only change forms. Meaning at some point, we all existed in the same form, regardless of who we are today.

We're all made of stardust.

Now I look at Zeke and think . . . maybe she had a point. I

feel closer to him. More connected. Like we truly have some kind of commonality. He revealed parts of himself he's not proud of. He probably would have taken those parts to his grave if it wasn't for this mission.

And I would have let him because I'm not brave enough to reveal the same darkness in my soul. I can't continue being a Sinner if I crack open those feelings. But if he can do it, surely I can find my way there too. As long as he doesn't give up on me.

The elevator bell dings, the doors open, and Zeke places his palm on my lower back to guide me into the car.

A bellboy inside asks, "Going up?"

"Penthouse." Zeke tosses him a key card. The bellboy glances at it, swipes the card over the receiver, and presses the penthouse button.

His jacket flops open to reveal one of the smallest machine guns around—the browning automatic. Definitely not just a bellboy. When we arrive, he takes us through a lavishly decorated penthouse to a round card table in a sunken area by some windows overlooking the city.

Already seated are four men: a middle-aged Asian businessman, an elderly white Southern gentleman sporting a bolo tie, a short man with glasses who reminds me of Rick Moranis, just as Raven said, and a millennial Middle Eastern sheikh. I'm sure I've seen him in the news for reckless spending and lifestyle.

There are seven places at the table. Four are taken. Zeke wasn't lying when he said I was the good luck charm. I quickly look around the penthouse and see no other women. The two Romanians standing by the bar watch Zeke like a hawk. Both are in expensive suits, but the roughness on their skin and around their eyes proves they're not afraid of doing their own dirty work.

Andrei must be the shorter one, with the slicked hair and mole above his eyebrow. Emotion flares in his eyes as he watches Zeke. His wary distrust remains as he takes me in.

Leaving a possessive hand on the small of my back, Zeke walks me over to them and smiles tightly. "Andrei, I'd like you to meet my good luck charm, Lei—"

I smack Zeke over the head, much to his surprise. "Pet, that's not my name."

He hits me with a confused look. I make a show of putting my hands on my hips and tapping my bullwhip impatiently. To his credit, he looks suitably abashed.

"Sorry, mistress." He bows his head. "I'll do better."

"Good," I purr, then trace his tie with a finger, starting at the belly and moving my way up until I tip his jaw back so he looks me in the eyes. I turn my voice deep and husky. "Don't fuck up again unless you want to be punished."

Zeke's eyes darken with unmistakable desire. But to the others, he clears his throat and starts the introduction again as if nothing happened.

This is the first time we've worked together in this capacity. I haven't even prepared him for the kind of behavior I usually portray. So the fact he rolls with it without question is a little overwhelming. I almost let my mask slip.

"Petrov, Andrei," he greets. "Please meet Madam Mina."

"A pleasure to meet you, Madam." Andrei takes my offered hand and makes a show of kissing my inner wrist.

I'm not sure what he expected, but it's not my glower for

assuming he has permission to kiss my skin. Like a good little guard pet, Zeke honors my distaste and snarls.

"She's mine," he snaps at the dangerous man. "Touch her again, and you'll die."

Andrei bristles at Zeke's declaration but lowers my hand. I immediately press against Zeke's side, slide my palm down to cup his buttocks, and whisper just loud enough so the others can hear, "Good pet. I'll enjoy rewarding you tonight."

Amusement dances in his hazel eyes, but he plays the part of someone enthralled.

Petrov doesn't know how to respond to me for insulting his boss. But my show is for the man sitting at the poker table, drooling at me with lust-filled eyes. We're all good as long as Andrei doesn't lose his shit. He sees Zeke become a puppy under my touch, stays Petrov as he reaches for his gun, then slides a curious gaze my way. "Duly noted."

They must really need Zeke to up the bets for them if they're so eager to accept my domineering behavior. Either that, or Andrei also secretly loves being dominated. I turn the full force of my attention to Zeke. His eyes sparkle with pride, lust, and something else I can't decipher. But it's enough to make me think that, even though this is an act for me, it's not for him. He'll kill anyone disrespecting me.

A flare of need rocks through me. I grab Zeke's tie and tug him in for a passionate kiss. When we break for air, he echoes the same possessive obsession I feel. We gaze into each other's eyes like lovelorn teenagers. Zeke wipes my smudged lipstick, and I do the same to him. I can't fully remove it, but I like that he has me all over his mouth. It's my very own stamp of ownership.

I face Andrei and see something appeased in his eyes. He no longer looks at us like the enemy. He should. I thought if I gave in to my feelings for Zeke, it would make me weaker. But I feel stronger. Deadlier.

"Darling," I say in a bored tone to anyone listening. "Who do I need to spank to get a drink around here?"

"While that's an appealing offer"—Andrei smirks—"no spanking necessary. Help yourself, Madam."

He nods to the kitchen bar next to us.

I almost sashay away, but then remember the second part of my plan—I need to spike the drinks with poison. Just enough to dull their senses, make their tongues loose, and make it easy for us to escape in case shit goes sideways. There's still a possibility I'll have to drag our target out and torture him for information.

I face Andrei with a sly look. "You seem like a whiskey kind of man. Am I right?"

He darts a nervous glance at Petrov. Probably has other tastes. I stroke my bullwhip as I wait for his reply.

Zeke drawls, "The correct answer is yes, my friend. Tonight you drink whatever she pours."

"Whiskey is good," Andrei answers, his curiosity in me renewed.

"And your friend?" I barely glance at Petrov. I'll also dismiss every other man in this room except for our antiquities collector. Mind games are what I do best in this role. Soon, those who don't have my attention will beg for it, and those that do will preen.

Before I leave, Andrei says to me, "He tells me you're here

for one thing. So long as you leave my city tomorrow, you have my word that you're safe."

I glance at him from beneath my lashes. "Duly noted."

He chuckles as I walk to the kitchen. Before I'm out of earshot, I catch him mumbling to Zeke, "Now I understand why you've been gone for so long, *sifon*."

While introductions are made at the table, I quickly pour whiskey into empty glasses, adding a dash of poison from my ring to each for good measure. I pile them all onto a tray and bring the bottle to share with Zeke.

As I approach the now seated group, his eyes crinkle, but I see the strain in them already. Whatever they were discussing, he's not happy with. I move to stand between Zeke and our target, then place the tray on the poker green. Ludovic's eyes go straight to the red thong at my hip. Zeke hooks his hand around my waist and drags me to his side. I stroke his hair as he introduces me.

I let my eyes gloss over the sheikh, the Southerner, and the businessman, but when I land on the antiquities dealer, Ludovic, I boldly hold his stare until he glances away. Good. Submitting already. As a reward, I deposit a glass of whiskey before him with a wink.

Petrov tries to take another from the tray, but I swat his hand and glare until he uses his manners. Each of the others must offer similar respect before I allow them a glass. To Zeke, I lick the bottle's rim suggestively.

His eyes heat, and he slides his hand along my thigh. "You're making me thirsty, babe."

"Quite the opposite, darling." I press the bottle to his lips and order him to drink.

The sudden notion that I'm actually having fun hits me like a ton of bricks, along with a sense of foreboding. Every Sinner knows fun never lasts.

The game commences with a conservative round. Everyone is wary of each other. Bets are light. Poker faces are grim. I top up the whiskey glasses using the bottle in my hand, getting a replacement when it drains dry. By the third round, the men are all suitably slurring and have no idea it's the additive I put in their two drinks each.

Time for the second act of my show.

"You're all so boring." I yawn, stretch until my breasts almost pop from the corset, then toy with one of Zeke's money chips. "Does no one talk at these things?"

"Talking means it's easier to reveal a tell. You find it boring?" Zeke hands his cards to me. "You play." Then he stretches back and puts his hands behind his head. "I'll watch."

He's not looking at the table but at me as he gestures to the chips. "Have some fun, kitty cat."

"But I don't want to lose your money." I nudge his stack of chips.

"I don't care about the money." He pinches me on the ass and waggles his brows. "You can punish me later."

I laugh despite myself but decide to do as he suggests. It's a good segue into the next part of my plan. My patent leather creaks as I sit on his lap and face the table with a broad smile. Andrei doesn't care. He's happy for me to lose money. The Southerner is wary, and the businessman is impatient. Ludovic still drools over me, but no one is talking. The poison makes them all feel a little too drunk, and as Zeke said, no one wants to reveal their weakness.

"Another drink, pet." I click my fingers and wiggle my ass. Zeke groans as I rub against his groin and then reaches around me to feed me a sip from the bottle. After he settles back in place, I ask the table, "Now, who can tell me how many cards we all get? Do I have enough?"

"You have all you need," Zeke murmurs hotly against my ear. "Just place your bet."

"I'd rather bet on more interesting things."

Andrei burps, then says, "No. Money is what we use."

"Like what?" the sheikh asks, his interest piqued.

"Like you?" Ludovic's drunk eyes are full of gross intentions. His gaze dips to my chest.

Zeke tenses behind me.

I scoff. "You can't afford me. Even if you can, you couldn't handle me."

"One Rolex," blurts the Businessman and drops his watch onto the table. "Limited edition."

The Shiekh gasps, suddenly having fun. I see now why he's in the papers for risky behavior. "Two weeks on my private yacht! Clothing optional."

"How about an entire cattle farm," says the Southern gentleman, surprising me. I thought he was annoyed with me all night. Maybe all he needed was a little liquid courage.

"Now, now," Zeke raises his palms, his tone sharpening. "Let's not get ahead of ourselves."

I glare at him. "Don't you trust me?"

He takes in my hard stare and licks his lips nervously. "You'll spend the night with one of them in return for a cattle farm?"

"Have you forgotten who makes the decisions in this relationship? I'll sleep where I want, fuck who I want." I reach down and grab his cock, snarling into his face, "Touch who I want. Understood?"

Just play along, Zeke. I can feel Ludovic virtually busting from his skin watching us.

Zeke's eyes say he's almost done with this game, but he nods.

I face the table and pretend I'm bored again. "But you're right, pet. Nothing they've offered is worth a night with me."

"I might have something." Ludovic slaps the table. His Romanian accent is thicker now that he's inebriated. "It's so rare and old that it was lost for hundreds of years."

"What, like a Viking horn or something?" I act unimpressed.

"A helmet said to have been crafted from the true nails that killed Christ himself."

Zeke barks a round of harsh words in Romanian at Ludovic. I twist to look at him, surprised to see fury on his face. I'm equally surprised that he speaks fluent Romanian. My gaze darts between Ludovic and Zeke. Andrei and Petrov follow the conversation with amusement.

Zeke has completely slipped from the role we're supposed to be playing.

I can't understand the argument, but it seems like they're discussing the validity of such a claim. Zeke rolls his eyes and then says in English, "You're wasting her time."

Ludovic slams his hands down with outrage and stands. "I am telling the truth. I know where it is."

Zeke dismisses him with a gesture, shares a look with Andrei and then tells the others, "We use the chips."

He pinches me surreptitiously beneath the table. It feels like a signal. Did he get the information we need? But before I can feel an ounce of triumph, the ceiling lights flicker. It hits everywhere, from the kitchen to the lamps, to the chandelier over the poker table.

The light on the Mustang's radio had flickered.

Goosebumps break out on my skin, and I hear a faint whistling that's steadily getting louder. Where is it coming from? I recognize the song as the tune becomes clearer and the elevator dings.

It's "The Gambler" by Kenny Rogers.

Twenty-Seven

Leila

I always thought that if I stared true evil in the face, I'd see the tortured souls straight from hell. But as Asmodeus steps out of the elevator, all handsome charm and debonair suaveness, I look into his black eyes and see nothing but emptiness. The yawning chasm is at odds with his charisma. I feel a strange sense of pity. What kind of creature has nothing inside? How lonely would that be?

Am I seeing his lack of soul?

He prowls into the penthouse with an eerie sense of delight, as though it can fill that emptiness or distract us from the truth.

It's everything I feel sometimes, but suddenly, seeing it before me, I realize I don't want to end up the same way. I don't want that empty look in my eyes forever. I don't want Madam Mina to be the most character I have. I want to figure out who I am without all this Sisterhood business.

"Puck?" Zeke mumbles in surprise.

My gaze darts to the three men walking behind Asmodeus. They're the bikers from the bar. My heart stops . . . No, that's not completely true. Demonic features cover their own. The monstrous and contorted faces are a macabre mask only I can see with my supernatural *sight*. One man has a feral, animalistic visage with whiskers and burning embers for eyes. Yet, strangely, Asmodeus still appears as human, despite what I glimpsed on the CCTV.

"Possessed," I warn Zeke under my breath. "All three."

He moves almost imperceptibly, but I hear the metallic sound of his pistol cocking.

Wait . . . did Zeke say Puck? As in, the old bully from our group home? I shift my gaze back to the redheaded biker's face. He's indistinguishable to me from the demon inside, so it's hard to place the features. But it can't be a coincidence Zeke called him Puck.

Once that part of my brain clicks, I recognize something far more troublesome than a childhood bully. Puck is possessed by the demon with whiskers and burning eyes. Could this be the same demon who killed Zeke's sister? Didn't it look like a leopard on two feet with burning eyes?

"Flauros possesses Puck," I mumble, twisting on Zeke's lap to look him in the eyes.

His gaze darts between Asmodeus and the biker. He can't see what I can, but he's undoubtedly assembling the same puzzle pieces. This is too much of a coincidence to ignore. Zeke's bronze complexion pales.

Asmodeus points between Flauros and us. "You know each other? What are the odds of that?"

"What do you want?" I growl.

"Same thing as you, most likely."

To kill him? I highly doubt that. Then I see his black gaze swing to a red-eyed Ludovic. *Shit.* Asmodeus wants the helmet. Of course, he does.

"What's going on here?" Andrei stands up, sways, and scowls. "Who invited you?"

The sheikh shouts to Asmodeus, "Come inside, my friend. The game is not done." Rosy-cheeked and glassy-eyed, he gestures at me. "The bossy lady is making this more fun and giving us all her money."

Zeke is a rock beneath me. His hand splays on my stomach, holding me to his front. His breathing is shallow but steady. He still holds the cocked pistol in his right hand down by the seat.

"Fantastic." Asmodeus barely glances at me as he rubs his hands together gleefully. His eyes are locked onto the card game like each piece is a diamond. "I, too, have money to burn. Of course, unless anyone objects to another player?"

Looks pass around the table. Ludovic glowers at the intrusion but holds his tongue. The Southern tycoon is falling asleep at the table. The businessman is blinking at his cards—I don't even think he heard the question. Petrov has one eye open and the other on his swaying boss. I may have overdone it with the alcohol and poison. They'll all be lambs to the slaughter.

Andrei sits down with dollar signs in his eyes.

This is where it gets strange. Asmodeus recognized Zeke and me. Surely he knows we intend to kill him, but he walks over to greet his . . . friend? "I've been *dying* to let loose a little."

"Sit, sit," the sheikh slurs.

Asmodeus shoves the Southerner off the seat. The man

falls hard on the floor beside the table and doesn't get up. Unperturbed, Asmodeus takes the seat, whiskey, and picks up the Southerner's card hand. He joins the game as though he truly wants to have fun. My mind scrambles to make sense of this.

Asmodeus is the demon prince most known to fraternize with humans. Lust, parties, gambling. I recall his irritation at Lilith. This could be a temporary cease-fire. Don't get me wrong, I know he's after what's inside Ludovic's head. I know he's our enemy and could spread his war sickness or sic his demonic minions on us at any moment. But I think he's feeling so cocky about his power that he believes he has time to play.

He's not wrong. I have no angelic relic. But I do have a blessed dagger strapped to my thigh and the hairpins in my hair, thanks to Zeke's last-minute alterations.

And poison.

And one weapon all Sinners have—underestimation.

If I can calm my beating heart, I might be able to get us out of here alive.

The opportunity presents itself when, full of excitement and booze, the sheikh snaps his fingers at me and demands, "Boss lady, another round of drinks."

My brows raise at the order. Zeke bristles beneath me. Asmodeus barely glances our way as he puffs his cigar and studies his cards, shifting their positions to suit his game. I suppose there's no point holding onto the Madam Mina charade. That ship has sailed.

I smile sweetly at the sheikh and reply, "Of course."

Zeke tries to stop me from standing, but I pinch him on

the thigh, much like he did to me earlier. Questions are in his eyes, but I keep mine full of calm.

I've got this.

As I stand and straighten my skirt, I take a sidelong glance at the demonic bikers around the table. Two watch Asmodeus, but Flauros watches me.

Ice-cold fingers run down my spine. The demon prince might be preoccupied, but this one is not. He knows what he wants, and apparently, it's me. I force my legs to walk smoothly toward the kitchen and narrow my eyes with a thought . . . Lilith mentioned she wanted one of her own up here with Asmodeus. It must be Flauros—the same demon that killed Zeke's sister. Zeke said he had suspicions the demon was after me all along.

Lilith also failed to tell Asmodeus what closed the cracks on the seals to the gates of hell—Sinners working with Saints. I don't know what Lilith is fully up to, but it's not something Asmodeus is a part of. She's manipulating him. If Asmodeus learns Lilith has undermined him, then this could be another opportunity.

The more I act like this is normal, the easier it will be to slip poison into the drinks and feed them to the possessed hosts. We kept Prue sedated when Pestilence possessed her. It wasn't a foolproof plan, but it helped us contain Pestilence for a few days. Maybe a good dose of poison will give us a few hours. I'd be happy with a few minutes.

Flauros's hungry gaze follows me as I walk about the kitchen collecting fresh glasses. Unable to find the freedom to dose each individual glass, I settle for dosing the entire whiskey bottle. Every last drop of the poison in my ring is added, making it a potent concoction. As long as none of the inno-cents drink, we'll be fine. I give the bottle a little swirl and then start pouring.

I serve Asmodeus first, slipping the demon prince's glass next to him, before moving to Flauros and the other two biker demons. I can barely breathe from the stench of rot on their breaths. The people they've possessed might be dead inside those bodies. It feels like their souls are long gone.

Fear presses down on me. Flauros's eyes bleed flames. If a spark lands on something flammable, we're all dead. This pent-house will burn in seconds, and with the elevator the only way down, we could be sardines in a can.

"Pretty little doll," he hisses to me under his breath. "We have unfinished business, you and I."

I smile tightly and hand him a drink. "I don't know what you mean."

He hesitates. "Don't you know me, little china doll?"

"Do you want the drink or not?"

Again, he hesitates, clearly confused over my lack of interest.

I shrug and say loudly, "Oh well. I'll drink it if you don't want to join the party."

Asmodeus glances up suddenly and glares at Flauros. If he is truly the demon of fun times, then he'll be pissed if his minions aren't participating. As predicted, Flauros scowls in chagrin, takes the glass, and shoots it back. He gives me a very human *Happy now?* look before tossing the glass over his shoulder.

It shatters loudly on the floor.

Now that all the demonic entities have been fed the

whiskey, I glance at Zeke and get ready to run. We're out of here when any of them drop or stumble. Asmodeus was the first to drink, but he's a prince of hell. All he does is cough and tap his chest as though something is caught. A moment of panic pierces my mind. Maybe I've misjudged. Maybe the poison won't work after all. I could have used too much on the others.

"Read 'em and weep," Asmodeus drawls, grinning from ear to ear. "Royal flush."

"You cheated," Ludovic slurs, pointing his finger at Asmodeus. "I saw you."

"Only rats dare accuse the great Asmodeus of cheating." Flauros snarls at Ludovic.

Rat . . . didn't Raven say something about a rat in her warning for Zeke?

One of the biker demons falls with a loud thud.

"How much did he drink?" Asmodeus asks the sheikh, who shrugs in return.

Zeke turns to me, his eyes full of something unreadable, yet frightening. Then he shoots Ludovic between the eyes.

All hell breaks loose.

"No!" Asmodeus roars, standing so suddenly that he tips the poker table over. Chips, glasses, and cards tumble everywhere. Furious eyes dart between Ludovic bleeding out, the remaining demon bikers swaying from the poison, and Zeke with his smoking gun.

Asmodeus gestures in the air. Lights flicker, the temperature drops, and the atmosphere pops in my ears. Every human apart from Zeke and myself becomes infected with his war disease. Poisonous chaos spreads from their eyes over their skin, covering their cheekbones with a black web. This is the first time I've seen the evil take root. This is pandemonium in its rawest form.

I duck in time to miss a fist swinging for my head. Thank God for muscle memory because it's the only thing saving me as I deflect blow after blow from Petrov as he tries to take me down, snarling something about never trusting me.

"Fucker," I grunt, as I block his next strike with my forearm. My fist connects with his midsection, but he barely registers the blow.

Time to get serious, then. I back up. Petrov snarls and launches at me, hands out. I release my bullwhip and use the length to capture his outstretched arms. I wrap once, twice, around a wrist and yank him until he stumbles. He knocks me around, but I use his weight against him. In the next second, I have him face down on the ground with my knee pressed to his shoulder blades. One of my sanctified hairpins is in his soulless black eye before he can buck.

The sigils do their job, and Petrov stills. I want to feel bad, he's innocent just like Sister Agnes was, but another body rushes me. I glimpse the whiskey bottle on the floor with the rest of the poker cards and chips. I crawl toward it. Something grabs my ankle. I glance back and see it's Flauros. Sound warbles. Smoke stings my nose. The demon crawls to me, hissing and crackling like the brimstone in hell. The poison has barely worked to slow his host's body. Perhaps he's too powerful.

The carpet catches *fire*. My training flies out the window, and I freeze. Fire. We're all going to burn. I smell the smoke and remember it's the same scent Snuggles always seemed to carry. It invaded my dreams.

This is it. I'm going to die surrounded by flames, after all.

Then I hear the sound of heaven. Gunshots. Three in quick succession. *Zeke*. He's alive. He needs me. The need to get to him trumps my fear. My hand flails out behind me and blindly searches the floor until my fingers wrap around the hard neck of the whiskey bottle. I swing it at the burning demon.

He takes the hit to the head with barely a reaction. He hisses and snarls. "China doll."

"Fucking call me that again, I dare you."

He licks his lips. "I'm ready for my snuggle, little one. I'm going to fuck you hard while your body burns. Do you think he'll do nothing, just like when I killed his sister?"

His words fill me with rage. I pull the final sanctified hairpin from my bun with trembling fingers.

Flauros starts laughing. It's an odd, sizzling sound that drills fear into my soul. "It was only a matter of time before I caught up with you again. You're mine."

"Like fuck, she is." Zeke's voice rings clear in the room. He's over by the kitchen, bloody lip, jacket off, the businessman dead at his feet. He raises his pistol to the ceiling. The gunshot snaps me out of my daze. Water sprays like rain. The demons suddenly scream as though it's acid. What the fuck?

"It's not holy water, you imbeciles," Asmodeus barks as he shoves the sheikh out of his way and steps over the sleeping Southerner. But even Asmodeus has a glimmer of fear in his soulless eyes.

"Not holy water . . . yet." Zeke rolls up his white sleeve,

glances at a tattoo, slices a knife across his forearm, and uses his blood to paint a sigil on the waterlogged carpet. He stares at Asmodeus and mumbles a spell.

"Don't just stand there," Asmodeus roars at the cowering biker demons. "Attack them!"

But they scramble to hide from the water spray, their movements sluggish from the poison.

Water runs down my face, soaking into me, and all I can think is: thank God I'm not going to burn. Zeke saved me. But then I see Ludovic's blood pooling in a dark stain beneath his body. Asmodeus steps toward us, focused on me.

I rip the split on my skirt and release the hidden dagger, but Zeke's voice stops Asmodeus.

"If you want to rifle through his memories," Zeke warns, pointing at Ludovic's body. "You'd better be quick. He's bleeding out."

Zeke stalks toward me and tugs me toward the elevator. I stumble because I keep glancing over my shoulder to where Asmodeus crouches over Ludovic's body, water dripping down his hate-filled face. Flauros snarls as he writhes on the water-soaked carpet, steam billowing from his body. "Everyone you love will burn, china doll."

Before I can breathe, we're down the elevator and jogging out the lobby door, hailing a cab. We're both too stunned and cold to speak for the entire journey until we enter the motel room where a certain kind of safety exists.

It all happened so fast. The demons. The fire. Zeke shooting Ludovic—an innocent.

"You shot him," I whisper, my eyes darting over his face. Like me, he looks like a drowned rat. His eyes are bleak. Wild.

Is he okay? He barely moved in the cab. I freeze as a new fear rears its head. "Are you infected?"

Stupid question. He would have attacked me by now. I would have seen the black chaos spiderwebbing from his eyes.

"No," he answers quietly. He pulls his hand from his pocket and opens his palm. A set of rosary beads dent his skin from how tightly he held onto them. "I think this protected me. But I transferred the blessing to the water. They were a gift from Cisco."

"You shot Ludovic before Asmodeus cast his spell."

He gives a grim nod. "Raven said gods don't worry about the rats they step on to protect the innocent. When Asmodeus called Ludovic a rat, I knew I had to kill him. It was the only way to keep Asmodeus from coming after us."

"The CCTV footage," I mumble, remembering how Asmodeus used the barmaid's blood to gather the information he needed about the ancestors of this Sarah woman who betrayed him centuries ago.

"I can't believe that was Flauros," he mutters, running his fingers through his damp hair.

I go to him and cup his face, turning it until his eyes lock with mine. "You were right. It was after me, not your sister. I'm so sorry."

His brows meet in the middle, and his eyes screw shut as if he can stop the flood of emotion taking over his body. He swallows hard. "I should have screamed. Flauros had my baby sister, and I hesitated."

"Hey." I pull his head down to my chest. "You were a kid. It's not your fault."

His palms slide up my back. His embrace turns hard and

desperate as he rasps against my chest, "*One thing,* wildcat. That's my real one thing. Not you, not me, but her. I fucked up. I hated her because she cried so much. But—" he chokes up.

"I know." My eyes burn with tears. "You loved her."

He nods. I feel his tears against my skin.

"Breathe, Zeke." I stroke his hair. "Breathe."

We move to the bed, and I tighten my embrace, coo soft words to him, and wish I could turn back time to the moment I was conceived. Without me, none of this would have happened. I know it's a fool's notion. A stupid one. But it's there, dancing around the edges of everything I do.

"I'm so sorry," I murmur.

I keep holding him until his breathing settles, all the while looking outside the tiny slit in the curtains, watching for danger. Nothing is outside but a half-filled parking lot, the night sky, and the urgency that we need to get out of here as soon as possible.

"What happened to Snuggles?" I ask.

Zeke is reluctant to let me go but clears his throat and straightens. He won't look me in the eye, and I hope it's just his embarrassment from letting his emotions out. I hope it's not hate for realizing the pain in his life is all my fault.

"I carried it around with me for a while, hoping to draw the demon to me. After I thought you were dead, I still carried it. I think I tried to throw it out but couldn't."

"Is it here?" My eyes widen. Does he still have it?

"I left it at the abbey."

I exhale. "That's good. I think. I should probably warn the

Rev in case it really is some kind of beacon for demonic activity."

"I know where the helmet is." He wipes his face and inhales deeply.

"That was why you pinched me."

"Ludovic boasted about it when we argued. I accused him of lying. He said he almost has it. That it's in a temple in the Carpathian Mountains."

"That conversation . . . I didn't realize you speak Romanian."

"When I worked with Andrei, I often visited the country." He gives a self-deprecating shake of his head and stares at the rosary in his fingers. "Do you remember the first time you changed your *one thing*?"

"What?" I almost jolt from the sudden change in subject. I don't know how to answer.

"You said you would go back in time and stop Vlad the Impaler from doing his thing." He frowns. "I went to Romania thinking I could visit that castle and somehow be closer to you. That's how I learned to speak it. You."

Exhaustion sinks in, and I rub my eyes. "Raven said she saw Dracula in her vision."

"So we must be on the right track."

"We just need to get there before Asmodeus."

"He can manifest demonic wings and teleport."

I think about our odds. "Do you think he got the information from Ludovic's blood?"

Zeke's brows furrow in thought. "I think if it were easy to get, Asmodeus wouldn't have given up attacking us for the chance to get to Ludovic. Maybe once the blood goes cold, he can't read the blood."

"What if he did?"

Zeke doesn't move. He stares at his rosary beads with a vacant look.

I don't know if this is a delayed shock, but I finally feel more like myself. I'm ready for action for the first time since this demon thing started, and I have no idea why. Thirty minutes ago, I was petrified, frozen stiff, ready to go to hell and face my eternal damnation.

But then Zeke was there. He acted when I couldn't. He really was my man, my huckleberry in every sense. I have to believe that look in his eyes has nothing to do with regret for being with me. We're a team. We work. We're Wyatt and Doc, two halves of the same coin.

If he's stuck, I'll pull us both out.

"Let's go," I say, heading into the bathroom. I quickly strip off my wet clothes and dress into my Sinner uniform. We'll get on a plane and head to Romania.

Our false passports will get us into Europe. It will have to do for now. While we're in the air, I'll contact Thea and see if she can coordinate the rest of our travel arrangements.

When I leave the bathroom, Zeke is still staring at his rosary.

"Zeke?"

"Somehow," he mumbles, "I came into this night thinking I was invincible. I'd bypassed the law. I'd cheated death with Andrei. I actually thought we had God on our side. But then I looked into the soulless depths of Asmodeus's eyes and realized this has nothing to do with sides. It's not about a bargain we make or a lucky charm. It's not about justice. It's about who wants it more."

"Who wants what more?" The relic?

He doesn't answer, just clears his throat and grabs his backpack. "Let's go."

He's not even in dry clothes. I grab his arm as he turns to leave. A harrowing look haunts his eyes as he meets my gaze.

"Thank you," I murmur, softly touching his face. "You saved our lives."

He swallows and frowns, seemingly at a loss for words, but it's okay because I can take over from here. I'll be his huckleberry.

Twenty-Eight

Zeke

Whenever I kill a man, I step further from the light and closer to the dark. It was a fluke that we got out of there alive. I reacted when I saw the carpet in flames, the demon from my past, and Leila's frightened eyes.

I pitted my will against Asmodeus's.

I pitted mine against Flauros's, against Lilith's.

I won. For now, until the next time we meet again.

Love makes us better, Cisco said.

Better is a subjective word. Better at killing? Better at protecting? Better is not good. Better is not holy. Better is simply winning.

Our flight is crowded, so we can't discuss what happened without being overheard. The long hours across the Atlantic are spent sleeping fitfully. I keep dreaming of flames, Ludovic's startled eyes when I pointed my pistol at him, and Puck crawling after Leila. I wake frequently and check she's still sitting next to me. For most of it, she's out like a light. The rest of the time, she's making plans and messaging her team back home.

I like to think she's not messed up about this because she feels safe with me around. I've finally been able to put to use all the demonology knowledge I spent years gathering instead of being with her. I try and latch onto that. Nothing else matters.

A private charter plane will be ready for us when we touch down in Romania. This one will take us as close as possible to the small village near the temple Ludovic mentioned. We'll parachute in and then question the locals about the helmet.

Leila organized everything. I don't tell her I have absolutely no clue how to skydive because I'm worried, despite everything that's happened to draw us closer together, she'll find a way to go it alone. If I had the choice to leave her, knowing she'd be safer, I'd probably take it.

I already did that once.

I guess I haven't changed that much at all.

WIND BLASTS into the fuselage through the open hatch. Probably just as well that I'm freezing my ass off. Otherwise, I'd be too worried about the twelve-thousand-foot drop onto a snow-covered mountain. Leila is strapped into her chute and checking her bags and supplies. We're both wearing insulated skydiving suits, but there's no escaping this frigid temperature. Hell has frozen over, and we're diving into it headfirst.

"Check your chute!" she shouts through the roar of the wind and points to my backpack.

I peer over my shoulder and tug a few straps but have no idea what I'm doing. Now might be a good time to confess to her about all this. But when I face her again, she's giving me a smug look.

She knows.

I shake my head in disbelief, then lean closer so she can hear me shout, "You know I have no clue how to do this, don't you?"

"Of course I do." She scowls. "You don't know the difference between a ripcord and a ribbon."

"Don't go without me," I beg, feeling my heart strangle.

Her eyes widen. "I wouldn't do that."

I would.

"Good," I reply. "Because I'd jump after you anyway."

Something passes between us. For most of the journey, we've kept our conversation to a minimum and focused on our plans. Asmodeus shocked her. The fire demons and Flauros freaked her out. Then it all freaked me out. The only thing keeping me sane right now is her being with me.

I have the sense that even if we're really dropping into hell, it wouldn't matter as long as she's by my side. I think I could weather any storm with her. She takes control of the situation and tethers me to earth. She checks my pack and chute. I'm so in love with her it hurts. I need her to say it back.

This can't be our life—catching frozen moments from a paradise with teeth. We deserve better.

"We'll tandem jump," she tells me. "Your backpack doesn't even have a chute in it."

My cheeks heat as she points out the straps on her own suit.

"You really knew from the start."

Her wry smile leaves a twinkle in her eyes. It makes me warm, despite the icy air biting my face.

"Come on, Huck," she says, gesturing at her front. "Strap in."

My heart soars. *Huck.* Then my stomach flips. We're going to fucking jump out of a fucking plane. Into snow. I didn't think I had any phobias, but now I'm unsure.

I take her face between my hands. "If we survive this—"

She plants her lips on mine, swallowing my words. I've forgotten now. All I have is her intoxicating taste flooding my body with more endorphins than I need. While I'm embarrassingly stupefied, she manhandles me to fit against her front.

"Turn. Arms up," she orders. Tugs hard on a strap, squeezing us together. My spine pushes against her soft chest, and I stifle a groan. "Arms down. Good. Stop fidgeting." She reaches around my body and pats me, testing that all ties are secured properly.

Fuck, I love it when she gets bossy. Never thought I had this kink, but she's behind me and making the decisions. I'm so fucking turned on that I can't think. She latches us together using the tandem ties and shuffles us to the hatch.

"Oh shit." I glance down, snapping out of my daze. White. Gray. Clouds. Can't even see the ground. How will we know where we are? Panic strangles my lungs as I realize what we're about to do.

She pinches my ass and shouts in my ear. "You'll be fine, pet. Just don't breathe."

"What?"

She pushes us out of the hatch. Icy wind punches my face. We fall face-first into clouds. Terror floods my system, but then Leila *yeehaws* behind me.

"SEE?" Leila grins as she unstraps us from each other. "Nothing to worry about."

We're already lying on the snow, but when the straps release, I fall onto my face with a groan. Ice cold seeps into my skin. I'm unsure if my muscles are stiff because of the landing, my recent injuries, or the temperature. I roll onto my back and blink at the blue sky, trying to work out if I'm beyond repair.

"I think my knees are broken." I grimace, trying to bend them. Honestly, it's my ribs aching more.

Leila's beautiful face appears over mine with concern. "For real?"

My lip curves on one side, and she punches me in the arm.

"Ow." I rub the spot. "Go easy on me, slugger."

"You're such a wimp. Suck it up."

My grin widens. She sniffs and shields her eyes from the glare to search our snowy surroundings. Her cheeks are wind-blown, but her complexion is bright. *So fucking beautiful.* I can't help it—I grip her collar and yank her down to me. Her body flattens against mine, and an *oof* of air puffs from her lips.

"Kiss me." It was supposed to be a request, but there's no question in my tone.

She licks her lips and then lowers. I cup her head and pull

her the rest of the way until our lips clash, and I drive my tongue in deep. I sweep her mouth with long, hot strokes. She moans at my intrusion. Our kiss is hard, fast, and hungry. I need more. Something about falling from the sky has wiped the last traces of the fear our run-in with Asmodeus left behind. How can I complain about anything when Leila kisses me, making little feminine whimpers as I slide my hands down her back and squeeze her ass.

She is warm and alive. I'll never get enough of this.

When she pulls back, I almost groan at the loss. I drink in the sight of her flushed and happy face. I try to freeze time. Right here, right now. If it wasn't so fucking cold, this is where I'd stay forever. I won't need food—I'd feast between her legs daily. I won't need heat—I'd warm myself by fucking her senseless.

For fuck's sake, I'm so hard right now. When we finally get somewhere warm and dry, I'm going to—

"What?" she whispers, her brows lifting in the middle. "Why are you looking at me like that?"

"Because," I answer gruffly. "I want to do wicked things to you."

I nip her chin, tugging her hips against mine and flexing until she feels the hardness waiting for her. My wildcat blushes, and I might make some kind of desperate whimpering sound no man should make.

Her eyes are full of hot desire, but she climbs off me and then does that beautiful thing where she cares for me. This is the old Lei Ling I remember. The sweet, caring heart that would cut my hair with rapt attention to detail. The one who made sure I ate.

I could probably detangle myself from the chute, but I don't want to. I want to watch her fuss and check my knees. I relish her tiny touches as she prods my bruised ribs, pretending she's not blushing from how deeply I look at her. I want to take her hand and guide it south, but what I want isn't important right now. Her safety is.

Asmodeus could be hot on our tails. He could be at the temple already.

I grumble as I collect our pack. I truly am a bit stiff. At least the snow softened our landing, but, Christ, jumping out of a plane isn't my first choice for a mode of transport. We narrowly missed the wrong side of the mountain. Leila had expertly steered us through the wind and landed us in a valley between snow-capped forests. The sky is now bright blue and clear. We left the clouds somewhere behind.

"There it is." She points in the distance.

I squint and see smoke from over the horizon of the valley. "The village?"

She nods. "Thea booked us a place at the local hotel—"

Warm and dry. "Say no more."

She laughs and hurries to catch up to me. I think her laughter is the sweetest sound I know.

"Thea said reviews online mentioned the villagers are usually very welcoming. I figured since you speak the language, we might be able to arrange an invitation to dinner with one of the families so we can ask about the helmet. Local folklore could help us find this temple."

"Good idea. I think Ludovic struggled to find its exact location. If that's true, then we'll need more information."

"If he wasn't lying."

The walk into the village is across treacherous terrain. Snow sometimes has ice beneath it and can hide rocks and deeper drifts or sinkholes. We're lucky we landed not too far from safety.

I offer to carry her backpack, but she refuses and soon walks ahead of me while I'm wheezing to catch up. I'm not terribly upset. At least with her in front, I have the perfect view of her pert ass flexing in her tight skydiving pants. Plenty of fodder for my fantasies.

But after an hour's walk, not even my dirty thoughts can keep me warm. The cold nips at my extremities, and I begin to worry my cock will fall off. Then I really will be in hell. Miraculously, we clear the hard terrain and walk up a sludgy footpath with hoof prints in the muddy snow.

The village is small and mainly consists of farming structures and log cabins. We receive strange looks from locals as they go about their afternoon, collecting logs for their fires and feeding farm animals. I don't have the energy to summon an approachable smile. Leila does all the talking. A local geriatric walking a donkey gives us directions to the hotel Leila booked.

I'm a little sad that my gun-running trips to this country have never taken me somewhere this isolated. This place has a certain charm and honesty missing from the city. It's the furthest thing from godless and dark. It's hard to imagine anything bad touching the fresh air and huts painted with colorful flowers.

If Asmodeus gets here and we can't stop him . . . all these happy, innocent people will die.

We see no sign of foreigners or anyone who might be considered a treasure-hunting mercenary team. I hope it doesn't mean Ludovic lied. Since Leila mentioned it, the doubt has been circling my thoughts.

Eventually, we find the hotel. It's more of an inn and another log cabin with a porch and veranda. Somehow, news of our arrival traveled faster than us. An older man with white hair waits on the steps with a big goofy grin on his rosy, broken-capillary face. The hand-knitted jumper stretching over his portly torso is covered in the same brightly colored flower patterns I glimpsed on some of the houses.

"Welcome!" he bellows in a voice big enough to cause an avalanche. "I am Orlov."

"Bună ziua," I greet in Romanian.

His eyes widen. "You speak Romanian?"

I nod but gesture to Leila. "She doesn't."

"So we will speak in the English for you."

"Thank you." She smiles.

He takes her hand and shakes vigorously. "You must be the nun. I speak with your holy woman. She has good things to say."

Nun?

Leila doesn't blink. She rolls with the cover the Sisterhood set out for her.

"Very nice to meet you, Orlov," she says. "Thank you for accommodating us on short notice."

"Oh, is okay. No problems. We don't have many visitors this time of year. But come, you must be cold. You look like you fell from the sky!" He frowns at our wind suits.

Leila gives me a wink and then smiles at him. "It's defi-nitely been a long journey."

"Food and a hot shower, yes?" he decrees boisterously. "This way to your rooms."

He takes us down the porch and around the cabin. A path leads through the muddy grass to another cluster of cabins. As we walk, I note an open garage door. Inside, a burly blacksmith pumps the bellows, adding air to a fire. Perhaps he makes shoes for the donkeys. Through the window of another house, a family sets a long wooden table for dinner. My stomach grumbles.

Leila sees the same thing. Orlov catches us both staring and announces with gusto, "We will eat in thirty minutes. You are most welcome to dine with us."

"Thirty minutes?" That's not enough time for the hot, steamy shower sex I dreamed about giving Leila on the journey over.

Leila hits me in the stomach, then smiles politely at Orlov. "We'd love that, thank you."

Twenty-Nine

Leila

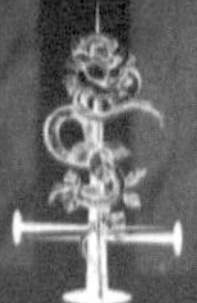

Orlov hands me a key and explains housekeeping rules as he takes us on a quick tour of the folk-decorated cabin—everything has flower patterns. The oven, the tiny two-person dining table, and the couch before the lit fireplace. Even the ceiling and windows have flowers. A ladder leads up to a loft where Orlov says the bedroom and bathroom are.

When he leaves, Zeke drops his backpack and turns to me with a scowl. "Now we only have twenty minutes."

"What are you talking about?"

"I promised myself while we were walking that as soon as we get somewhere warm and dry, I'm going to have hot shower sex with you."

"Oh, you did, did you?"

He nods.

"You can barely stand up. You need rest. We could be headed back out into the wilderness tomorrow. If we're lucky."

The cheated look on his face makes me laugh. It's like I've told him no Christmas gifts this year. I roll my eyes and head toward the loft ladder. He takes my hand and pulls me to him with a serious look on his windblown face.

"You'll get lucky," he mumbles, wrapping his hands around my waist. "I'll see to it."

"Were you always this horny?" I smirk.

His eyes glimmer with amusement. I'm sure a roguish reply is on the tip of his tongue, but his gaze gets lost around my mouth.

"I love seeing you smile," he says, brushing a thumb across my lower lip.

Heat flares where he touches, and I sigh, almost giving in to the urge to stay here. I want to shower, get dressed into something cozy, then sit by the television eating popcorn and chocolate chip cookies.

"Do you remember," I say hesitantly, "when we would stay up and watch movies?"

He nods, gaze still lost on my lips. "We would pretend to go to sleep, then sneak out once the matron was snoring. We'd sit right up close to the screen so we could hear it with the volume down. Sometimes we'd put a blanket over our heads and the TV, like our own private little fort."

"You let me watch Dracula."

"You let me bore you with Westerns."

"We were happy, weren't we?"

His eyes finally flick up to meet mine. "Yes, we were."

"I want to find our way back to that place." My throat is thick and tight. Saying it out loud feels scary. It's like the moment it left my lips, it became a tangible thing—something vulnerable and out in the open. Something that can be stolen.

I'd like to blame the demons and Lilith, but there was the Sisterhood too. For so long, that was my reality, and Zeke was a dream. I'm not sure it's possible to switch them again. We might not even survive . . . and then there will be hell. My reckoning.

I shiver.

"Hey," he whispers tenderly, chucking his finger under my chin. "We'll get there. I promise."

Cross your heart? I want to whisper, but the words conjure pain instead of hope.

"Wildcat." His forehead drops to mine, and he shakes his head. "I broke a promise to you."

"I know."

"Never again."

All I can muster in response is a nod.

"Come on," he says, a tone of regret in his voice. I feel like I ruined the moment with something that should be left in the past. "You're right. We need to shower, eat, and rest."

Twenty minutes later, we're in dry and warm clothes, walking to Orlov's cottage in the near dark. I'm even wearing the brown complimentary knitted pullover with pink floral patterns. We found the knits in the closet. I made Zeke wear the man-sized one.

"Wish I took a picture," I mumble to him. His sweater is still two sizes too big, and he's wearing a matching beanie. Also a little too big.

"I feel like a crochet doily."

I chuckle. "But I'll bet you're warm."

He shrugs, smiling. We stomp up the steps, shaking the snow from our boots. Voices inside are as boisterous as Orlov. I hear younger voices mixed in with the older. Zeke barks a sudden laugh.

"What are they saying?" I ask, curious.

"Someone is telling the other they're annoying. The mother says they're both annoying."

"They're laughing."

He nods. "Sounds like a normal family."

We both become lost in our thoughts when we should be knocking on the door. With the conversation and the quaint cabin with herbs and flowers in pots, this feels . . . domestic. Foreign yet familiar. Addictive. And we haven't stepped a foot inside.

I clear my throat and lift my fist, ready to knock. "Remember, I'm a nun."

I knock. Zeke again gives me a look that says I've stolen Christmas.

A teen girl opens the door.

"Hello," she says. Then goes on to speak Romanian at me.

Zeke explains I can't speak Romanian. She pouts and then looks at him. She blinks, blushes, and mumbles something before rushing into the house. I hide a smile.

"I think we can go inside," Zeke offers, confused.

"You're such a lady killer," I tease.

His eyes sparkle. "I know."

"Also arrogant."

"That too."

I scoff and head inside. Zeke closes the door behind us. It's also covered in painted flowers. We find our way to the kitchen.

This cabin is similar to ours, with a lot of shared space. I don't see private bedrooms, just the loft upstairs and a glimpse of multiple beds. The whole family lives here?

The dining table is by the window. A fireplace burns and provides heat along with the oven in the kitchen. They live simply, without much space, fanfare, or luxury. It reminds me a little of the abbey in its simplicity and honesty. I guess the colorful flower patterns painted everywhere are to brighten the small area on gloomy, snowy days.

I'm happy to see a painting of the pope hanging over the fireplace—it means they will be more inclined to know the local folklore surrounding the church. They might know if there's any validity to this helmet being made from the nails that crucified Jesus. Hopefully, we will get answers.

A brunette woman with a scarf in her hair stirs something on the stove. The girl who let us into the house is there. She mumbles something to the mother, takes a bowl of mashed potatoes, and ducks her gaze as she hurries to the long wooden table.

The mother smiles warmly at us before gesturing at the table. "You sit."

Orlov arrives with a teenage son, each carrying bottles in their hands. It's not wine, but some kind of homebrew.

"Is good to see you again," Orlov says. "This is my family. My daughter Paula, my son Matei, and my wife Claudia. All good strong Catholic names. I am the only one who is the bad one." He laughs heartily. "Good thing my family will keep reminding me."

It takes me a moment to realize what he means, but then I see he's trying to connect with me being a nun. Some of us joined the Sisterhood and took religious names. I, however, couldn't completely let go of mine.

"I'm afraid I'm in the same boat as you, Orlov. Sister Leila isn't quite a biblical name, but I don't think the Lord will mind as long as our hearts are in the right place."

Matei has been studying me curiously since they arrived. He listens carefully, and then, just when I think he needs Zeke to translate, he blurts, "You do not look like a nun."

I laugh. I seem to be doing that a lot lately. "Modern nuns look different worldwide, but I am a special nun. I travel far and wide hunting for relics of importance to the church. So sometimes I must dress differently."

Zeke takes his beanie off to hide his growing scowl. I know he doesn't like how easily the lies fall off my tongue. But he's no saint, despite the men he arrived with at the abbey. I guess, what I understand about that reaction is that he's trying to be. Sinners wouldn't be needed if more people tried to be honest.

"Are you looking for something here?" Matei asks. "In our village?"

"First, we serve our guests pálinka and food, Matei. It is rude to question before."

A blush hits Matei's pale cheeks, and he dips his gaze.

"Oh, I don't mind." I smile at the boy. "Really. We have lots of questions too. But we wouldn't say no to a glass of that. It looks amazing. What is it?"

"We make this ourselves. It is like the brandy but from plums."

"Sounds delicious," Zeke says.

Paula snatches the bottle from Matei and fills a small shot glass for Zeke with a shy smile. Matei snatches it back and fills mine. They bicker a little—something that makes Zeke's lips twitch, and Orlov smacks Matei on the head. What he says draws another blush from Matei's face as he darts a horrified glance at me. I'll have to ask Zeke about it later.

Through all this, the smells from the kitchen are slowly crawling into my lungs and filling me with delicious longing. Not long after I sip the potent but delicious brandy, I'm off my seat and into the kitchen.

It's intoxicating inside the small space. Herbs of all kinds hang from the ceiling. Lavender, dill, parsley. Little pots of fresh flowers sit by the painted windowsill. A mortar and pestle is filled with ground seeds. The raw simplicity of the place reminds me of the abbey. The nuns there use as much as they can from the walled garden.

"Can I help?" I ask Claudia.

She wipes her sweaty forehead with the back of her hand and darts an annoyed glance at her daughter, who is enthralled with Zeke.

"I don't mind." I smile. "I enjoy working in the kitchen."

Claudia gives a curt nod and directs me to dish up the soup into six waiting bowls. It looks like chicken soup, but she called it *ciorba rădăuțeană*. I think it's the same thing. While I'm ladling, I can't help but notice the polenta mix she's busy with. Looks like dessert. As soon as I've served the soup to the hungry people at the table, I'm back and inquiring about the dish. It's sweet, rich, and smells delicious.

When I taste it, I moan at the burst of flavor. "Please tell me you will give me the recipe," I ask, grinning at her, then nodding back to where Zeke sits with the others. "He needs more meat on his bones. I will bake this for him."

She gives me a judgmental once-over. "You must eat too. Even the soup."

"Of course!" I realize I've not had a spoonful.

"But yes, he is not fit for this weather." After she puts the polenta dish in the oven, she collects a basket of bread in one hand and gives it to me. We settle at the table to eat. The food is so pure and good that I feel nothing but satisfaction.

Claudia returns to the kitchen and brings over the second course—vegetables, cabbage rolls, and stew. She dishes up an extra serving for Zeke with a look that says he needs to eat it or else.

I grin as I rip a chunk of bread in two and soak up the stewy sauce. "This is delicious," I say to him.

His eyes are a little glassy from the pálinka as he replies, "I'm in heaven."

Our eyes lock for a moment. Beneath the table, he slides his hand over my thigh, then passes his compliments to the chef.

"Eat, eat," she says, motioning for him to stop chatting and to feed himself.

We're halfway through the meal when I remember to ask about the folklore tales surrounding the nearby temple.

"Ah yes," Orlov says. "We have many visitors for the temple. Is old and dangerous so you must be careful for when you journey, yes?"

I nod. "We are always careful. But tell us, the stories point to this temple, but no one ever finds the helmet."

Orlov and his wife share a look before he says, "Is for a good reason."

"It is?" Now I'm intrigued. "What is it?"

He leans in and raises his brows dramatically. "Ghosts

haunt the temple. There are dangerous traps that steal the soul of anyone who enters."

Traps. I can handle that. Ghosts? I'm sure they're not real. Just a scare tactic to frighten away anyone who might want to steal what is inside. But, interestingly, no one has found it yet.

"You said others have been here to search?"

"Yes. They go in—" He gestures one way through the air. "They don't come out."

"They are searching the wrong place, anyway." Paula shakes her head with derision.

The family goes quiet. I catch Orlov slicing his daughter a disapproving glare and she ducks her head.

"What is the right place?" I ask.

"It was the frozen lake by the temple."

They all laugh as if it's the most obvious reason, but I feel as though it's a cover-up. The laughter is too forced. Orlov adds a story about a prideful soldier who drove his men into the water to prove that he could make them walk on it because he wore the protection of their savior. But they were weighed down by the iron they carried, and most did not survive. They are still resting at the bottom to this day. I join them, smiling, but can't say I share their humor. How the hell are we supposed to search the bottom of a frozen lake?

"Would you like to hear more stories?" Orlov asks.

"Sure."

"We have a story in our village," Orlov says, turning his tone somber and dramatic. "Many years ago, a Poland pastor came to our tiny home, searching for something touched by the Lord to help him fight against evil."

My neck prickles with anticipation. "Did he find the helmet?"

Orlov shrugs. "Village does not know, only that this man hunted down the world's most dangerous monster."

I'm leaning in by this stage, enthralled. "What was the pastor's name?"

"This man is called Georg Andreas Helwing."

I sit back, confused.

Zeke squints at Orlov. His cheeks are ruddy with the effects of the pálinka. "You wouldn't happen to be talking about Dracula and Van Helsing, would you?"

My eyes widen. *Helsing and Helwing.* So similar.

I stare at Zeke with wonder. I'm the one who made him watch that damned movie, but he remembered the details.

"Story goes," Orlov says, "he came here, to this very tiny village, and my ancestors helped him."

"*Our* ancestors," Matei corrects.

"Yes, yes, you too."

"So he took the helmet? How did that kill Dracula?" I ask hopefully.

"The many tales of the demon Dracula say many different weapons were used to kill him."

"Mmm," Claudia adds, still as dramatic with her tone as her husband. "A knife. A stake. Potions. A pistol with silver bullets."

"What do you think was the real weapon?" I ask.

"I think our ancestor was a gun maker. To this day, we use the same forge as him in our workshop."

"A gun."

They nod.

"And where do you think this gun might be today?"

"Not here." They laugh again. But my humor is coiled tight like a piece of barbed wire. I feel like we're so close to finding the answers. Maybe the helmet was turned into a gun. Or maybe the prophecy was intended to point us here so we found this story. Orlov called Dracula a demon. Little details like this in local lore can mean everything.

"Any idea?" I press.

Orlov scratches his peppered chin. "We talk about this many nights, and it is Matei who I think has the best answer, yes?"

He looks at his son, who blushes at the attention. "It's just a theory."

"I'd love to hear it," I say.

"Well," he replies. "I think there is not much we know about Helwing when we search online, but our village speaks of the church he was the Pastor for . . . It is not a well-known church, but not far from where Vlad Țepeș was a prince. It is in ruins now and is also said to be haunted, and amaranth grows around the grounds. People say they hear gunfire, but no one is there when they go to look. I think Helwing was there when he died. Or he left his special gun close by in case Dracula rose again from the dead."

"Do you think this might be the place Ludovic spoke about?" I ask Zeke.

"We won't know unless we look, but it's possible."

A church haunted by a ghost who fires a gun. I tap my chin. And there was something else he said. "You mentioned amaranth."

Claudia answers. "It is a special flower that protects against evil spirits."

A Pastor who used a holy relic to kill a demon . . . and maybe magical flowers. Our lead is getting stronger.

"I think we would like to visit this church," I tell our host family. "How far away is it?"

Matei is pleased he helped us out and pulls out his cell phone to show me the map. It's about half a day's drive south . . . not far from the ruins of Vlad's real castle. A tingling in my blood remains. I can't help the feeling we're on the right track.

I turn to Zeke but find him struggling to keep his eyes open. The potent pálinka got to him. Claudia kept refilling his glass. He's also exhausted and probably sore from the journey. I have to remind myself he's not as fit as me.

I thank our hosts for the amazing hospitality and organize a lift in the morning to the nearest town where Zeke and I can either rent a car or find a bus. Then I make our excuses, and we leave.

Zeke fumbles up the loft ladder when we get to our cabin and falls onto the bed. There is only one. I'm less upset about that than I would have been two days ago. I find myself eager to join him, but first, I must complete my checks.

This is a new place with new hazards . . . especially the fireplace still burning downstairs. Everything in the cabin is flammable. I don't like the idea of leaving it unattended while we sleep. I *know* logic says an ember won't likely fly over the barrier and burn the place down. But I have to check.

I look around the house for electrical hazards, ensure all

windows are shut, and return to douse the fire but don't want to fill the place with unwanted smoke. So I sit on the flower-covered crochet couch and watch the flames warily, hating how I'm still a slave to this fear, hating how Flauros is one of the demons in Asmodeus's entourage. At least Snuggles is far away. If that was truly a beacon, then I can sleep safely knowing it's nowhere near us.

My phone buzzes with an incoming message from Thea. Something about the new prophecy. I'm not one for studying pictures, so hit the call button instead.

"Hey," Thea answers.

"Hey."

"You in Romania?"

"Yep."

"How's it going."

"Okay."

"You gonna say more than one-word answers?"

I chuckle and then tell her everything we learned from Orlov and the poker game.

"You guys were lucky to get out of there alive."

"I know."

"None of the Holy Nails are authentic. At least, Mercy and Tawny didn't react to being near them. You two are our best bet right now."

"I think we're in the right place. Can't explain it, but it feels right."

"And . . ." Her voice trails off as the baritone of male mumbling increases. She asks, "And how are you and Zeke doing?"

"What do you mean?"

"I mean, you know. Are you enjoying the ride?"

"We're on a mission."

"You know what I mean. He's hot. You're hot. Letting off steam with each other is not unheard of." Her salacious undertone makes me suspicious. I'm not ready to divulge the details of Zeke's and my relationship. I don't even know what we are yet.

"We're fine."

"That's it?"

I frown. "Why are you so interested?"

"I'm not. It's just . . . Wes told me you guys used to know each other."

"Did he?"

She sighs. "You could have talked to me, Leila. I'm probably the only one who knows what you're going through."

It's none of their business. "Like you talked to me about healing Zeke from certain death?"

"Wasn't my story to tell. Okay, fine. Look. If you won't talk about it, then I may as well tell you more of the prophecy we've worked on. Sending pictures now."

I rub my eyes as I read it.

In the tapestry of time, foes become allies, allies turn to foes, and betrayal creeps from within righteous hearts. Yet, fear not, for salvation, like a gentle smoke, shall whisper from unexpected corners, burning forgiveness into the darkest of hours. Amidst the crucible of treachery, hold fast to the unwavering path of truth, anchored in divine providence. As the inferno subsides, wounds shall mend, and the light of truth shall triumph. The soul is forged in trials, and redemption awaits, guiding the greatest of sinners with grace to ultimate victory.

"I'm too tired to decipher this shit," I mumble. "Just tell it to me straight."

"When we first started translating the gospel, there was a line about the enemy being within. I thought it was about me dealing with my own inner critic, but maybe it's much more literal. Maybe one of our own who goes bad."

"Zeke?"

She hesitates. "Why do you say that?"

"No reason." Just . . . protecting my heart.

"I think he's the last person you need to worry will betray you."

Unless he's done it before. But I don't say that because I think she's right. I know where my loyalties are before she finishes speaking. Every time Zeke touches me, talks to me, or looks at me, I see the truth of his emotion. He's done lying to me. I believe him.

I yawn again.

"I think it might be Mercy," Thea whispers.

I sit upright. "What? Why?"

"Has she been acting weird lately?"

I think back to her irritation at being judged by Team Saint for her sexual needs. But she directed that all inward. I tried to make her feel better. I don't think she'll turn those feelings against us. "She's a little antsy, but that's to be expected. She doesn't have the freedom to be herself."

"Yeah. You're right."

"Why do you think she's the one?" I press.

"There was this picture in a book—of Lilith. It looked like Mercy."

"Coincidence."

"Possibly."

I think about it for a minute. "It could be one of Team Saint. Could be Raven—she's been extra headachey and stand-offish. Could be Tawny after Asmodeus kissed her. Could be one of the nuns, if they don't heal properly from the war sickness. Could be Jinx. Could be one of our Sinners who haven't returned from extended missions."

"You're right." She sighs. "Could be anyone."

Wes's voice rumbles again, just out of earshot. When Thea returns to me, she says, "You should get your rest. Let me know what you find at Helwing's church."

"Yeah. Got it."

"Enjoy the ride, bitch."

"You too."

The last thing I think of before I fall asleep are the words Flauros said when we left him. *Everyone you love will burn.*

I wake in a cold bed with a slight headache and a dry mouth. It's still dark, but something is wrong. My hand runs over cold sheets. Leila's not here. I sit up, and my head swims.

Christ. That pálinka was potent. I could barely keep my eyes open when my head hit the pillow. I'm still dressed in a knitted sweater and jeans.

The dizziness settles as I go to the bathroom, take an awkward piss, then wash my face. I drink gallons from the tap and then return to the bedroom with a shiver, wondering where my girl has gone.

I check my cell phone. Nothing from her but a thousand messages from Wesley. It seemed Leila chatted with Thea while I was out. She apprised them of the new information but said nothing about us being together. Half the messages were drilling me for details.

> Has everything gone according to plan?
> Wes asks. Have you kissed and made up?
> Give me the details.

The final message was:

> Sorry, mate. Thea stole my phone. I don't
> need details. But if the cracks are bigger,
> we need to know. It's imperative you take
> advantage of this situation with Leila.

I frown as I stare at those words. I don't like the idea that what I feel for Leila has some kind of ulterior purpose. She still doesn't know about that part of the prophecy. And if she wasn't comfortable enough sleeping next to me, then I'm not finished thawing the ice between us. But at the same time, Wes should know Leila and I aren't fighting. We're far from it now. I think.

When he and Thea worked against each other, the cracks in the gates of hell were big enough for the demon Vepar to manifest in this realm completely. I have no idea what makes us special enough for this honor, but I'm long past denying it. I just want Leila.

If Flauros ever fully manifested in this realm again . . . I close my eyes and see him crawling through my childhood window. The snuffling. The sulfur. The sizzling. I shake my head. I don't think any spell on my body or bullet to the head will stop him. But the relic might. Somehow.

I catch a ghostly whiff of Leila's fruity scent, and my mind wanders to everything I love about her. She's so fucking beautiful. Last night, she was happy. I don't think she realized how much she smiled when she helped Claudia with that dish in the kitchen.

Thinking of Leila's smile triggers a reaction in my body. My blood heats and heads south. Fucking hard again. *Jesus*. I need to find her. She must be close.

I glance over the loft's edge into the shadows beneath. The fire in the fireplace is out. The only light comes from moonlight sneaking in through the frosty window. A bootless foot dangles over the edge of the couch. I frown—why wouldn't she feel comfortable sleeping in bed with me?

I sniff my pits—my breath. Not that bad. But then I realize with a shiver why it's so cold. She had to watch the fire go out before she felt safe. Probably did her nightly checks, too. Something in my chest squeezes, and I quietly climb down the ladder.

She sleeps with a frown and a blanket up to her chin. But her long legs don't fit. Her lips are blue.

"Come on," I whisper, slotting my arms beneath her legs and shoulders. "Let's get you to bed."

She murmurs something I don't quite catch, but her tone sounds concerned.

"Don't worry," I say. "I've got you."

"Promise," she mumbles sleepily.

"Cross my heart," I rasp through a tight throat. The last time I said that to her, I lied. "Hold tight."

I guide her hands around my neck, shift her weight to one hand, and climb with the other up the rungs. I feel her looking at me halfway up the ladder, but she doesn't speak. She watches me as I carry her awkwardly. When we crest the top, I almost drop her trying to maneuver my knees onto the platform. I end up with one knee on the ground, one foot planted, and carrying her just shy of the wooden floor. Not exactly the smooth move I was imagining. A curse word slips past my lips, and she giggles.

She fucking giggles.

My eyes flutter closed, and I groan as that sound ignites my blood.

"You okay?" Her worried tone has my eyes opening.

The moonlight gives her features an ethereal quality. She glows. It reminds me so much of how she used to look when we were children, watching secret movies in the living room, the two of us against the world, the blue light from the television flickering against her face. How did I get so lucky to have her in my arms, staring back at me with all the trust I don't deserve?

"Do you remember," I mutter, staring deep into her eyes, "just before the fire, we had that movie marathon on the couch?"

Her brow pinches, and she nods.

"I think that's when I fell in love with you."

"But you pushed me away. I thought you were annoyed at having a little girl following you around."

"Leila." My voice deepens. "I was a horny teenager who already had wet dreams about a girl far too young for me. A girl I treated like a sister. When you came in for a cuddle, and my cock twitched, I knew. You were it for me. I didn't want to see you as a sister anymore and . . . I had to get some distance."

Her grip tightens around my neck. She's so quiet I don't know what to think. Then she whispers, "And now?"

"Now the sound of your laughter is my favorite wet

dream," I rasp. "The smell of your shampoo gets me hard. You're all I think about."

In the dark, the sound of her shallow breathing is too loud. It fills the silence along with my beating heart.

"Zeke," she breathes. "I've always loved you."

We don't make it to the bed. I crush my lips to hers and kiss her with all the longing I've locked inside.

The floor is hard. The air is cold. None of it matters as we collide and fall. I cover her body with mine, spear my fingers into her soft hair, and invade her mouth with my tongue. Every inch of that hot, wet space is mine in seconds. I stake my claim. I make it my property and groan as she sighs in response.

She tears at my clothes, kissing me, wanting me. We're ravenous beasts with each other. Our mouths are open, kissing and biting any surface of the other we can touch. I yank her knitted sweater over her head. She unzips my jeans. I don't know what comes first, my hand on her naked breast or her fingers around my cock, but we both release an agonized groan into each other's mouths.

"Fuck." I thrust into her hand. "Your fingers are cold."

"Yours are ice," she gasps, arching into me. I pinch her nipple, swallow her gasp with another kiss, then drop my head to take her breast into my mouth. I want to give her heat, to give her comfort and—

"Zeke!" she cries out as my warm mouth hits her cold, sensitive flesh. I glance up, see the pleasure blooming in her unguarded expression, and swirl my tongue around her hard little bud. I kiss and lick down her naked body, taste her goosebumps, and explore every inch of her flesh with insatiable hunger.

All I can think of is how hot she makes me, how I'm going to love her and touch her and sink inside her. And how I desperately hope this time she believes it's forever.

Zeke's mouth blazes down my body. The stark contrast between that heat and the ice in the air is dizzying. I don't know where to focus. All my nerve endings are alive—my mind buzzes. My breasts feel heavy and tingly. My pussy pulses and throbs, impatient with the need to have him touch me down there.

He loves me. Always has. I gasp as his hands find my bottom, and he yanks my pants down my hips to my knees.

"Spread your legs, kitty cat." Charged, erotic thunder has replaced his usual carefree tone.

He plants his hands on my thighs when I'm too slow and opens me. My ankles are trapped in my pants. Cold air rushes in to kiss my wet center, and I suck in a breath.

"Bed," he grumbles, tugging my pants completely off. "We're finishing this in bed."

He picks me up, takes two steps, and drops me onto the mattress. Also cold.

"Don't worry, darlin'." He keeps his eyes on me as he slides his jeans down his hips. His erection springs free, jutting toward me with all the eagerness I see in his eyes. "I'll keep you warm."

He tucks the blanket around us so we're in a cocoon of sorts. Then he sweeps another blanket over our heads until we're in our own little fort. As he braces himself over me, I look into his shadowed eyes.

"Just like old times, huh?" His eyes crinkle.

"I don't think we were doing this back then." I reach down and capture his erection.

He groans at the contact, thrusts hard into me, and murmurs, "I should have stayed." The shadows don't hide his pained expression. "Should have been your first. Should have shown you everything there is to know about a man's body."

"We can pretend." I whimper as his fingers glide through my slick, needy flesh. "Pretend I'm sixteen and you're twenty-one. Pretend you've had enough of denying yourself. You want me, and no one will get in your way."

"Yes." He sinks a finger into my core, then traces his fingertip around my folds, teasing me with his touch. "So fucking wet for me, babe."

"Mmm."

"Say it's for me."

"It's all for you, Zeke."

"Fuck." He explores me with his fingers, learning every inch down there. "I don't think I would have waited for sixteen. Fifteen. Maybe fourteen."

"Fucking pervert." I giggle. "No, you wouldn't have."

He thrusts against my hip. He's so hard that his cock

bruises me. "Giggle again, and I'll come all over your sweet, smooth belly."

I bite my lip, grinning down at him. I love that he's so into me. Every trembling touch he makes is a battle between reverence and need. Passion. Obsession.

"You're too honorable." I rub my thumb along his stubbled jaw. "You would have waited until I was older, ready."

He scoffs. "You think I'm honorable."

"With me, yes."

His gaze turns serious. I think I catch glimmering there. "I would have made it so fucking special, Leila."

"Tell me," I whisper.

"I would have pampered you first. Bought you clothes. Taken you to the movies. To a fancy restaurant where they make those stupidly expensive maroon cookies—"

"Macarons."

"—yeah, macaroons. That's what I said. Then when we would have come home—to *our* home—and I'd have undressed you slowly, got down on one knee, and . . . asked you to marry me before I worshiped every inch of your body."

"What?"

"I would have married you first."

My heart swells. I almost think it will burst from my chest, but then he drops his face to my neck, breathes heavily through his nose, and growls deeply, "But now I can't wait for that. Right now, I need to fuck you so good, we'll erase time."

He slides down my body. I lose sight of him in the shadows beneath the blanket but need to see him. Tossing the covers off me isn't much better, but there's enough moonlight to catch the wicked gleam in his eyes as he plunges his tongue into my pussy.

I cry out as he fills me. Grasp the sheets as he grips my ass and forces me to submit to his punishing mouth. All I can focus on is his tongue, sliding, probing, and feasting on me. My nerves spark and shoot like fireworks. I clutch his hair to stop myself from burning in sensation. It's not until stars float before my eyes that I realize I'm not breathing. I gasp. Pant. He snarls against my intimate flesh and then pushes a finger deep inside me. Then another.

I fall back on the bed and give myself over to him. It's a surreal experience, handing control of my pleasure to another person—to Zeke. At first, I'm too lost in my head. I can't get myself there. But then he starts talking to me.

"Tell me, kitty cat." He rubs his fingertips over my needy flesh. "Tell me what feels good."

"I . . ."

"This?" He pinches my clit. "Or this." He sucks on the little bud and curls his fingers inside me. "You gotta tell me what you need, baby." I moan as he spreads my folds and flicks me hard with his tongue.

A bolt of hot pleasure spears through me. I arch into him, slam my hand on the back of his head, and hold him there.

"Yes," I gasp. "Don't stop that, Zeke."

He makes a satisfied growl and continues his assault but doesn't come up for air. He gives me what I need until I feel pleasure coiling, tension rising, and my climax building. A keening sound slips from my lips as the pressure keeps building. It's building. Climbing. "Zeke," I cry out. "I'm . . ."

He pulls off me.

The pressure dies. I whimper at the loss, glaring down my body at him, ready to demand why he stopped, but his cock is inside me before I can utter a word. He thrusts hard to the hilt, slamming the bed against the wall.

"I need to be inside you. Need to feel you come on my cock."

His eyes open and lock onto me. I inhale at the desperate lust in them.

"I don't know if I can this way," I mumble. Never have I ever fucked a man like this until I orgasmed. It never mattered. Some women never do it.

"Yes, you fucking can." His eyes flash with determination, and then he flexes his hips, hitting me hard. "For me, baby."

I moan with every clash, but it's not enough. He sees the self-disparagement in my eyes and leans over me, kisses me hard, and then changes the angle of his entry.

"Tell me, Leila. One thing." He thrusts.

"What?"

"Tell me one thing that makes you feel good." Another thrust.

"I want to be on top."

His lips curve, and we switch positions.

"Now, tell me one more thing." His voice is thick as he watches me sink onto him.

"I like it when you touch me."

His thumb goes to my clit and rubs. "What else?"

"Let me—" My words cut off as I see the bruises on his ribs.

"Uh-uh." He brings my eyes to his. "Keep going. What were you going to say?"

"I—"

"Leila," he clips. "Tell me."

"I was going to say, let me lose control, but I don't want to hurt you."

He grips my hips, lifts me off him, then slams me down hard. His eyes roll back in his head, and we moan in pleasure together.

"Fuck." I shudder. *Too good.*

"Use me, wildcat."

"Shut up. I love you."

I said it again. He locks eyes with me. Looks like he's going to cry. I swallow the lump in my throat and then slap my palms to his chest, lean forward, and start fucking his cock like I own it.

There's nothing left to hold back from him. He's got it all now. My body. My love. My soul. Together we become a sweaty mess of tangled limbs. I keep finding new positions that hit me right. He keeps helping me by teasing my clit. Finally, we hit an angle that works. I'm on top again, riding him hard and fast. He's lying back, looking at me like I'm a goddess. My thighs burn, but I'm not giving up. I can't. I need this.

"Almost there," I whimper, my hands sliding to my breasts, trying to ease the ache.

Zeke sits up and takes one into his mouth. It's the angle, the sensation, the attentiveness that I need. My orgasm hits so hard that I can't see, breathe, or move. I am the wave of pleasure rolling over me. It's everything. It's heaven.

When I finally come down and back to my senses, we both breathe in hard, ragged bursts. But he's not moving. His head is buried in my neck.

"Zeke," I gasp. "Are you . . . did you?"

He pulls back, eyes drunk and so full of smug satisfaction that I melt.

"Oh yeah," he says, his lips curving lazily.

"When?" I frown, trying to remember, but I was so in my head that I don't think I can.

He chuckles and falls on his back with a flop. "That good, huh?"

"I mean, sure, you're okay. It was fine."

His eyes crinkle, and it's the sexiest thing I've seen.

"Babe," he purrs, reaching between us where we're still joined. He plunges his finger inside me, past his cock, and I moan at the stretch of my inner walls. Still so sensitive. Still so good. When his hand comes back, his finger is covered in our sticky combined release. "You came so hard you don't even remember me doing the same."

"Shut up."

"You said that too." He laughs. It's deep, hearty, and I hope I never stop hearing it. "I think you scratched all down my back, too."

"I will murder you if you tell anyone about this."

"Why are you embarrassed? My wildcat has claws." He snarls, nipping my shoulder. "I love it."

"I'm not, I'm just . . ." I don't know.

"Leila, it's okay to want to be fucked so hard you can't think of anything else. In fact, I'm getting hard again thinking about it. I want to fuck you again while you're full of my cum." His breathing becomes shallow as lustful thoughts darken in his eyes. "I loved seeing you use me to feel good.

After this time, I want you to do that while you're sitting on my—"

"Zeke!" I cover his mouth. I can't believe my cheeks are heating right now. I'm not a prude. Am I? I mean, I can't be. I've been with too many men. But this was different. It wasn't just fucking. It was letting myself go with someone I'm not ashamed around. It was making love and all that sickening bullshit. I said I *love* him. During sex. My hand is still over his mouth. He mumbles something, so I slide it off.

He starts rocking his hips, hardening inside me again.

"Say it again," he pleads softly.

I don't need to ask what he means. "I love you," I moan.

Even if that means he's in the firing line. I'll just have to work twice as hard to keep him safe.

Thirty-Two

Time is erased.

There is nothing but us for long sweaty minutes as we languish beneath the blankets until finally, Leila moans, "I need to go to the bathroom."

"Later." I chase her lips.

"Zeke." A warning tone.

I give a reluctant groan but let go of her and lie back on the pillow. "Okay, fine. But then you're coming back to the same spot. We're fucking again."

She laughs but doesn't answer my demand. Just gives me a look that could mean yes, it could mean no. I have no clue and don't care. As I said, there is no time. I'll wait here forever.

While she's gone, I drag a blanket over my body and sigh. I don't think I've ever been this happy. I'm still staring at the flowers painted on the ceiling with a dopey grin on my face when Leila cries out in surprise from behind the bathroom door.

A chill runs through my veins. There's no reason for me to be alarmed. That was just a sound of surprise. Confusion. Could mean anything. But my hand is hunting near the floor beside the bed, groping for where I left my Colt.

I'm on my feet, gun pointed at the door, when it bursts open, and she runs out with wide eyes.

I grip her shoulder, tugging her close. We twist so my body is in harm's way—gun pointed at whatever threat is inside the bathroom. My lungs heave hard. My mind scrambles to catch up.

What the . . .?

Snuggles—the toy I swear I left at the abbey—sits beneath the sink, facing us with its one-button eye. The smokey scent hits me.

Leila covers my hand on her shoulder. Her heart pounds so hard that I feel it against my fingers, despite being inches from her chest.

"Leila," I say slowly. "Did you bring the toy from the abbey?"

She shakes her head. "I thought you did."

I slam the bathroom door shut. "We have to get out of here."

Fuck. Fuck. Fuck. I scramble to find my clothes and shove them on while thinking of the millions of protection spells Wesley tried to drill into me. Which one on my body was it again? Wasn't there a demonic containment spell? Shit. I think it keeps demonic entities out or in. I was better with the physical weapons. Brainy stuff was Wesley's area.

"Maybe we can burn it," I suggest. "Toss it into the blacksmith's forge, then protect this cabin with a spell. Put salt around the exterior boundary."

"We can't just lock ourselves in. The others in the village will be at risk."

"You're right. Dammit. Get dressed." I race around, gathering anything I can find to help me mark a magical safety boundary with the right sigils.

"We can't stay," she repeats, voice calm. "We should head out to Helwing's church. Bring the toy with us."

"I'm not fucking touching that thing again. It's probably possessed." I shudder.

"Then we really need to bring it with us."

I stop cold in my tracks. Leila's somehow fully dressed before me, in her black Sinner uniform—hoodie, red cross on the front, tight leggings with hidden places for weapons. Her katana is strapped between her shoulder blades, and her Smith & Wesson is holstered at her hip. I gape.

"How did you dress so fast?"

"You're too slow," she admonishes.

"Jesus." I hasten my movements.

"We'll help the villagers safeguard themselves," she continues, all businesslike. "And then we'll take the toy and leave on the bus in the morning. No demons will come here with any luck, but instead, follow us."

I glance at the bathroom door and feel like Snuggles is watching us through the wood. I lift up the hem of my T-shirt and twist my torso to see the Enochian sigil I think we need for the protection spell.

"This one." I tap it. "If we paint it on the doors with our blood and say the words around that tattoo, it will contain the demonic entity inside the room and keep it out. It's like the one Wes used to keep Prue in the pentagram when Pestilence possessed her. We also need salt to make it foolproof, but maybe this will work enough if we paint it on all exits."

"The bathroom window too." She nods.

"And then we go and warn the village."

THE SOFT-PINK LIGHT of dawn touches the sleepy village as we walk toward Orlov's house. I keep one eye behind us while Leila focuses on the front. Danger might come from anywhere at this point. A rooster crows from somewhere, but its sound echoes, and I can't pinpoint the location.

Snow hasn't fallen overnight, but remnants of ice collect in random piles, and the path is muddy. Our breaths mist before our mouths. We squelch loudly. But I'm alert, awake, and ready.

We trudge quietly up the steps to Orlov's porch. I turn to survey the village street with my Colt in my hand, spelled bullets loaded, ready to fire at anything that moves. My wrist is wrapped with a hasty bandage, as is Leila's from a shallow cut we made for the containment sigils. Leila's fist lifts to knock on the door, but she pauses.

"Zeke," she whispers. "Look."

Before I follow her instructions, I check our surroundings one last time, and eye off some smoke curling from a chimney. Satisfied we're not in danger, I face her.

She points at newly painted flowers on the wooden door. "They weren't there before."

At first glance, the painted flowers are the same as all the others around the village, but this new lot on the door have familiar shapes and ligatures.

"Enochian Sigils." The language of the angels.

Her shrewd gaze hits mine, and she steps back to take a better look at the cabin's exterior. Freshly painted flowers hide more sigils along the walls and windows.

"And look." She points down at our feet where tall red flowers grow in pots along with other herbs and varieties. "Don't those flowers look familiar?"

"I've seen the red ones painted in the cabin. And these sunflower ones." I crouch and touch an empty pot. The soil is upturned, like something was freshly pulled out. "Looks like we weren't the only ones busy last night."

She thumps her fist on the door. I turn my attention back to the village paths—sweeping my gaze from cabin to bush, from pig stye to garden. My neck prickles like we're being watched, but it could be just remnants of my nerves from Snuggles turning up unexpectedly. Another shudder runs through me just as the door opens.

"Is true! You are the Vânătoare." Orlov's reverence spins me around.

The tall, robust man looks at Leila's Sinner uniform with wonder in his eyes. A military vest covers his knitted sweater. The pockets are filled with tinkling vials, bullets, and . . . is that a grenade painted with flowers? A floral wreath adorns his neck and an ammunition belt rests around his hips.

He is a man prepared for war, and he called Leila the Hunter.

"What the fuck is going on here?" I ask in Romanian.

Before he can reply, Leila says, "Your village is in danger, Orlov. This might sound weird . . . " She takes in his strange military attire. "Okay, maybe not so weird going by your clothes. But I'm afraid we've led demons to your village. We have to protect it."

Claudia calls from somewhere deep inside, "Shut the door. Sun is coming."

"Come. I explain." Orlov waves us inside, glances warily behind me at the road, and bolts the door once we're in. "Time around dawn and dusk are most vulnerable for strigoi attacks."

"What's going on?" Leila asks. "Strigoi?"

I holster my gun but keep my hand on the hilt. "He thinks you're a vampire hunter."

"Follow me. I explain as we walk," Orlov says. Instead of heading to the kitchen and main living area, he takes us toward the bathroom. "Strigoi are not just vampires like common perception. But evil spirits. Demon. We have been waiting for you, Vânătoare, for a very long time."

Leila glances warily at me, and I frown.

A trap door on the bathroom floor opens. Matei pokes up his head, grinning. He also wears a floral and herbal wreath around his neck. The smell of some kind of familiar garlicky, smokey, floral bouquet wafts up from the basement.

"We have been much working for long," Matei says, his voice cracking with excitement.

"Matei," Orlov chides. "Let us get down."

Matei flattens his lips, glances shyly at Leila, then disappears into the basement.

"After you, Vânătoare." Orlov gestures for Leila to go first.

"Wait a darn minute." I hold Leila back. "Orlov, just exactly who do you think Leila is?"

"She is the one Helwing told our ancestors would come. A holy woman hunter who will harness the weapons he created."

"Weapons?" Leila's eyebrow arches.

"Yes." He nods enthusiastically. "We have much to show you."

Leila and I share a look, both of us weighing whether to trust this new information.

"They have Enochian sigils on their doors," I point out. "It's too much of a coincidence."

"Okay," Leila says. "I'm going down."

Thirty-Three

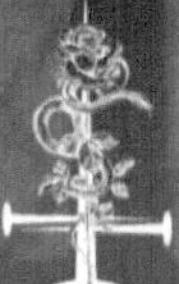

The basement is some kind of doomsday bunker spanning the width beneath the entire cabin. I stand in the center of it and turn slowly, my jaw dropping as I take in my surroundings. Wooden support posts covered with nails and herb bouquets hold up the ceiling. The walls are painted with Enochian sigils between botanical illustrations. Shelves with old musty books to my right. Ammunitions and workbenches to my left. Laboratory. Antiques.

Claudia works at another table with Paula, tying wreaths and sewing bouquets between patches of white gauze. Another picture of the Pope hangs over a potbelly stove where a cauldron bubbles away. That's where the familiar smokey aroma comes from.

"What is this place?" I ask as Zeke stands behind me.

Orlov shuts the trapdoor and climbs down to meet us, huffing from his exertion. The women stop their preparations and look at us. Matei already stares from his ammunition workbench.

"Our village and family have been keepers of Helwing's story for generations." Orlov points to a shelf of old books and antiques. "He left much information for defeating the strigoi when one day it would come to visit us again."

I ask, "Is the gun here, in this village?"

"No. But something else is." He walks to an old wooden chest beside the stove and unlocks the five padlocks holding chains. More sigils are carved into the glossy surface. My finger comes away sticky when I touch it. *Curious.* Orlov talks as he unlocks. "Along with being an expert in hunting monsters, Helwing was also a Pastor and botanist. He understood much of the supernatural properties of certain plants. We have kept the recipes safe within these walls. Have learned, practiced, and always told our children the stories. We had thought, perhaps, our ancestors were not right in the head when nothing came to us for years. No strigoi. No holy hunter. But . . . ah, yes. Here."

The last chain falls away, and he opens the chest with a creak. Inside, a small tinder box is wrapped in gauze. He glances at me as he unwraps it, revealing a surface featuring the same red cross that's on my Sinner uniform. The rest of the tinderbox is painted with strange leaves and flowers I've never seen before.

"The Hildegard Sisterhood logo." I frown and touch it. "This is where I come from."

"Yes." Orlov rocks proudly on his feet. "Helwing's wife was called Dorothea Hildegard before she married him."

"And the plant?" I point to the flowers.

Claudia comes forward. "Is called *Helwinga*. When

prepared right, it can become protection against unnatural fire."

My gaze snaps to Zeke. "A flame retardant?"

His brows lift, impressed.

"Open it." Orlov hands me the tiny box. "Please."

I lift the lid. Inside, a lone tarnished bullet sits on a threadbare pillow. A Romanian word is engraved onto the metal surface. It smells funny. Old. I show the cartridge to Zeke, and he translates for me.

"It says *Forgiveness*."

"The prophecy." I pull out my cell phone and scroll through pictures until I find one of Thea's translations of Mary's gospel.

That which was the tool of the greatest sin in passion shall be forged by saintly fire into a chamber of forgiveness against the greatest of sinners.

A chamber is the part of the gun where the bullet cartridge is loaded. Thea always warned us the translations were a little wonky. Some words are so ancient that today we have multiple variations of them. A chamber *for* forgiveness could mean the chamber where this bullet labeled *Forgiveness* is placed. I slide to the next prophecy picture on my phone.

"And I saw a rider, with a mouth of flames and a heart full of vengeance, riding forth upon a black

steed. His name was War, and he sought to spread
his flames and burn all in his path."
But then a voice spoke to me, saying, "Do not be
afraid. For like all who repent, he who rides upon
the black steed shall be forgiven, for he shall take
unto himself the helmet and bridle of passion."

"This bullet is for Asmodeus." I show Zeke. "Orlov, does this bullet have a special purpose?"

"Yes. The holy gun was forged here and made from the helmet you seek. Bullets were made from a bridle found with the helmet. They must be used together to stop the strigoi Dracula. Only one is left, but only one is needed."

"Orlov," I ask, looking up at him. "Who killed Dracula? Helwing or Dorothea?"

He grins. Claudia grins. Paula and Matei grin. They point to an ancient, leather-bound journal on the bookshelf. A faded red cross is painted on the cover.

Claudia says, "No one believed a woman to be so strong in those days, but we have the true story here . . . in her own words."

"And all this"—I point to the herbs and weapons—"is based on what Dorothea wrote?"

Paula rushes over to collect the book and hands it to me. "She wrote much. Including how to make more bullets." She frowns. "Not so magical as the one you have, but they will kill demons."

"We have made you many demon-killing bullets." Matei proudly swipes his hand over the ammunition table where a reloading machine sits, along with herbs, engraved casings, and gunpowder.

I look back at the journal. It's all in Romanian, but the diagrams tell the story of a monster hunter of a demon with black eyes and wings and a tail. It looks eerily like the demonic form Asmodeus took at the bar. I turn a few pages and find more demons. More names. More protections and wards. And finally, I find a diagram of the gun. Time slows as I study every detail. It looks similar to Zeke's long-barreled Colt Lightnings. They're double-action. This might be single. I'll have to cock the hammer with each bullet I fire. Six chambers. The holy nails of the cross stick out of the barrel at odd angles like thorns. No. I squint, looking harder. I think the nails contain the barrel, maybe even penetrate.

I can't understand the inscription, but going by some other small diagrams outlining a process, I think the gun barrel and chamber was forged from the helmet. The spiky nails on top are the nails that Constantine used as decorative validating proof of this divinity.

"That's it," I breathe reverently. It's the relic we're after. This journal had the information the entire time. We might have been prepared for Lilith if something like this existed at the Sisterhood. "I can't believe Dorothea isn't mentioned in the Sisterhood archives. I've never heard of her."

"As I say, we are the secret keepers of this story." Orlov bows his head. "And, when you read her journal, you will see she argued much about her Catholic faith with her Lutheran husband. She stopped Dracula but was mortally wounded. They fought before she left on her hunt. Distraught, Helwing buried his wife in the church crypt, along with her gun. But he returned here with her teachings and the remaining bullet. He instructed our ancestors to hang the picture of the Pope and said one day, one like his wife would come for her things. After that, he wanted nothing to do with this story."

Time to let this family know everything. "Orlov, the demon prince Asmodeus is hunting us. He is very powerful and dangerous. He knows we're after a weapon that will kill him. He looks like this"—I find the page and tap the demonic diagram—"and I don't think he's far behind us."

"We think a possessed toy might be leading them here." Zeke scratches his head. "I know that sounds strange, but for years it haunted Leila with fires as a child. It somehow turned up at our cabin here, even though we're both certain we left it behind."

"Mmhm." Claudia's eyes flash. "Then we must destroy it."

She gives instructions in Romanian to her children, and they rush to gather supplies from around the room.

"Also," I add quickly, "Asmodeus might have learned about this village from the same man we learned it from. His name was Ludovic. Do you know of him?"

"Ludovic." Orlov spits on the floor. "He did come here once, yes. He came with many men who plundered and defaced the old temple in the mountain. When he found no helmet, he returned to us and threatened to burn us to the ground." He shakes his head. "Since it had been so long for us to keep this Helwing story, many here do not believe it to be true. Even we had lost faith and allowed our flowers of protection to fade and peel on the walls and windows. One of our people told Ludovic about the church and the ghost who shoots the gun."

"He could be there now." I frown. "Did Ludovic mention that to you, Zeke?"

"No." He tapped his chin. "Maybe he didn't believe it."

"He did say he would return here." Claudia pointed out. "He said he would bring more men and machines. They would look in the lake."

"Maybe Asmodeus won't come here," I tell Zeke hopefully.

"Even if he doesn't, Snuggles still turned up. We're not safe here. No one is."

I swallow. "You're right."

The wooden floorboards above us creak. I still. Halt my breathing. Listen hard. Another creak. *Footsteps or the wood expanding and contracting?*

"Someone is here?" Orlov's eyes widen in disbelief. "But we protected the house."

"Unless you used blood to paint the sigils, the protection might not work."

I'm surprised they didn't know this, but now worry about how much of their story is authentic. Whatever the case, it's the only lead we have. We'll have to see it through. I put the special bullet in my pocket and nod at the ammunition they've been making. "Will they work in normal guns or just the relic?"

Depending on the caliber, demon-killing bullets would come in handy now.

"They will only kill demons in the venerated Helwing gun."

Shit. I scrub my face, thinking of my options.

"I have five spelled bullets in my Smiths," I tell Zeke.

"I've got a few." His jaw works as he taps his pistols and

jingles his pockets. He crosses the floor and inspects one of the casings the family has been working on. "Similar markings. If used in a normal gun, they might do the same thing as mine—exorcise the demonic entity but kill the host."

More creaking overhead disrupts sand and dust stuck between the floorboards.

"Sounds like they're in the kitchen." Orlov's voice trembles.

"Hurry." Claudia gestures for us to come to her. "We will give you what we have made for your journey."

"We'll stay and fight," I insist. We can't leave them here.

"No." She hands me vials of something liquid to put in my backpack. "This is our destiny. It is what we have trained for all our life."

But their protection sigils didn't work.

Zeke and I are jostled, pulled this way and that, instructed, and lectured about the weapons. Claudia tells me about the flame retardant vials before spraying me all over with the same concoction. It's made of the same smokey origin I can't quite put my finger on. Paula sprays Zeke. Matei fills our bags with bullets until we can barely carry the weight. Orlov collects weapons for his family—shotguns, crossbows, and homemade grenades. Nails stick out of all of them. *Jesus Christ*. They mean business.

"Here." Claudia tugs me back to face her and waggles a white lumpy gauze square in my face. It smells funny too. "This will prockect *you* from bullets."

She yanks my top down and unceremoniously shoves it into my bra. With all that sticky, smokey gunk dripping down me, it actually stays in place. Paula shoves a similar sewn patch down Zeke's shirt.

"Whoa." He laughs nervously, taking over. "I got it."

"Must stay on your skin," she warns him.

"Got it."

He meets my eyes. Something passes between us. A shared warning. I can't let these people die from the danger I've brought to their doorstep. Only the bullet in my pocket and the Helwing gun are in Mary's prophecy. All this other stuff might not work at all. And if it doesn't, these innocent people will be lambs to the slaughter.

Zeke and I barely escaped with our lives.

"Orlov." Zeke strides to the ladder leading up to the bathroom. He points at the closed trapdoor. "When Leila and I go up, I want you to paint your protection sigil on that surface with your blood. Doesn't have to be big."

He lifts the hem of his hoodie and shirt to reveal the tattoos on his sculpted torso. He points to one. "It should look like this."

Orlov pulls spectacles from his pocket, puts them on, and leans close to Zeke's abdomen to study it. "Is like ours."

"Do you say these words?" He taps at the script on his tattoo.

"Yes."

"So it's just the blood." He drops his shirt. "Get that part right and your spell will work."

I catch Paula pout as Zeke covers his abs, and her mother nudges her with a frown. I smile and turn to watch Zeke show Orlov how to paint the sigil correctly. As pride expands in my chest, I know exactly how Paula feels. Zeke's ruggedly handsome, charming, and brave. He's a catch. And he's mine.

"You ready, wildcat?"

Zeke releases one of his pistols and starts climbing the ladder. I unsheathe my spelled katana and am right behind him. But as he opens the trapdoor, the rest of the family start climbing behind me.

"No," I hiss, waving them down. "You guys stay here."

They all scowl at me and hold their ground, even the teenagers.

"Oh fuck," Zeke mumbles as his head breaches the trapdoor.

"What?"

"Snuggles."

"You're fucking kidding me?"

He glances down at me, shaking his head.

"Fuck. Go." I poke him in the ass. "Hurry."

My heavy backpack straps dig into my shoulders as I climb after Zeke. When I lever myself up and onto the bathroom floor, Zeke has his gun pointed at Snuggles. The creepy toy still smells faintly of smoke and stares at us from the doorway.

My heart clenches. "I used to cuddle him in my sleep. He doesn't *feel* evil."

Wouldn't I know with my special *sight*? But then again, I see things. My feelings are usually based on what I see. Even with Sister Agnes, I couldn't explain how I knew she wasn't possessed. Father Angelotti has the supernatural ability to sense evil in people. It's what made him a highly sought-after exorcist.

"He doesn't look possessed." I shake my head, dumb-founded.

"Because he is not." Claudia's voice has me spinning to find her climbing out of the hatch.

"I said to stay down," I growl.

She shakes her head stubbornly. The rest of her family joins her, squeezing into the small space. *Goddammit.* They're brave. I'll give them that. Brave or reckless.

"Look." Claudia hesitantly steps toward Snuggles, looks warily at Zeke, and then picks up the floppy stuffed bear. She shows me the pads of the paws. They're shaped like . . .

"Flowers," she says, holding the toy to her nose and inhaling deeply. "Yes. I smell Helwinga. Inside is spiritual protection."

"What?" Zeke takes the toy from her and turns it over in his hands, scowling at the rough stitching and stuffing poking out. "I sewed this damn thing up so many times and never thought to look inside."

"But it just showed up," I point out. "It followed us."

"It followed *you*." Claudia tugs Snuggles from Zeke's grip with a motherly scowl and then hands him to me. "Someone who loved you very much made this charm to keep you safe."

"We heard footsteps."

"Could be the footsteps of your ancestors, bringing your protection back to you."

Tears burn my eyes. I look upon Snuggles in a new light—how I used to—with all the innocence and love a child has for something her biological parents left. I was abandoned with Snuggles on a church doorstep as a baby. I'd always hoped he was from my birth parents. I'd always prayed he was a sign that they loved me and never wanted to give me up. "Is it possible Snuggles kept me *safe* from the fires?"

"I thought he was a beacon for Flauros." Zeke looks heartbroken. "I thought taking it and leaving you was the right thing to do." His eyes dart from side to side as he resifts the sands of his past. "My sister died because she didn't have it. But it kept you *safe*. I was so wrong."

"We don't know that for sure. There were no fires when I joined the Sisterhood."

"Like Wes said, maybe they'd lost the strength by then."

"Zeke." I reach for him, but he shakes his head. The self-doubt in his eyes is harrowing, and when he meets my gaze, I see how ashamed he is. "Stop. Stop that right now. You are *not* to blame."

He scrubs his face and looks away.

"I mean it, Zeke."

Outside, a bell rings erratically.

"The village alarm," Orlov gasps. His usual jovial face turns hard and menacing as he pumps his shotgun.

Panicked shouts on the street hit us first, and then a blood-curdling scream.

"You must go to the church," Claudia says hurriedly. "Take the toy with you."

"I have no room in the pack." I shake my head. And I need my hands for fighting.

"We will hold them off." Orlov's big boots thunder across the wooden floor as he crosses to the front door.

"Matei," Claudia calls him over. "Give Vânătoare the map. I will tie the toy charm to her."

The teen's eyes are saucers as he jogs to the kitchen, yanks open a drawer, and pulls out a paper map. Suddenly I'm surrounded again by a bustling Romanian family barking orders and instructions. Claudia secures Snuggles to my backpack with string. Matei rambles about how to get to the church. Paula shoves the keys to their truck into my palm. Zeke. Where is Zeke?

Outside, gunshots ring out in quick succession. My heart leaps into my throat. Orlov is still by the door. With a map in one hand and keys in the other, I run to meet Orlov. Outside, along the muddy path, Zeke steadily walks away—a pistol in each hand, firing ahead at villagers who have black spider veins webbing out from their eyes.

"They're newly infected."

Thirty-Four

Zeke

I focus on the feel of reckoning in my palms, the twitch of my trigger fingers, and the *bang* of gunpowder igniting. My pistols recoil simultaneously. Bullets slam into the heads of two infected. The double action reloads like lightning.

We don't have time to worry about innocents. We can't both save these people and get to the church. I might have royally fucked up my life and Leila's, but I can do this. I can shoot. I can clear a path.

My pistols twirl in my trigger fingers as I retarget to find two new infecteds running from different directions. I shoot one, twist and drop to a knee. Shoot the other.

"Zeke, you bastard!" Leila is by my side, her left arm wide and pointing her Smith & Wesson, her katana twirling in her right. I tense, expecting her to berate me for shooting these people but she fires her gun, putting a bullet in another infected. "You could have waited."

"You worried I'll take all the glory?" I smirk.

"Don't be cocky."

"But I am."

"You still could have waited."

A snarl behind me. Leila lifts her gun and shoots but then lets out a curse word. My body reacts before my mind catches up. I spin as an infected woman in a terry-toweling bathrobe leaps at us. I fire, hitting her between the eyes. She falls inches from our feet, splashing mud.

I nudge Leila. "I wouldn't be your huckleberry if I waited."

"For the last fucking time, you're not Doc Holliday."

I shrug. "You don't know that."

"And here I was thinking you were all wounded over Snuggles."

A slice of self-loathing flashes through me, but I shake it off. "We don't have time to bleed."

More villagers appear down the path. Their eyes are all crazy and dark as they stumble toward us like zombies.

"Leila," I mumble with a bone-chilling realization. "I can see the black web coming from their eyes."

"You can?"

I nod gravely. "With the infected nuns and at the poker game, I didn't see. I knew they were infected because you told me they attacked. I'm not supposed to see."

"What do you mean?" she breathes, eyes wide.

Wes said that as long as Leila and I are together, the cracks on the seals holding the gates of hell will remain small. If we fight or are enemies, the cracks grow bigger. But I haven't told her that part of the prophecy—how us entering a relationship is supposed to stop any of that from happening. Now's not the time. Maybe I see this because half of our teams still aren't quite working together yet. Maybe with each passing day, the cracks still grow until we all work in harmony. I reload my pistol chambers.

"Zeke? What do you mean by that?" Leila repeats.

"I just meant that I thought you five Sinners were the only ones with the supernatural sight." The white lie tastes bitter on my tongue.

"Whatever the case," she says, aiming her gun at an infected family shuffling closer. "They're infected with the war disease, but I don't see Asmodeus. He must have popped in and infected everyone to slow us down."

"We hope."

Orlov walks up to us and fires his shotgun at the infected. I grimace as a body goes down.

"You must get to the truck," he says, pumping, reloading, and releasing a spent shell. "Take that path behind our house. The truck is the blue one with one brown wheel. *Go now.* We will hold them off."

"But—" Leila's protest is cut off by Orlov.

"This is our destiny, Vânătoare. Do not take it from us."

I glance over my shoulder and see his family standing on his porch, armed to the teeth with guns, crossbows, and grenades. Claudia has just finished pouring salt around their house. With the correct sigils, they'll be safe inside if they can't control or contain the infected. The war disease eventually wears off, but it could take weeks without Thea's healing relic.

We don't have time for this. Not if Asmodeus is already at the church.

"Let's go." I grab Leila by the arm and drag her down the

path Orlov pointed out. Pigs oink. Goats bleat. Chickens cluck. But no demons as we run. No Flauros. No Asmodeus.

I don't like the knot of dread forming in my gut. As we get to the truck, I put my guns away and hold my palm out to Leila. She slams a set of keys into my hand with a grim look. I see my own panic reflected in her eyes. The sadness.

"We can't stay." I open the driver's door and get in.

She knows I'm right because as I start the engine, she's already in the passenger seat, peeling off her pack.

With a tight jaw, she unfolds the map. "Drive."

I plant my foot on the gas. "Don't look back, kitty cat."

Her fingers crumple the map, but her eyes stay focused ahead. As we hurtle down the beaten track, splashing mud, I glimpse flames in the rearview mirror. Matei's cracking war cry slices through the morning air.

Don't look back.

AN HOUR LATER, we're still on the same bumpy dirt road. The weather is warmer. The snow is gone. The countryside is green.

"I'm hungry." Leila's first words are strained.

"Check in the back." I keep my eyes on the road, my hands on the wheel.

She unclips her seatbelt, leans over the back of the bench seat, and searches the narrow cavity behind us. I'm sure I saw some bags left there when we got in the cab.

My bravado evaporated about a half-mile back. Since then,

in the quiet bumpy cabin, I've been re-enacting our escape. Orlov and his family have to be okay. I'm almost certain Asmodeus wasn't there, and if he wasn't, then Flauros probably wasn't. The more I think about it, the more I'm certain Asmodeus infected the villagers to slow us down. Or maybe they were actually demons. *Christ*, I don't know. All I can do is go with my gut.

I glance at Snuggles laying on his side beside me in the middle of the bench seat. The fluffy maniac is still tied to Leila's backpack, staring back at me with his single unblinking button eye.

"You really here to help?" I raise an eyebrow at him, daring him to speak. When no answer comes, I return my gaze to the dirt road and shake my head in disbelief, mumbling under my breath, "A fucking teddy bear protector. All these years I thought it was that red bracelet."

"Maybe it was both." Leila slides back to face the front with a scowl on her face. "No food."

The passenger window is open a crack, shooting air into her shiny dark hair. A little tuft keeps catching and lifting, sending snatches of her fruity shampoo into the air. It's enough of a hit to my soul that my endorphins flare. I feel slightly better.

"Check our packs," I suggest. I think I had some protein bars in mine.

She sighs dramatically and starts rifling through our bags. I hate seeing the defeat in her eyes.

"They'll be okay, wildcat."

"How can you be sure?"

"Faith."

She scoffs.

"I'm serious. They know the right way to cast the spells now. I saw Claudia running salt around the house. She's badass."

"She is . . . but the spell didn't work for Snuggles."

My jaw clicks shut. We thought the blood was the missing factor in why their wards didn't work. But failed to realize ours didn't contain Snuggles either. "Maybe he truly is good. I mean, that spell was for demonic entities."

"You're right." She finds a protein bar, unwraps it, and takes a bite before handing it to me.

I bite straight from her offered hand. "Thanks."

Another few minutes of silence pass as we eat. The dirt road turns to asphalt. Houses and farms dot the countryside as we pass. Ahead in the distance, a winding road leads up the hill to where Helwing's church is supposed to sit.

As I turn onto the road, Leila frowns. "I missed."

"What?"

"The infected back at the village. I missed."

I shrug. "It happens. Don't worry about it."

"I don't think you understand." She taps her pocket. "I have one bullet. If I get this relic against all odds, manage to load the bullet into the chamber, and fire—I have one chance. I can't miss."

My hands tighten on the steering wheel. "You'll be fine. Focus on your breathing. Take the time to line up your target. Keep your stance stable and your eyes on the prize, even after you squeeze the trigger."

"Follow through." She nods thoughtfully. "I think that's where I go wrong."

I glance at her. "I watched you run one day at the abbey. You attacked that path like it was just another obstacle in your way, while Mercy ran as though something chased her. You've always been able to do anything you set your mind to. I believe in you."

She scoffs quietly.

Finally, as we turn onto that road and climb the steep incline, Leila mumbles, "I don't know how much longer of this life I can take."

"Any time you want out, you let me know." I glance at her. "I'll go to a deserted island with you. I'll go anywhere."

She smiles at me with sad eyes. "I love you."

"I love you t—" Another car slams into us, rocking us to the side.

MY BODY IS a bag of pain as I hang upside down in the truck, the seatbelt cutting into my thighs.

Leila! I look her way and my heart leaps into my throat. Her body is half outside the broken passenger window, motionless on the ground.

"Leila!" I roar, adrenaline pumping into my system. She had taken her seatbelt off to search for food. She never put it back on. Fuck me. "Babe!"

I hate the sound of raw panic in my voice. I don't want to feel fear. Don't want to acknowledge what might be happening. But she doesn't move. *She doesn't move!* What if the half of her outside the cabin, the half I can't see is—I squeeze my eyes shut and take a deep breath. Then I unlatch the belt securing me to the seat. I fall and bump my head. Heat sears my chest and I hiss. Weird reaction to hitting my head.

I try to wiggle myself free, but I'm half-folded and cramped in the crushed cabin space. My body is too big to maneuver out of the busted driver's window.

Leila's moan is the sweetest sound I know.

"Babe," I call.

She tries to push up but hits her spine on the window frame and flops down. "What the fuck?"

"We had an accident." I bend my knee, but I'm stuck. "Another car hit us."

"Zeke?" She gasps and cranes her neck to peer into the cabin at me. "Are you hurt?"

I take a moment to process the aches and pains in my body. It's not so bad. The worst is the burning at my chest. "Unless I'm having one of those shock moments where I don't feel my amputated leg or something, I think I'm good. You?"

She wiggles her body, testing it. "I think I'm good too."

I try again to twist my body to get out but hit the other side of my head on the dashboard. Fire flares at my chest again. *Fuck.* I slap the burning spot.

"What's wrong?" she asks.

"It burns there every time I hit myself."

I reach in and pull out the sewn, lumpy gauze square Paula shoved beneath my shirt. "I think this saved our lives."

Leila tugs hers out. "Mine is hot too. But I thought it was protection from bullets."

"I guess it protected us from high impact." I twist to meet her eyes. "You know what this means?"

"They'll be okay."

Relief courses through me. Thank fuck for that. Outside the truck, something sizzles behind Leila. The back of my neck prickles and my gaze snaps to the road behind her—Biker boots.

"Hello, china doll."

Leila looks outside. But she's too late. She's dragged from the cabin before my eyes, and I can do nothing about it. I'm stuck.

Flauros drags me from the cab by my hair. I drop the protection square when my arm scrapes broken glass in the window frame. Tiny white-hot pokers stab my scalp. I feel like it will rip off from the brute force of his pull versus my weight.

But it won't.

I'm fucking made of stone. I've honed this body into a weapon, including my neck and head. When I trained with the Shaolin Monks, I had to walk for hours daily with a heavy laundry basket on my head. I didn't break then, and I won't break now.

The demon's true leopard-like visage flickers over the body he occupies. I don't know if he chose Puck's body because he thought it would intimidate me, but when I look at him, I only remember how Zeke kicked this psychopath's ass.

I grind my teeth, reach up and take hold of the hands that grip me. I latch on like a vice, scissor-kick my legs, and twist his arms with the force of my body. Breaking free, I roll to my feet like a cat with nine lives and immediately flow into a Kung Fu *ready* stance.

Flauros can't do much but drip flames from his glaring eyes. He's not really here in this realm. He's just a spirit occupying a human vessel. Here, on the asphalt, nothing can catch fire. Not even me with my sticky, Helwinga-covered body. Nor the wrecked car he must have been driving as it hit our truck.

Interesting. Either Asmodeus can't teleport others with him, or Flauros stole a car just to crash into us like a petulant child playing with toys. The demon huffs smoke as he watches me circle him.

"Clever little doll," he hisses, tracking me with his eyes. "But not clever enough."

"For what?"

"For figuring out why I'm here."

"Oh, I know that already." I scoff as if it's obvious.

He returns a smug, feline smile and I laugh. My reaction makes him hesitate.

"That's right," I tease. "I know who really pulls your strings, and it's not him."

Whistling to my right turns my focus to where Asmodeus casually strolls up a winding path on the boulder-littered hill. I follow the direction of the path up and see a church steeple over the top of the hill. The arrogant demon could teleport himself up there if he wanted. He wants to rub salt in my wounds.

"I'll bet this accident was your idea, huh?"

Flauros snarls.

"I'll bet you have something else up your sleeve, too. And

I'll bet your buddy up there has no idea what it is. And I'll bet you just can't wait to get rid of him."

The flicker of acknowledgment in the demon's eyes makes it all start to make sense. Lilith has never cared for the so-called individual horseman of the apocalypse. The real ones, she somehow locked up in hell. Asmodeus said it himself at the bar. Lilith only cares about making the cracks bigger. But she's too late for me and Zeke.

Scraping behind me indicates Zeke is on his way out of the car. Our road must curve around the hill and enter the parking lot from behind, but the fastest way to the church is on foot—up that steep incline. Good thing I love running marathons. I can take that distance, barely breaking a sweat.

My gaze bounces between Flauros and Asmodeus, sizing up my chances, then I bolt.

Grunting, I pump effort into my legs and use my hard-earned strength. Running has always been something I've loved. It's just me and the terrain, an easy target. Flauros will either chase me, or he'll stay and fight Zeke. Either way, I can't let Asmodeus get a head start. Zeke can handle himself with this shell of a demon.

I need to get to that crypt first. Running, I close the gap between Asmodeus and myself. It gets to a point where I don't think he hears me coming. We're almost at the top, and I still have energy to spare. For a split second, I even consider spear-tackling him to the ground. But then he flickers out of existence.

I stumble to a stop at the top of the path and survey my surroundings. Cool air brushes past me, lifting my hair. Glorious green grass and beautiful spiky red flowers sway. Red

Amaranth—the same flower Claudia used to make the protection pouches. The old stone church looms ahead, fifty feet away. It's about the size of the one back home. Enough for about a hundred people inside. The roof has holes in it. Gargoyles with broken noses loom over us from the eaves. A sinister vibe lives in the shadows, but the tiny flowers painted on the gravestones beside the church are just like the ones in the village.

This is definitely the Helwing church.

Dorothea was buried in a crypt. *Heavy breathing behind me.* I reach for my gun, but it's not there. I also left my katana in the truck. Shit. My only other weapon is a blessed dagger strapped to my ankle. I spin and duck, ready to release it, but stop when I see it's only Zeke. Alone.

"Where is Flauros?"

"I saw him," he huffs, wheezing. "His fiery eyes were there instead of Puck's."

He said before that he witnessed the infection manifest as black webbing spreading from their eyes. Now he's seen Flauros's true face. I frown, disconcerted. There must be discord between the teams at home, unless . . .

"Did Flauros say something to you?"

A flash of guilt hits his eyes, and he shakes his head. "Nothing I can't handle."

Fuck. I don't have time to deal with this now.

"But where is he?"

He searches behind him, down the hill, and points. "There."

For some reason, Flauros also takes his time walking up the path. Why are they so confident?

A sharp, whistled tune catches on the wind. Asmodeus is in the graveyard, kicking over headstones, having the time of his life.

The crypt isn't there, dickhead. It's in the church.

"Did you know," Asmodeus shouts at me, "that he's been lying to you from the start?"

I glance over my shoulder, wondering who he's talking about. I feel sick when my eyes land on Zeke's pale face. That guilt flashes again in his eyes.

Not now.

I start walking toward the church, refusing to acknowledge Asmodeus's words. One purpose fills my brain. *Get the gun.* But Asmodeus teleports to block me. He slides his hands into his suit pockets and looks down his nose at me with black eyes. His slicked black hair barely moves in the breeze. A slow smile curves up his handsome face.

"Did you know?" he repeats.

"You'll have to be more specific." I sidestep.

He blocks. "Oh, darling. That can be arranged."

I bite the inside of my cheek to control my temper. Letting it out now will only cause trouble. Asmodeus gestures at Flauros. The fire demon tosses something Asmodeus plucks out of the air with finesse. When he turns it to his face and stares, I realize he's holding Zeke's phone.

"Do I need to embarrass you with the proof, Gunslinger?" Asmodeus squints as he taps the screen. His forked tongue pokes from his lip as he concentrates on making the phone bend to his will. "I must admit, these little shiny bricks are clever. Just need to remember how to get to the—oh yes. There it is."

"Leila, it's not what you think." Zeke stalks toward me in my periphery. He should be shooting these demons between the eyes, but he's looking at me with barely veiled fear.

His expression tips me over the edge of paranoia. "What's he talking about, Zeke?"

He tries to answer, but Flauros covers Zeke's mouth with his big, meaty paw.

"Aw, come on." Asmodeus scowls at Flauros. "Let the man speak."

Flauros resists complying. Asmodeus's black eyes narrow to slits. Tension thickens the atmosphere. I was right. Flauros is under Lilith's orders. Asmodeus senses something off but impatiently shows me the cell phone.

"He's lying about why he's with you. You see, the prophecy not only needs Sinners to *work* with Saints, but for members of each team to fall in love. Well, that's the inference your friends have made. See for yourself."

My gaze dips to the text message conversation between Wes and Zeke. It's dated from last night . . . before we made love. Every word I read stabs a knife into my heart and then repeats it in my back.

Wes asks:

> Has everything gone according to plan? Have you kissed and made up? Give me the details.

> Sorry, mate. Thea stole my phone. I don't need details. But if the cracks are bigger, we need to know. It's imperative you take advantage of this situation with Leila.

"Gotta love that word choice." Asmodeus points to the

message. "*Situation*. They think you're a *situation* that needs to be taken advantage of."

I'm cold. Numb. My brain isn't working. Nothing flows but Asmodeus's words. Is it true? I'm right about Lilith and Flauros . . . was I right about Zeke abandoning me because he was annoyed to have a little girl hanging off his every word? Am I a situation to be taken advantage of? Or is this all wrong?

"Is this fake?"

"Oh, it's not fake. Believe me." Asmodeus is smug as he tosses the phone to Zeke.

Flauros lets go. Zeke catches the phone but doesn't look at it. His hazel eyes plead with me. Guilty.

"Zeke?" I whisper.

Some distant part of me shouts a warning. This is Asmodeus we're talking about. The demon of lust and gambling and games. This is a sick joke. He's playing with me. I should run—get into the church. Find the crypt entrance. Kill the son of a bitch.

But when Zeke's lips move, and all I hear is his confession through my warbled hearing, I can't move.

"It's true," he says. "The prophecy says it's more than our teams working together. We're fated to be together. In love."

"You lied to me."

He reaches out, but I step back, shaking my head. *He lied.*

Loud thunder cracks, splitting the sky. But there are no clouds over us. Asmodeus grins as he looks behind me. It wasn't thunder but a widening crack in the gates of hell.

Flauros is gone. Puck is Puck again, blinking at us with confusion. But a red line has sliced straight down the center of his face. Blood seeps out. The line widens to reveal his internal musculature and bone. Flauros crawls out of Puck's splitting body like a monster being born.

The fully manifested Flauros eyes me like I'm dinner.

Zeke stares at me with a look that installs fear into my soul. Not because he's gloating or he hates me or anything else. But because I see sacrifice. I see love. He opens his mouth but then shuts it. No words. He just launches at the demon with all his might, tackles him around the midsection, and keeps pushing until they stumble back to the hill's edge.

"Zeke!" I scream as they disappear over the side.

I run after him, barely stopping in time to avoid toppling too. My worst nightmare unfolds. Zeke and Flauros are locked together as they roll down the steep decline, hitting boulders and sharp rocks like rag dolls. Little fires catch and smolder. A leopard's tail whips about. Within moments they come to a rest on the road between the two wreckages, unmoving. Zeke's leg is twisted at an odd angle. My eyes blur. My throat clogs. He must have left the protection patch behind as well.

"What a shame," Asmodeus croons behind me. Then adds jauntily, "Oh well."

I spin and snarl at him. "You think you've won, but you've been played. Lilith had that demon doing her bidding for years while you were imprisoned. She planted him in your entourage to manipulate you. She's been moving you around like a pawn in her own private game of chess. You can't even see that you're a puppet. *Weak.*" I spit on the grass. "You've been so caught up in your macho revenge ploy that you've failed to see the worst truth of all."

His intelligent eyes blaze with fury. Despite my words, he's not weak. He knows it. But he can't resist asking, "And what's that?"

"She probably orchestrated your imprisonment in the first place. How else did she know about Tobit?"

We all know the story. It was in the Bible. But I knew something had to be off for Asmodeus to look so confused, dazed, and suspicious at that line. A flicker of recognition in his eyes means I'm right. He's only now putting the puzzle pieces together.

I cackle like a madwoman and continue taunting him. I don't care. He can rip out my heart for all I care. It's dead now, anyway.

"You were her puppet no matter what you chose to do when you escaped prison—hell, you only escaped because it was part of her plan." I wield the special bullet from my pocket like a shield. "This is the only bullet left in the world that will work with that gun to stop you. You could get to the relic before me, but it won't matter. It's worthless without this bullet. Lilith knew our chances were slim. She used you to grow the divide between Zeke and me. To grow the cracks. You're a *pawn*."

His eyes darken. I feel the shadows drawing nearer. But still, he doesn't speak.

"So long as Flauros is in this realm," I snarl contemptuously, "fully manifested like you, your power is threatened. Who knows how strong he's grown while you've been stuck in a rock."

Asmodeus's upper lip curls. I see my death in his eyes. But it's not my death he envisions. Great demonic wings tear from his back. Horns sprout from his head. Muscles swell in his

Italian suit, ripping the seams with their girth. He takes to the sky, breathing fire from his mouth like a dragon. He swoops over the hill's edge, sights his prey, and dives.

Zeke.

I run down the path to Zeke. My clumsy boots slip. I almost lose my balance but steady myself with my hands, grazing my palms. I keep going, but sobs wrack my chest. My body won't work in my grief. I'm taking too long. But I try to keep Zeke's body in my line of sight. Even if he's dead, I won't let Asmodeus ruin him. Fuck my stupid temper. Zeke loved it. He loved when I let it out. Called me his wildcat. But now it's going to ruin everything.

I'll never hear another stupid reference about being Doc Holliday. I'll never hear his voice.

My vision blurs with each stumble. Flames burst at the base of the hill, but I'm too teary to see straight. I wipe my eyes and skid to a screaming stop on the road. Asmodeus stands over Flauros like a god of vengeance, breathing fire over the impudent feline demon. I wince and shield my face from the scorching heat. When Flauros tries to escape, Asmodeus effortlessly pins him to the ground with his taloned hands, grinning at his prey's useless thrashing.

"Leila." Zeke's croaky voice is the hand of God turning my head.

A sob bursts from my chest when I see him sitting against the truck's crushed cabin. While I was too teary to see, he must have crawled toward the truck, away from the dueling demons. His bloody hands grope for his guns, but his leg still sticks out awkwardly. I go to my man, fall to my knees, and take his face between my hands.

"You bastard."

"I prefer Huck."

I laugh. Cry. Kiss him as my heart bursts from my chest. His palm smooths up my spine to pull me closer. When we break, I press my forehead to his.

"You just ran." My voice is tight. "You pushed him over the edge without a word. I thought . . ." That sacrificial look in his eyes had broken my heart.

He rubs my back soothingly. "I wanted to promise you I'll be back, and that I love you, but after last time . . . after what Asmodeus said—"

"Promise?" I pleaded.

The last time he made a promise, he broke it.

"Cross my heart and hope to die."

"It's okay." I stroke his face, smiling through my tears.

"I didn't tell you because I wanted you to believe in us. If you knew, I was afraid you'd think I only loved you because of the prophecy. But I've always loved you."

"I believe you."

A deep, rumbling voice intrudes. "Aww. So sweet."

My sanctified dagger hilt meets my hand. I spin to face the great demon standing over his burning prey. His leathery wings are flared wide—their wingspan is enormous. Embers burn and spark down the fabric of his suit, charring from his own destruction. But just as quickly as it burns, he somehow fixes it. The suit knits back together.

The sheer soullessness of his black eyes sends a shiver down my spine. That yawning chasm is terrifying when I realize he has nothing to lose. But I do. I move to shield Zeke with my body and prepare for the fight of my life. If this is the end of my ride, I enjoyed it—at least the last part.

Asmodeus's face crumples with loathing as he looks down at me. "Fools. Bleeding hearts lost my soul in the first place. I don't need to kill you. You'll do that yourselves."

The rustling of his great leathery wings fills the air, shadowing us briefly before he returns to the church. I watch him retreat to ensure Zeke is safe.

"Leila." He taps my leg. "Take Snuggles and go."

"What?" I drop to face him again. "I'm not leaving you."

Anger flashes in his eyes. "Don't you trust me?"

"Of course, I do, dickhead. But I'm not leaving you."

"Then I'll climb the path myself." He stubbornly uses my katana to lift himself, putting weight on his good leg. He scoops up my backpack from the cab and leans on the sword like a walking stick. He hobbles toward the hill path, determination hardening his face. I don't want to look down at his leg, but it's not flopping around. It's not falling off. "I won't get in the way of your destiny, Leila."

I run to fit myself under his arm. "You dumbass. It's because of you I have a destiny."

He shakes his head as we walk. "I messed up so much. That's what Flauros said to me while you ran after Asmodeus."

"Shut up." I grunt, shifting his weight to walk better. I glance at the smoldering remains of Flauros. He's so dead that ash crumbles from his corpse. "Without you, Zeke, Puck would have made my life hell. He would have destroyed my soul. Raped me. Ruined me."

A reluctant sound of agreement comes out of him.

"Every time I was fostered out, and the fire was blamed on

me, you waited for me at the group home. You dried my tears . . ." I swallow a lump in my throat. "You taught me how to get up every time I fell."

I keep listing all the good things he's brought into my life. People forget that saving lives can be as simple as stepping in and telling a bully to go to hell. It can be the moment you make up a silly game about eating horse manure pie. It can be a hug. It's the little acts of kindness that add up. I'm still talking when we finally reach the hilltop.

But my mouth clicks shut when I see Asmodeus pacing the church, burning tracks in the grass. His demonic form is shifted away, and he's back to being the suave businessman in a suit. No. Suave is the wrong word. He looks unhinged as he attempts to get inside but can't walk through the decrepit open doors.

"The church is on hallowed ground," Zeke mumbles. "Even the devil can't get in. I think."

"Maybe not." I point to flowers painted around the foundation bricks. "Protection sigils."

Asmodeus's head snaps our way. Then he glares at the flowers and grins. He opens his mouth and breathes fire at the church. Flames lick up the sides of the building. They burn so hot and fierce that they catch the roof and ignite.

Fear pounds in my blood. *Fire.* I'm paralyzed as flames engulf the church, blinding me. Smoke burns my nose. When I close my eyes and pray, I don't hear the voice of doubt in my mind. I hear Zeke's as we drove up that bumpy road.

"You've always been able to do anything you set your mind to. I believe in you."

I open my eyes and tighten the straps on my backpack.

"Wait here," I say.

He grabs my hand as I leave, stopping me. "Leila. You can't be serious. It's an inferno."

I smile at him. "I'll be back."

A moment of silence stretches. I'm sure it's only a second, but it feels like an eternity. He has to trust me, or this doesn't work.

"Promise?" he croaks.

"Cross my heart."

His hand slides down my arm, then I run into the flames.

Thirty-Six

Leila

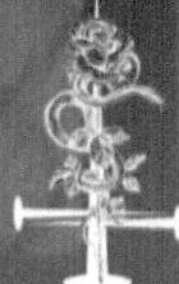

I'm unsure which keeps me safe, Snuggles or the Helwinga concoction, but I emerge unscathed from the wall of flames outside the church. The inside is empty except for a stone altar shrouded in smoke at the end, and the shadow of a man disappearing there.

The funny thing about being afraid of fire my entire life is that now I know everything about surviving it. I cover my mouth with my sleeve, keep low, and move toward the altar.

Behind it is the crypt. A heavy concrete lid has been shifted to the side, revealing steps leading down. As long as there's air down there, I should be able to wait out the fire if it worsens. But it's mainly stone. I don't expect the flames to last long.

Steeling my resolve, I descend the steps, twirling my sancti-fied dagger in my hand. The musty smell increases. I hit the bottom and keep walking down a dark narrow tunnel covered in cobwebs. A flash of fire ahead brightens the corridor from about thirty feet away. I shield my eyes as Asmodeus burns the tomb door to cinders and then walks inside.

Something stops me from rushing after him. Now that the door is open, I feel something strange in the air. It's almost electrical. Magnetic.

The relic.

I wasn't entirely sure it was meant for me. But now that I feel its power calling out to me, I have no more doubts. I swallow my fear and put one foot in front of another. I keep going until I enter the large stone room. Magnetic electricity buzzes against my skin. It's so strong I can't tell where it originates.

Candles flicker in brass wall sconces around the tomb. Asmodeus must have lit them before walking toward the sarcophagus on the raised dais. Helwinga flowers are carved into the stone coffin. On the wall behind, an inscription is carved onto a plaque. It's in Romanian, German, and English. When I read, a slow smile splits my face.

> *Here lies Dorothea Helwing, who never stopped being a Hildegard.*

I let Asmodeus climb the steps to the sarcophagus. Instead of chasing him, I check my surroundings, looking for clues and feeling out the holy energy source. The walls are painted with figures watching over Dorothea's body. Sigils are everywhere, hiding in plain sight behind the painted flowers. Some of them I recognize, some I don't. This tomb has been booby-trapped. I just need to figure out what and how it will help me.

The sarcophagus lid grates as Asmodeus slides it open, but

I don't look his way. My gaze snags on something that doesn't belong before the wall beside me.

Snuggles sits on the floor before a particular painted figure, his floppy head bowed. I reach behind me and find the string that held him has been broken . . . or cut. He either fell, or Claudia was right and my ancestors did their thing. I choose the latter because I feel the power thrumming behind Snuggles like waves of hot air pulsing against my face. It must be fate.

I study the peeling painting above Snuggles. It's of a fierce woman in black robes. She holds a sword in one hand and a rosary in another. The faded red cross on her chest slides the last puzzle piece into place. She's a Sinner. And she's looking down at Snuggles.

Not Snuggles.

The loose brick beneath her foot—where she steps on a dead dragon. Power thrums through that brick. My heart leaps into my throat. Dorothea was a Sinner who never quit her mission. She wouldn't leave a holy relic capable of killing our enemy somewhere obvious. She would let her Sinner sisters watch her back, even in death. Hearing Asmodeus preoccupied with ransacking the coffin, I drop to my knees and stab my dagger into the gap between the loose brick and the next. Driven by the energy calling me, I jimmy the brick forward. When it's about to fall, I grab Snuggles to save him from being crushed.

A shadow looms on the wall before me, flickering from the candlelight. *Asmodeus.* I gasp, turning and raising my hands as a shield. But it's no use. Fire engulfs me. Heat blisters my skin, burning away the last remnants of Helwinga like it's dust. I'm dying. Burning alive. But somehow, when the flames extinguish, I still kneel with my hands held out. And Snuggles in them.

Unburned.

We're both safe. I'd picked him up just in time. He truly is my guardian angel. Through the smoke ahead, Asmodeus's body slowly takes shape. His black eyes widen when he sees my toy.

"That's absurd," he snarls.

"Think quick." I toss Snuggles at him, twist on my knee, reach into the wall cavity, and pull out the holy relic.

My blood sings as we connect. Unseen energy booms outward from me, creating a wave of dust like the ripples in a pond. I swear the pistol sighs as though it's finally home. It's as magnificent as I imagined. Spiky nails on the long barrel—the same nails that pierced Christ's skin. The gravity of this moment is not lost on me. The relic chose *me*.

I'm glad I studied Dorothea's diagram because I know how to open the chamber, drop my special bullet, and lock it. I spin and cock the hammer, aim—Asmodeus' eyes widen. He flickers and jolts. Frowns. Flickers again. Nothing. I laugh.

I think he's trying to teleport, but the sigils have trapped him.

My laughter was a mistake. A taloned hand swipes at me, and I jerk backward. The back of my head hits the wall, and I see stars. He tries to take the gun, but I have it in a death grip. We end up rolling and grappling along the tomb floor.

As we near the dais, we run out of room to roll. I end up on top and straddle his waist to strengthen my purchase to pull the gun from his grip. His fingers hiss with smoke as he grips the spiky barrel and tries to squeeze the trigger. But I'm ready. I follow through with my other elbow when he tugs, smashing it into his nose.

Shocked, his head whips to the side.

"Fucking bitch!" he spits.

Demon noses bleed just as ours do.

"Love it when they talk dirty," I say, as if he's just another notch on my demon belt. I pull back my elbow and body slam his throat. He chokes, but as I climb off him and aim the gun down at his chest, he kicks my feet from under me. I flip back, glimpse sigils on the ceiling, and land hard on my spine. The wind knocks out of me. The gun skitters from my hands, spinning away on the dirty stone floor. I flinch, expecting the hammer to drop. But it doesn't.

Asmodeus pushes himself off the floor.

I scramble and crawl to chase the relic, expecting him to fight me for it. But he runs through the door. *Hurry.* My blood sings as my fingers wrap around the gun's grip. I get to my feet and stand in the doorway, widening my stance. My gunslinger's deep voice whispers instructions in my mind.

Focus on your breathing.

I exhale.

Take the time to line up your target.

I look down the long barrel of the gun and realize each spiky nail acts as a sighting device. I lock onto the center of Asmodeus's back as he runs away.

Keep your stance stable and your eyes on the prize.

I make sure the hammer is cocked.

Even after you squeeze the trigger.

I fire, holding the pistol steady through the recoil.

Asmodeus jerks forward. He falls. Lands hard on his face

inches from the steps leading out. Smoke curls from a hole in the center of his back, right over where his heart should be. But he doesn't get up.

I blow away the smoke curling from the barrel, then holster it where my Smith & Wesson usually sits. The relic fits perfectly. I walk back into the tomb and pick both the special bullet casing and Snuggles off the floor. Smiling at him, I dust him off.

"Saved me again, buddy."

It all happened so fast. It's over. Asmodeus, a demon prince of hell, the Horseman of War, is dead. I put the spent casing back in my pocket. It's almost too good to—

Groaning in the corridor snaps my eyes back. My lungs seize. Time stops as horror sets in. He's not dead. *Not dead.* Panicking, trembling, I drop to my knees and riffle through my backpack. I fumble. Struggle to grasp Matei's bullets in my numb fingers and reload the gun's chambers. But as I swing my aim back to the corridor and cock the hammer, Asmodeus raises his palms.

"Don't shoot!"

I hesitate. Breathe. And study the man before me on his knees with agony on his face. He clutches his chest, cries out in pain, and rips his suit and shirt open in one fell swoop. Buttons spray. He claws at the unnatural wound at the center of his sculptured chest. Instead of blood, light bleeds from the puck-ered hole. Lightning surges through his veins, illuminating the skin, and reaching further to his extremities with every strike.

"I can't . . ." He hisses. "I can't breathe."

I slowly walk to him. The smell of flesh burning mixes with something floral and coppery. Asmodeus crumples forward, clutching his chest. He glances up at me, brow furrowed. Candlelight from the tomb is enough for me to see his eyes flicker from demonic black to human brown.

"What have you done to me?" he snarls.

I pull the casing from my pocket and turn it in the light until the engraving is visible.

"Forgiveness," I mumble.

His brown, human eyes suddenly flick to black. He snarls, baring fangs and a forked tongue. Black-tipped taloned fingers take a swipe at me. I dodge, but he scrapes my midsection, tearing my clothes.

"Fucker." I press the barrel of the relic against his forehead and pull the hammer down with my thumb.

But he's in even more agony than before. His attack cost him more than it did me. It's like a repulsion beneath his skin.

"Do it," he spits, leaning into the cold metal pressed against his forehead. "Shoot me."

I holster the relic again and step back.

"*Shoot me!*" His eyes leak water.

But I turn my back on him, stroll to the tomb and collect Snuggles and my backpack. After fitting them both, I walk past him. He reaches for me, but not to attack, to beg.

"Please!" He gropes my legs weakly. "*Shoot* me. End my misery."

I kick him off me like a nuisance pest. I don't turn back until I climb to the steps.

"It hurts," he cries.

"It hurts because you feel guilt. Because you feel bad. All the sin you've ever committed is returning to haunt you."

He gnashes his teeth at me, trying to be the dragon one last time. His eyes flick to black. But it doesn't stick. It hurts him. I have no pity for him . . . only envy. Zeke and I always played the *one thing* game—asking each other what we would change if we could turn back time. And here he is, the demon prince, rotten to the core, and he's been handed his one thing in a silver bullet. He's been given a miracle that has turned back time to the moment Lilith fucked his life up.

"I'm still me," he rasps, thumping his chest like a gorilla. "Still a demon."

"A demon with a soul."

Thirty-Seven

Mercy

I bite my juicy, crisp apple and watch from the abbey steps as Leila helps Zeke out of the taxi. They return victorious in a blaze of glory under a setting sun. Asmodeus has been neutralized—he has a soul. She has the relic in her hands, and apparently, it makes her blood sing. We've proven, yet again, that we Sinners have what it takes to save this world. To be the saviors they tell us we're not.

I should feel good.

But I don't.

My eyes narrow on Leila's lingering touch as she helps Zeke hobble toward me. The others are on their way. But right now, it's just me here waiting. And I'm glad. Because there's no one to see the contempt on my face. My stomach curdles when he kisses her on the cheek, and she smiles. I must hide my feelings well because when they reach the base of the steps, Leila turns that grin my way.

"We did it," she exclaims, tapping a pistol now holstered at her hip.

I can't even look at it.

"Mercy?" Leila frowns. "Babe, you okay?"

"You warned me off him." I point at the gunslinger without looking at him. My accusation is for Leila only. "You told me not to go near him. That he's not to be trusted."

That they all lie and cheat. That these men are just like all the rest.

Her jaw drops. She blushes. "I . . . um . . . there's a story."

My brow arches. They look happy. In love. I shouldn't feel this envy clawing at my heart, but it's a poisonous snake wrapping around my Eden. I don't have feelings for Zeke. I don't even like him. But he would have been a willing release when I was in need, overcome with my urges and desires. I knew it. She knew it. And it wasn't only him she warned me off. It was all of Team Saint.

"So?" I ask. "What's the story?"

Zeke shuts her down with a warning look.

Lies. Secrets.

I'm already losing a battle of wills against my insatiable desires, but now I feel like everyone here is working against me. My girls always had my back. *Always.* Never once did I feel this unwanted and isolated.

"Congratulations," I grind out as footsteps thunder inside the abbey behind me. The door slams open, and Tawny runs out, eyes wide and full of her stupid, innocent optimism. Thea is next with her glowing fucking stick. But I can't stand here a moment longer. I jog down the steps, push past a bewildered Tawny, and start walking.

Somewhere.

Anywhere.

My feet keep moving until I find myself halfway to the church at the back of the estate. I stop. I can't go there. I refuse to. It's where *He* is—and he's the source of my insanity. I told Leila just how much of my mind he occupies, and—*argh!*

Forcing myself to breathe and dispel my anger, I try and think logically. I'm the only Sinner who hasn't taken the sacrament of reconciliation since Team Saint arrived. Father has been on my case. Every cell in my body wants me to go there, to him, to confess, to purge these feelings from my soul.

But I turn back toward the abbey, taking another bite of my apple. A sour taste hits me. Bile rises in my gullet, I spit and look down, revolted. The apple is rotten to the core.

Horror floods me.

Is that an omen? Am I rotten inside? Is that why I'm the only one here who battles with her inner demons daily?

Before I know it, I'm barging into the church—then I lurch to a stop. It's empty . . . and so quiet that I hear leaves brush against the stained-glass windows outside. A soft light glows from the open door of the special room set up for Sinner reconciliation. The Sin Bin, as we've called it, is carved into the door. I'm drawn to it like a moth to a flame.

By the time I shuffle inside the room, I'm already rippling with untapped arousal. My body reacts before I see him. It's like the awareness of his presence is a living, breathing succubus in the air between us.

The lightbulb in the center confessional cubicle is on, indicating the sacrament of reconciliation is in session. He waits inside. Just beyond that wooden door. He's here every night, listening to sin, granting absolution.

Fuck this. Fuck Leila for taking my chain cilices. Fuck thinking I'm a dirty whore whose only purpose in life is to drag men to hell with me.

I pace beside the confessional, flapping my hands. I can't do it. I can't face his judgment.

I spin and head toward the exit. But that old dark friend of mine, the insatiable lust, rears its ugly head before I'm two steps away. I turn back.

I have to. I can do this.

Don't want to be rotten to the core.

If I don't confess, I'll burst from my skin. I don't trust myself or my urges. Confession is the only thing that keeps me grounded. That and pain. Penance gives me focus. It doesn't work if I do it on my own. As Leila witnessed, I go too far. There is no line. I need someone to guide me, and Father Francisco McHottie is the right man.

Stop it. I smack my head. He's a regular man. A devout catholic with fuckable lips I want to sit on.

A frustrated whimper shoots from my lips, and tears burn my eyes. I'm ready to pull my hair out. I can't stop. Can't bottle this up anymore.

"Are you coming in?" Father's deep, Italian-accented voice rumbles from inside the confessional. The baritone tickles my skin like a feather.

Of course he heard me. Probably knew I was here the entire time, beating myself up. Damn it. I have nowhere to hide now. It's either face my shame or spiral into the lusty pits of hell.

And he hasn't seen me yet. His door is closed. I can still do this anonymously.

I yank open the wooden door and stumble inside. Turning, I sit on the tiny wooden bench and watch the privacy door close, darkening the cabin until the only light comes from a crack above the door and a ray through the window of lattice to my right. Just enough illumination that I can see my fingers, legs, and dust motes dancing in the air. And the kneeler beneath the lattice in case I want to get down and face my judgment.

The priest sits behind a thin wall separating us, ready to act *in persona Christi*. Through the lattice, I see the curve of black-robed knees, and a scarred, tattooed fist thumbing a set of rosary beads. The crucifix inked beneath the knuckle of one finger catches my eye. *Fuck me.* Those hands are hot. I imagine seeing that finger sliding in and out of my pussy, that tattoo disappearing into me. I squeeze my thighs to ease the ache, but I'm already wet. He's a mafia enforcer turned exorcist, and for some reason, that's my crack. He let God act through him even before he took his vows.

Those large hands would have seen their fair share of death. Danger. Blood. Throats. I bite my bottom lip to stifle a moan. Why the fuck was I born like this? I screw my eyes shut, hating myself.

"Whenever you're ready," he says.

I shake my head. I'm afraid that if I speak, I'll embarrass myself. For the past few weeks, I've been fantasizing about him. Because I can't have him. He's untouchable. *Bad, Mercy.* I slap my head.

"You can start with the reconciliation prayer, or just—"

"Bless me, Father," I blurt a little too loudly. "For I have sinned."

His breath hitches. I straighten. Did he just gasp? Is it because he recognizes my voice already? He knows I'm the only one who hasn't seen him. The silence between us is deafening. If he hasn't guessed it's me . . . I suppose he will now.

"It's been weeks since my last confession, and these are my sins. I fucked a married man a few months ago. My regular release wasn't at the bar when I needed him. So I seduced the chef. It didn't take long. Just a pout here and a touch there. Before I knew it, he was railing me from behind in the Coolroom. But that was weeks ago. I haven't been able to release this tension since Team Saint arrived." I cough, trying to stop myself but the words keep falling out. "I can't help it. I fantasize about sex all the time. I masturbate whenever I can. *Jesus Lord, do I.* In bed. In church. In the gym. In the pool. In the shower. In the fucking toilet. It's worse when I don't fuck someone. I just can't stop. I know this isn't right. Many priests, nuns, and people better than me have told me that my urges come from a sinful, evil place. That's why I'm here, right? To turn that rotten core into something useful? But, fuck, I haven't been on a mission since forever—I can't even funnel these urges into something good. Do you know how hard it is to deny yourself the one thing your body *screams* for you to have?"

I flop back against the wall, defeated. Tears sting my eyes, but I hold them in. I always hold them in.

"*Sì.*" Father's soft, disembodied voice is a life raft through the lattice. I hear him licking his lips. Hear him breathe. And then he exhales. "I know what it's like."

"No disrespect to you, Father, but I don't think you get it this bad. I'm certified. Spent a few months in a psych ward. They tried to fry the sin out of me, but it didn't stick."

Silence is my answer. Shame heats my cheeks, and I brace for the hate I always get. So many of them can't help the righteousness they dish out. Whenever Father Angelotti sits across from me at a briefing in the archives, or looks at me from across the gym, his eyes simmer.

When the silence extends, I brave a look through the lattice. The priest's fist is clenched so hard around his rosary beads that a sliver of blood drips from his fist and stains his black clerics.

"They locked you up?" His voice is a raw, breathy snarl that sends shivers down my spine. "True?"

"I'm not lying." I blink. "Why would I lie to you? That's another sin I don't need penance for."

As if in response to the P word, my thighs burn. I yank my yoga pants down and inspect the circle of raw, creamy skin with a hiss. The welts from the chain cilice are as angry as they were when Leila stole them from me. I lick my finger and rub the wound. It's itching now. Needs air to heal, but I hide the wounds with pants. The tight fabric rubs and irritates me, giving me the pain I need to distract myself from my demons.

"I'm punishing myself enough," I mumble.

"Mercy."

"Yes, Father?" I lick my finger and rub my welt, wincing.

"Are your pants down?"

My spine straightens. My eyes widen and then shut. *Stupid.* If I can glimpse his knees through the lattice, he can see my pasty white ones with my black yoga pants around my ankles. My legs would be like a beacon in the shadows here.

"It's not what you think." I grimace. If this were any other place, if he were any other man, I wouldn't give a flying fuck. I'd kick my pants off and invite him in. For a split second, I entertain the thought of doing just that. Or, at the very least, sticking my fingers down my panties to ease my throbbing ache. But I slide my pants back up and over my hips. "I have cilice wounds. The pain helps me rein in my urges."

Wait for it.

Here comes the derogatory judgment.

"*Si*," he replies. "I understand. What else helps you?"

He's . . . not shaming me. He's . . . being nice. I touch the lattice with my fingers.

"Sometimes penance, depending on what it is."

"Go on."

I flatten my lips.

"I cannot help you if you do not share," he says.

"Honestly, nothing works for long. Pain helps me focus on something else. Missions give me focus. As long as someone else pulls my strings, I don't beat myself up about it too much." I survive. I flourish. I might even enjoy the ride. "And . . . confession. Letting something out, even talking about it, somehow seems to let off steam."

"And what happens when you . . . explode?"

"I, um . . . hurt people."

"You have forced yourself on someone?"

"No!" I shake my head, picking absently at the lattice. "But I'm hard to say no to. I find ways of getting what I need, even if that means someone wakes up with regrets . . . or . . . my steam comes out as violence."

"Mercy," he suddenly clips. "Put your hands on your lap."

The sharp authority in his tone is a bolt of heat to my clit. My fingers slide down the lattice, and I place my hands demurely on my lap.

"Where I can see them."

I slide them to cup my knees.

"*Molto bene*." Very good.

No. *Not* good. That voice. That dominance. I'm heating up inside, panting in this suffocating space.

"I don't think I can do this," I mutter, squirming.

"Yes, you can." His tone is hard, yet I don't think cruel. It's difficult to tell when I can't see his face. "You will come to this confessional every night, *si?*"

"Um. Oh-kay." I scoff. Whatever, Mr. Bossy. Every night is a bit much.

"Not *um*. Say yes, Father."

My humor dies beneath the control in his voice. All I can manage is a breathy, "Yes, Father."

"With regular confession and council, I can help you." He audibly swallows. "For now, that is your penance."

"That's it?" I frown.

"Unless you have more to confess?"

"I don't think so." I tap my lip. "I think I'm good. I was a little rude to Leila just now, but she'll forgive me. Anything else is clutching at straws."

"So . . . no killing. No steam explosions of violence."

I scrunch my nose at the lattice. "That hasn't happened in a *very* long time. It's not like I walk around stabbing people or cutting off dicks. Apart from demons, I haven't hurt a soul since my last confession."

He prays for my absolution in Latin, and then says, "You may go."

I get up to leave, hesitate, then sit back down. "That's really it?"

"*Sì.*"

"You're not going to tell me there's a special place in hell for women like me?"

"No."

"No flogging, or kneeling until I bleed, or begging Christ to forgive my sins?"

He pauses. "Mercy. Desire is not sin. Adultery, *sì*. This is why you have penance. But for your . . . urges. This is natural. This is normal."

I sit back, frowning. "Okay."

When I don't move, he reminds me, "You may go."

"Okay!" I jump to my feet and open the door. When I walk out, I feel lighter. I still have the same dark whispers bouncing around my head. But I don't feel bad about them. Not really.

The light in the confessional goes off, and Father's door opens. He sees me and freezes. I'm caught in the snare of his captivating brown eyes. Long, dark lashes surround them. He's both rugged and dangerous, yet somehow handsome and pretty. His skin is a beautiful golden-hued olive, like he spent his childhood sunbathing by the ocean.

We stare awkwardly at each other. I can't help noticing his short brown hair is ruffled, as though he's scrubbed it in frustration. Every instinct in my body begs me to look south, to check out those kissable lips, and then keep heading south. Is his fist still clenching the beads? Is he disheveled down there too? Is his robe crinkled at the groin from all the rubbing he's done through the fabric? Was he as turned on as I was, or was it just me doing my thing?

I'm proud of myself. I don't mention any of this but hold his intense brown gaze.

"Sorry. Just leaving." I spin on my heels and walk out of the sacristy. As I leave, I turn to read the carved words in the wooden door but find them patched over and stop. I glance back in the room and see him tugging his white collar off, kneeling on the one-person pew. His broad shoulders hunch over as he fingers his rosary and closes his eyes. A deep divot appears between his brows as he mumbles his prayers. I glance down at his fingers and see his blood glistening on the beads.

"Father." I step forward.

He opens a single eye and looks at me. "When the collar is off, it's just Cisco."

"Cisco." I take another step. "Are you okay?"

He goes very still.

"Do you want to talk? I mean, you looked troubled. I spilled my guts to you, but I'm also a good listener."

Both eyes open. I squirm under his attention and feel like he's about to reprimand me for the intrusion. But he slides his gaze back to the front and closes his eyes, dismissing me with a sigh.

"Thank you, but my penance is for me alone. You may go."

"I mean. It doesn't have to be listening." I crack my knuckles. Maybe someone hurt him.

He shakes his head, lips twitching before he scowls again. "Mercy, you may go."

The way he says my name. *Chills down my spine.*

"Right." I admire his profile for another hot second and then leave the church.

As I get to the door, I smash my hand into the holy water basin, pirouette, and make the sign of the cross at the crucifix over the altar. I give Christ a saucy wink. Maybe my penance won't be so bad after all. But I'm still pissed off about being lied to.

My bitches have some explaining to do.

Thirty-Eight

Leila

"What are you making?"

Zeke's voice behind me is a welcome sound as I crack an egg and separate the yolk. "Wouldn't you like to know?"

"Yes. Yes, I would. That's why I asked." His hands slide over my hips, around my stomach, and he drops his chin on my shoulder.

"How's your leg?"

"Better than new."

I straighten and twist to see him. He's no longer in his cast and grinning at me from ear to ear.

"Don't get used to Thea healing you every time you hurt yourself." I don't want him to think he's invincible and then go and run off a cliff again.

He sees the worry in my eyes, and his smile drops. "I won't. Promise."

I scoff and turn back to my bowl. He returns his hands to my hips and drops his chin on my head.

"Don't believe me?" he murmurs.

"Maybe I'm making a horse manure pie, just in case."

His laugh is deep and rattles my spine. My body reacts to his closeness—my nipples peak and my skin gets tight and hot. We haven't been intimate since the cabin in Romania before he broke his leg. A full-body shiver runs through me when he drops his lips to the tendon running from my neck to my shoulder.

"Mmm," he mumbles against my skin, inhaling deeply, sliding his lips toward my ear. "You just washed your hair."

I crack another egg but forget to separate it. Dammit.

He sucks my earlobe into his mouth. Another shiver trembles through me.

"Zeke," I breathe.

"Yes, wildcat?" His fingers start circling over my stomach. Even with an apron on, the effect is as though it's skin-to-skin. I'm on fire wherever he touches me and . . . I no longer run from the flames. Like every other challenge in my life now, I face it head-on.

I glance around the kitchen. It's empty, as is the dining hall beyond the open serving window.

"Checking to see if we're alone?" Zeke's eyes crinkle, and I think that's what seals the deal.

I need him as much as he needs me. But I don't tell him. I let him work for it. My lips slide into a secretive smile, but I don't reply. It was going to be a sponge cake, but now I've fucked up the eggs. I'll turn it into a pound cake instead. I lean across the stainless steel bench and tug the butter to me.

Zeke's hands slide up my ribs and cup my breasts. He squeezes until my nipples tingle, earning him a whimper from my lips. His groan draws a glance over my shoulder. I catch him staring at my rear end, biting his lower lip and frowning as though he's holding in the urge to touch me there.

"Right," I tease. "I see why you're here, and it's not to help me bake."

Hazel eyes clash with mine. He looks like such a mischievous devil that I can't resist. I tug him by the collar and kiss him quickly before returning to my bowl.

"I want to get this in the oven before dinner." I drop the butter into the mix. "We've all had such a hard time lately. Mercy too. I think something sweet for dessert will be nice."

"You're so thoughtful."

"Not really. Helping in the kitchen is part of my penance."

"Cisco gave you baking for penance?" He starts kissing my neck again, right behind the ear.

"I can't work like this," I moan, arching back into him.

"Yes, you can." His palms slide down my arms, cover my hands, and place them in the bowl. "Keep stirring. Or kneading. Or whatever you were doing."

The butter crumbles under my clenched fingers, mixing with the flour. But I'm not really paying attention. I'm too invested in where Zeke puts his lips next. He moves down my spine, kissing me through my T-shirt. When his fingers hook into my pants, I gasp as a rush of desire pools between my legs.

"Zeke," I moan, pretending I'm resisting despite wanting this all along. "Anyone could walk in."

He keeps sliding my pants over my ass cheeks, exposing my bottom to the air. "The nuns are in church, singing their hearts out. It's the only time they can break their vow of silence. They won't be back for an hour."

"But—" His fingers slide between my legs and glide through my slit, already wet. I bite my lip and whimper. "There are others . . ."

"They're busy," he mutters distractedly. I know he's staring where he touches me, concentrating and relishing. The knowledge makes my eyes flutter.

"Look at this pretty pussy under the lights," he murmurs. Almost to himself. His voice is coming from lower down, as though he's crouched and facing my ass while he fingers me. "Fuck, Leila. I can't believe I get to play with this whenever I want."

"That's a bold claim," I pant, unable to stop from pushing back, trying to force his fingers where I need them. "Stop fucking around and get me off."

"There she is. My wildcat." His tongue spears into my core. The sudden sensation bucks my hips forward. I plant floury and buttery hands on the counter with a gasp. Zeke pins my hips to the counter and plunges his tongue into my pussy. I'm a quivering, shaking mess as he works me hard. The suction and licks and twirls earn every whimpering sound I make.

We almost lost each other. Again. Everything has changed. We deserve every moment we can find. Never know when we'll get it again. My orgasm builds, and my whimpers become erratic.

"Give it to me, baby," Zeke growls against my folds. He pinches my clit, shooting fireworks through my body. "I want your cum on my tongue."

"Fuck," I gasp, rocking back on him. "Love it when you talk to me like that."

"I'm going to lap up every drop." His voice is gravelly and rough. Then I hear no more as he finishes me with hard and fast tongue flicks and I come apart, quivering on his mouth. The deep growls of satisfaction as he keeps working me past my climax, prove it's just as he wanted.

My bones are liquid as I lean on the counter, hot and sweaty, and catching my breath. I hear his zipper, feel the blunt tip of his cock notch at my entrance, but then he pauses. His ragged breath makes music with my own.

"Zeke?"

A hesitant touch against my anus, and I gasp. His voice is a secretive whisper when he asks, "You ever been taken here?"

I can't tell if I detect hope or fear in his tone. I glance over my shoulder and see him fisting his cock hard, staring at my ass like it's something he wants to devour, despite the remnants of my last release still glistening on his lips. The sheer lust drenching his gaze has my pussy clenching again.

"No," I breathe. "Never."

His desperate eyes meet mine. "You mean I can be your first?"

"Now?" My eyes dart to the kitchen door, looking for signs that we'll be interrupted.

He spits on his finger and gently probes my puckered entrance. I moan as the new sensations trigger an onslaught of unexpected heat. "Not now," he mutters. "But when I can give you a proper first time. When I can turn back time and finally give you one thing we can claim together."

"Zeke." A sob catches in my throat. I twist and grasp his

neck, pulling his lips to mine. He kisses me with deep, devouring strokes that taste like me. But it only makes me needier. Stupid to be so worked up over this, but to have something that's just us, something new to explore, feels like we really haven't missed our chance. There's so much more for us to discover about each other.

He refits himself to my pussy and inches inside with short, sharp thrusts until I'm liquid again, clawing the counter with one hand, him with the other, facing the mess we've made with our passion.

With our faces so close, he can't pull out far but still manages to slam in hard, rocking me against the counter. Cutlery and crockery wobbles.

He's mine. He's got me.

He pumps with short, shallow strokes, then kisses my inner wrist and detangles from my hand.

"I need to fuck you hard right now, kitty cat."

He pulls out further and plunges in deep. So deep. I bite my lip to stop the moan.

"You love that, don't you?" he rasps.

I nod.

"Say it." He thrusts again.

"Yes."

"Fuck, you're so tight."

His hips piston hard, slapping against me with enough force to rock the counter. We're so noisy. Surely someone will hear. With my pants down my thighs and my hands clawing the counter, I can only submit to Zeke's hunger. I'm helpless to stop the pleasure coiling again in my lower belly.

"Shit," I mumble, biting my hand. "I'm close again . . ."

"What do you need?"

"Touch me."

He reaches around, toys with my clit, and keeps thrusting deep. I'm so relaxed, so centered on how he makes me feel, that I'm tipping over the edge again with an orgasm so intense it rips a sob from my throat. It doesn't take long before he seats himself and holds. He drops his head to my spine and groans. "You're so fucking tight that I'm done within moments of being balls deep in you."

He pumps a little, proving I'm all wet and slick inside.

"We have the rest of our lives for more."

"Damn straight."

My vision clears, and I witness our destruction.

"I have to throw this cake out." It's all over the counter now. I'm horrified at the mess when I should be horrified that he's still inside me, our naked rear ends out for all to see.

"I'll help you." He slides out of me, zips up, and finds a tissue to clean me before kissing my bottom and pulling up my pants. "See? Nothing to worry about."

I shake my head, smiling. "You're incorrigible."

"You love it." He slides his elbow onto the counter and looks at me with a flushed, smug face and swollen lips. His scruff has grown back. Combined with that messy, longish hair, I'm staring at the face of my perfect man.

"I do," I whisper, gazing into his eyes.

"Better stop with the eye fucking, Leila," he growls. "If you want this cake made."

I grin. He finger-combs my messy hair, then claps his hands and stares at the floury mess. "What do you need?"

"New bowl and ingredients for a pound cake."

He rattles off a list of items, impressing me with his memory. It's a simple cake, but he remembers it from our youth. While he collects fresh ingredients, I clean the bench and start again. We work in companionable silence for a while. It's nice. It gives me the courage to finally as a question that's been driving me crazy.

"Zeke?"

"Mm?" He looks up from where he greases a baking tray.

"What does huckleberry mean?"

He deadpans. "What?"

"I mean. I know Doc Holliday says it in the movie, but I don't get it. Is it Huckleberry Finn, or like—"

"Leila!" He gapes. "Are you telling me you've not understood all this time?"

I bite my lip, smiling.

His face turns serious, and he gesticulates between us as he explains. "It means I'm the guy you call when you need someone to back you up. I'm the one who gets to fight *for* you. Anything you need, I'm there. I'm your man."

"So... not Huckleberry Finn?"

"No!" Exasperated, he grabs my face and pinches my cheeks. "I mean. I don't know where it came from. It's a Wild West thing."

"I still don't get it." I pat his jaw. "But I love you too, Huck."

THE ENTIRE CREW sits at a long wooden table in the dining hall. Everyone from Team Saint and every Sinner. The Rev chose to sit with Magpies at another table, enjoying her silence. The only sound is clanking as dinner dishes are washed in the kitchen. And now the quiet conversation at our table.

"I can't believe we're all here." I smile at all of them. "We did it."

Raven's eyes are shadowed with pain. But she refuses to let Thea heal her. Dom sits awkwardly on the bench seat, darting a glance at Raven every so often. Zeke is by my side, looking at the slice of warm cake and a dollop of cream on his plate with hungry eyes.

"Now?" he asks.

"Not yet. I have something I want to say."

Mercy still isn't happy with me, but I talked it over with Zeke, and it's time for the truth. Wes and Thea don't know what I'm about to do. They're sitting at the end of the table, close together like newlyweds. Cisco is out of his clerics and in a hoodie and sweats. I can't get used to it. But I see him glancing at Mercy every now and again, almost as though he's confused about something.

Tawny whines and taps her fork on her plate. "Hurry. I'm starving! This looks so yummy."

"You just ate a full meal." Thea frowns. "How can you be *starving*?"

"She has hollow legs," Mercy sighs, casting an envious look at our tall blond assassin next door.

"I can't help it if I have a fast metabolism."

"Guys!" I stand and clang my fork on the plate, grabbing their attention.

All eyes shift my way. I don't want the entire dining hall to hear, even though I can trust them. I sit down and look at my cake as I speak. "I just want to take this opportunity to thank everyone. Even our absent friends, new and old. Asmodeus, and I dare say, the apocalypse was stopped because of all of us working together."

"And Snuggles." Zeke points to the toy sitting at the table's edge, watching us.

We all startle in surprise.

"Bloody hell, he really keeps doing that. Popping up." Wesley's eyes widen with alarm.

A clicking dolphin sound comes from beneath the table. Zeke's cheeks flush, and he drops his hand to pat the ex-demon clawing at his legs for treats. "And Jinx."

I look at Mercy. Here goes. "And I want to apologize. Firstly, for lying to you about my history with Zeke. Secondly, for lying about the part of the prophecy that predicts the merger of this team . . . romantically. I didn't know for long, but the lie almost cost us the relic, so I figured, better out than in."

Zeke puts up his hand. "My fault too. Sorry."

I look at our redheaded team leader. "Mercy, we should have told you the instant we saw you on the doorstep, but . . . there's been concern that some of us won't take the news well."

Thea and Wesley gasp. Someone drops a spoon, clattering loudly.

Mercy blinks at me, then Cisco, and then back at me as she asks, "The teams need to merge romantically? Like an orgy?"

I laugh and shake my head. "No. Just one Sinner and one Saint. Isn't that right, Thea?"

Her cheeks brighten. She knows they have to tell the truth now. She clenches her jaw but then nods. "It's not like we enjoyed withholding the truth. We weren't one hundred percent confident. But after Wes and I fell in love, and now Zeke and Leila have kindled an old friendship into something more . . . it's definitely part of Mary's prophecy. Five Sinners *for* Saints."

No one speaks. The silence is deafening. Dominic's brown skin looks greenish. Raven rubs her eyes. Tawny frowns.

"Wait," she says, counting us. "The math doesn't add up. Are we getting a new member of Team Saint?"

We all study each other. Cisco slides guilty eyes away.

Wes sees it and blurts, "They're coming, aren't they?"

"Who's coming?" Mercy asks, her voice tightening.

The priest doesn't answer, but Zeke does with bleak eyes. "The Entity—the Vatican."

"When?" Mercy stands suddenly, glaring at the priest with accusation. "They're coming to dismantle us? To condemn us?"

"Maybe the prophecy is wrong," I suggest. "Maybe we can refuse the Entity entry."

"It's not wrong." Wes taps his finger on the table. "Too much is right."

"Maybe they'll see the light," I suggest weakly.

"Can we eat yet?" Tawny whines, eyes already back on her cake. "I'm seriously hungry."

I sigh. "Guess the cake is going cold. We won't solve these problems at the dinner table. And I'm kinda starving still."

"Me too," Zeke mumbles.

A chorus of agreement rumbles around the table.

"Let's eat then."

I devour the cake and cream, but it tastes like cardboard. My emotions are too frayed right now. I probably should have dropped my bomb after we ate. After a few moments, Tawny looks at me with nervous pity.

"Leila, I don't mean to be rude, but this tastes like ash."

"What?" My blood runs cold. I thought it was just me who couldn't taste it. "Is everyone's bad?"

"Sorry." Mercy pushes her plate forward.

One by one, everyone gives me a guilty look. They all think it's my cooking. Zeke is the only other one who realizes something is wrong. Alarm enters his eyes as he whispers, "Leila's baking always tastes good."

I glance around the room and study the nuns closely as they eat. They're all playing with their food, shifting vegetables and meat around, filling and draining spoons. But not eating.

"Shit. Oh shit."

I run to the Rev's table, where her soup is untouched. I lift it to my lips and drink. *Cardboard*. I bite a carrot from Sister Agnes's plate but spit it out. *Ash*. When I finally face our table, all Sinners and Saints have risen to their feet, a grim look in their eyes.

One word comes out of my mouth: "Famine."

EPILOGUE

A homeless woman huddles in a desolate alleyway, her gaunt frame barely clinging to life. Her lips are cracked, and her stomach is in knots. But she is out of energy to shout warnings.

"Hungry," she begs. "So hungry."

No one stops to feed her. No one cares. Food rots in the street.

Hastily scrawled words on the long-forgotten signboard at her feet read: *When the soul starves, it is because evil feeds.*

Acknowledgments

This book was super hard to write. Not because of the content but because life was just crazy for me. I worked until the deadline, sent my structural editor Ann Harth a manuscript missing the last few chapters, and begged my Arc Angels Team and proofer Kelly Messenger to help me with only 48 hours to spare. Erika Robles brainstormed with me in the final hours, helping me figure something out I wasn't too sure about. They all rallied and in the end, we turned out a finished, bad-ass, demon-hunting book.

It takes a village!

I'm honored and grateful to have so many wonderful souls helping out.

And to my Patreon supporters, who give me inspiration along the way, and help keep me excited about all the projects, thank you as well.

Lana.

(Fantasy/Paranormal Romance)

Season of the Wolf Trilogy

The Longing of Lone Wolves

The Solace of Sharp Claws

Of Kisses & Wishes Novella (free for subscribers)

The Dreams of Broken Kings

Season of the Vampire Trilogy

The Secrets in Shadow and Blood

A Labyrinth of Fangs and Thorns

A Symphony of Savage Hearts

Season of the Elf Trilogy

A Song of Sky and Sacrifice

A Crown of Cruel Lies

OMG! How do you say my name?

Lana (straight forward enough - Lah-nah) **Pecherczyk** (this is where it gets tricky - Pe-her-chick).

I've been called Lana Price-Check, Lana Pera-Chickywack, Lana Pressed-Chicken, Lana Pech...*that girl!* You name it, they said it. So if it's so hard to spell, why on earth would I use this name instead of an easy pen name?

To put it simply, it belonged to my mother. And she was my dream champion.

For most of my life, I've been good at one thing – art. The world around me saw my work, and said I should do more of it, so I did.

But, when at the age of eight, I said I wanted to write stories, and even though we were poor, my mother came home with a blank notebook and a pencil saying I should follow my dreams, no matter where they take me for they will make me happy. I wasn't very good at it, but it didn't matter because I had her support and I liked it.

She died when I was thirteen, and left her four daughters orphaned. Suddenly, I had lost my dream champion, I was split from my youngest two sisters and had no one to talk to about the challenge of life.

So, I wrote in secret. I poured my heart out daily to a diary and sometimes imagined that she would listen. At the end of the day, even if she couldn't hear, writing kept that dream alive.

Eventually, after having my own children (two firecrackers in the guise of little boys) and ignoring my inner voice for too long, I decided to lead by example. How could I teach my children to follow their dreams if I wasn't? I became my own dream champion and the rest is history, here I am.

When I'm not writing the next great action-packed romantic novel, or wrangling the rug rats, or rescuing GI Joe from the jaws of my Kelpie, I fight evil by moonlight, win love by daylight and never run from a real fight.

I live in Australia, but I'm up for a chat anytime online. Come and find me.